ROMANTIC ... *TH,*
NEW YORK ... *OR!*

HALF-MOON ...

"Bobbi Smith is a terrific storyteller whose ... aracters, good dialogue and compelling plot will keep you up all night."

FOREVER AUTUMN

"*Forever Autumn* is a fast-paced, delightful story."

LONE WARRIOR

"Fast paced, swift moving and filled with strong, well-crafted characters."

EDEN

"The very talented Bobbi Smith has written another winner. *Eden* is filled with adventure, danger, sentimentality and romance."

THE HALF-BREED (SECRET FIRES)

"Witty, tender, strong characters and plenty of action, as well as superb storytelling, make this a keeper."

BRIDES OF DURANGO: JENNY

"Bobbi Smith has another winner. This third installment is warm and tender as only Ms. Smith can do. . . . Ms. Smith's fans will not be disappointed."

BRIDES OF DURANGO: TESSA

"Another wonderful read by consummate storyteller Bobbi Smith. . . . Filled with adventure and romance, more than one couple winds up happily-ever-after in this gem."

BRIDES OF DURANGO: ELISE

"There's plenty of action, danger and heated romance as the pages fly by. This is exactly what fans expect from Bobbi Smith."

More *Romantic Times* Raves for Storyteller of the Year Bobbi Smith!

WESTON'S LADY

"Bobbi Smith has penned another winner."

HALF-BREED'S LADY

"A fast-paced, frying-pan-into-the-fire adventure that runs the gamut of emotions, from laughter to tears. A must-read for Ms. Smith's fans, and a definite keeper."

OUTLAW'S LADY

"Bobbi Smith is an author of many talents, one of them being able to weave more than one story. . . . Ms. Smith creates characters that one will remember for some time."

THE LADY & THE TEXAN

"An action-packed read with roller-coaster adventures that keep you turning the pages. *The Lady & the Texan* is just plain enjoyable."

RENEGADE'S LADY

"A wonderfully delicious 'Perils of Pauline' style romance. With dashes of humor, passion, adventure and romance, Ms. Smith creates another winner that only she could write!"

BARE NECESSITIES

A sense of power filled Casey as she watched Michael Donovan standing waist deep in the water. She had him right where she wanted him. His pa acted like he owned the whole country, and it felt good to have the upper hand for a change.

"So, how's the water?" she asked.

"The water's fine."

"I was thinking as I rode up here that cooling off in the river probably would feel real good today, so there's no reason why you shouldn't just enjoy yourself a while longer. I'll be going now. . . ."

"Good."

"Yeah, I've got to get on back. . . ." Casey urged her mount across the low-running river.

"Why are you heading for Donovan land? I told you there weren't any strays around here."

Casey didn't answer. She just rode to the tree where his clothes were hanging, yanked them down and held them up for him to see. "I didn't find any strays, but I found these. I think I'll take them with me. . . ."

"You can't take my clothes!"

"Oh yes, I can. You said I needed new ones when you were making fun of me in town, so I'll just take yours!"

"You do, and you'll regret it!"

Other books by Bobbi Smith:

BAYOU BRIDE
HUNTER'S MOON (HALF-MOON RANCH)
FOREVER AUTUMN
LONE WARRIOR
EDEN
WANTON SPLENDOR
SWEET SILKEN BONDAGE
THE HALF-BREED (SECRET FIRES)
WESTON'S LADY
HALF-BREED'S LADY
OUTLAW'S LADY
FORBIDDEN FIRES
RAPTURE'S RAGE
THE LADY & THE TEXAN
RENEGADE'S LADY
THE LADY'S HAND
LADY DECEPTION

The *Brides of Durango* series by Bobbi Smith:

ELISE
TESSA
JENNY

BRAZEN

BOBBI SMITH

LEISURE BOOKS  NEW YORK CITY

This book is dedicated to all my friends in the Heartland Writers Guild in Sikeston, Missouri. You're wonderful!

And to Lynn Oris, the manager at Barnes & Noble in Crestwood, MO, and Connie Jeffries and Deborah Baldini at the University of Missouri, St. Louis. You're wonderful, too!

A LEISURE BOOK®

June 2004

Published by

Dorchester Publishing Co., Inc.
200 Madison Avenue
New York, NY 10016

ISBN 0-8439-5156-7

Printed in the United States of America.

BRAZEN

Prologue

The Bar T Ranch
Outside of Hard Luck, Texas
1874

It was a hot late August afternoon. Young Casey Turner had been out working with some hands from her family's ranch, checking on strays since early morning. She'd ridden away from the men to look for stock along the river that marked the property line between the Bar T and the Donovan ranch, the Circle D.

Casey stopped for a minute on the shady bank. She was hot and tired, and the water looked mighty inviting. The notion of taking a break was all too tempting, but she couldn't allow herself the luxury.

Times were hard on the Bar T.

Money was tight.

She had work to do.

There was no time to relax, no time for play.

Urging her mount on, Casey followed the river's edge. When she heard splashing from around the bend just up ahead, she expected to find cattle. She quietly rode closer, not wanting to spook the strays, ready to drive them back onto Bar T land.

Then she rounded the bend.

Casey's eyes widened in shock and amazement at the scene before her, and she quickly reined in.

There, standing in the waist-deep water with his back to her was none other than the Donovans' sixteen-year-old son Michael, and he was—as best she could tell—skinny-dipping.

Michael hadn't heard her approach, and she was glad. She'd never seen a naked man before. As embarrassed as she was curious, she took her time looking him over. His shoulders were broad and strongly muscled, and his waist was lean. Casey was really glad he was staying put, though, for she'd seen all of Michael Donovan she wanted to see.

The Donovans and the Turners had been feuding for years. Frank Donovan, Michael's father, had done everything he could to cause trouble for her and her father. He'd refused to let them join the trail drive to market, which cost them a lot of money, and he'd even accused them of rustling, which wasn't true. Casey knew she and her father had only managed to keep the Bar T in business because they had the best water in the area. She worked hard side by side with her father every day to try to make things better, but there were times when she wondered if they would ever start showing a good profit.

Suddenly Casey realized this was the perfect time to take a little revenge on Michael. He was pretty much helpless.

The thought of getting even with him made her smile.

Just a few weeks before she'd been in town picking up supplies, and Michael had walked into the general store at the same time. When he'd seen her, he'd made fun of the way she was dressed. She always wore boys' clothes because it was easier to get her ranch work done that way. She had one dress for church, but that was all. There was no money for extras like pretty dresses.

Casey hadn't wanted to admit it at the time, but Michael's comments had hurt her. Arrogant, rich Donovan that he was, he deserved what he was about to get as a payback for being so mean.

She smiled. Michael was still unaware of her presence. She looked around to make sure he was alone. Her grin broadened when she saw his horse tied up nearby and his clothes hanging over a low tree limb. True, the clothes were on the Donovan side of the river, but that wasn't going to stop her—not today.

A wild plan began to form in her mind as she stared at his clothing. He had made fun of her clothes in town; now she had the opportunity to take the perfect revenge. She knew exactly what she had to do.

Casey drew her rifle, then urged her mount closer to the water's edge. She stayed just far enough back to be out of Michael's reach in case he tried to come after her.

"Hey, Donovan!" she called out, enjoying herself tremendously.

Startled, Michael turned to find himself staring up at Casey Turner.

"What are you doing here?" he demanded as he moved into deeper water to keep himself shielded from her view.

"I'm checking for strays—but all I found was you." She was enjoying his discomfort.

"Well, just keep on riding," Michael ordered. "There isn't any Bar T stock around here."

"You sure?"

"Yes, I'm sure," he ground out as he glared up at her, not appreciating her amusement over his situation. "Go on—get out of here."

Michael wanted her gone, the sooner, the better. Everyone knew Casey was trouble. Though she was only twelve, she already had a reputation as a hellion. Her mother had died when she was five, and the lack of any female influence in her life showed. She was as wild and untamed as the land. She dressed like a boy, and acted like one most of the time, too. She kept her dark hair cut short, and the only time he'd ever seen her wear a dress was at church, and even then she'd had her boots on.

"I don't have to do anything you tell me to do, Michael Donovan," she shouted back. "I'm on Bar T land. I can stay right here all day if I want to. I don't have to go anywhere." She sat there staring down at him, looking quite relaxed in the saddle.

Michael's scowl deepened. He wasn't sure what she was up to, but he didn't trust her. She was Jack Turner's daughter. That alone gave him reason to worry. He was just about ready to challenge her, to walk right out of the water in front of her. He was almost certain that that would send her off at a dead run; he hesitated only because his mother had taught him to be a gentleman around ladies. Not that Casey was a lady, but . . .

A sense of power filled Casey as she watched Michael. She had him right where she wanted him. His pa acted like he owned the whole county, and it felt good to have the upper hand for a change.

"So, how's the water?"

"The water's fine."

"I was thinking as I rode up here that cooling off in the river probably would feel real good today, so there's no reason why you shouldn't just enjoy yourself a while longer. I'll be going now—"

"Good. Good-bye." Michael wished she'd stop talking and start riding.

"Yeah, I've got to get on back." Casey urged her mount across the low-running river.

"Why are you heading for Donovan land? I told you there weren't any strays around here."

Casey didn't answer. She just rode to the tree where his clothes were hanging, yanked them down and held them up for him to see. "I didn't find any strays, but I found these. I think I'll take them with me—"

"You can't take my clothes!"

"Oh, yes, I can. You said I needed new ones when you were making fun of me in town, so I'll just take yours!"

"You do and you'll regret it!" he threatened.

"I don't think so. What can you do about it?" Casey laughed out loud at him.

"You can laugh now, but you'll get yours! I'll see to it!" Michael started to charge through the water toward her, intent on getting his clothes.

It was then that she lifted her rifle for him to see. "Stay right there, Donovan."

He stood still, glowering up at her in silence.

"Enjoy your swim!"

Casey was still laughing as she rode to where his horse was tied up. She stopped just long enough to free his mount, then slapped it on the rump to chase it off. She crossed back to the Turner side and galloped away. She did not look back.

Michael climbed out of the water and up the riverbank just as Casey disappeared from sight. He swore loudly in humiliation and frustration. He wanted to chase her down. He wanted to teach her a lesson for doing this to him, but it wasn't going to happen—at least not right now.

Silently he vowed that one day Casey Turner would pay for what she'd done.

But first, he had to figure out how he was going to get home.

He looked around for something to cover himself with as he tried to figure out what to do. He spotted his boots and was grateful for that much. What he was going to do next, he wasn't sure. He only hoped that his horse would return to him on its own. If not . . .

* * *

After riding for about half a mile, Casey reined in and glanced over her shoulder toward the river. There was no sign of Michael chasing after her, and she was relieved. His threat of revenge had scared her a little, but she decided the risk had been worth it.

She dropped Michael's clothes on the ground. If he came that far, he was welcome to them. All that mattered was that she'd gotten them away from him in the first place. She was quite proud of herself.

Casey was smiling again as she rode off to join up with the ranch hands. She might not have rounded up any strays, but she'd certainly had an adventure. She almost regretted not keeping a piece of Michael's clothing, just to prove to everybody what she'd done.

Chapter One

Five Years Later
On the Circle D Ranch

The gunman smiled to himself when Frank Donovan rode into view. He had been waiting, hidden among the brush and rocks on the hillside with his rifle in hand. The hired gun took careful aim at the lean, powerful, silver-haired rancher, and when he came within range, the killer got off his shot. He watched as Donovan was hit and fell from his horse. The boss had said to make it look like a robbery, so he mounted up and rode down to where the rancher lay unmoving on the ground. He took what money Donovan had on him, then rode away without a backward glance.

* * *

"Mrs. Donovan!!" called out Tom Richards, the foreman on the Circle D, as he led the boss's horse up to the main house.

Fifty-year-old Elizabeth Donovan was busy in the kitchen when she heard Tom's call. She knew it had to be important if Tom had come looking for her, so she hurried outside. Elizabeth was surprised to find the foreman waiting for her at the foot of the porch steps with her husband's horse. "What is it, Tom? Where's Frank?" She looked around for her husband.

"His horse just came back in without him!"

She went down to check the mount. It was obvious it had been running hard and fast. "You'd better get some men together and ride out to look for him. He said he was going to check stock in the south pasture when he left this morning."

"We'll head out right away."

Elizabeth wasn't too worried about her husband as she went back inside. Frank was an excellent horseman. It wasn't often his horse got away from him. She found herself smiling at the thought of Frank being forced to walk home. The hands would find him, but she knew he wasn't going to be a very happy man when he did get back to the ranch.

A good two hours passed before Elizabeth heard the riders returning. She went outside, expecting to see Frank riding in along with them. Instead, she was shocked to see the men bringing him home on a makeshift travois.

"Frank!" She ran frantically to her husband's side. He was unconscious, and his shirt was blood-soaked. She looked up at Tom in horrified disbelief. "What happened?"

"He must have been ambushed. He was shot in the back and robbed," Tom quickly explained as he dismounted and went to her. "I already sent Harry to town for the doctor—and the sheriff."

"Who did it? Did Frank say anything?" Elizabeth asked tearfully, kneeling down and taking her husband's hand. His grip was usually strong and firm, but now his hand was limp in hers.

"No. He was unconscious when we found him."

"Let's get him inside," she directed quickly, desperate to do all she could to save him.

With great care, the men lifted Frank off the travois and carried him inside and upstairs. It wasn't easy, for he was a big man. They laid him carefully on his bed. Tom stayed on to help Elizabeth, while the other hands went back outside.

Elizabeth stripped off Frank's shirt and removed the makeshift bandage Tom had put on the wound when they'd found him. She cleansed the wound as best she could, but there was little more she could do. The bullet was still in him.

They waited anxiously for Dr. Murray to arrive.

"Why would anyone do this?" she whispered to Tom.

"I don't know, but whoever did do it was a coward—back-shooting him this way," Tom answered solemnly.

Tom left Elizabeth with Frank then and went downstairs to wait. He had been the foreman on the Circle D for five years, and he admired and respected Frank. If he'd had any idea who'd ambushed his boss, he would have been riding after the culprit to seek revenge, but he had no clue. There had been no talk of trouble in the area or of any outlaw gangs around.

Tom knew the Donovans had had some run-ins with neighboring rancher Jack Turner over the years. Old man Turner had no use for Frank, and Frank felt the same way about him, but their hatred for each other had never resulted in bloodshed—before.

Elizabeth stayed by her husband's side, anxiously awaiting the doctor's arrival. Each minute seemed an eternity as he lay so deathly still before her, his breathing shallow and labored. She desperately offered prayers that the doctor would be able to save him.

The moment Elizabeth heard the sound of a carriage pulling up, she hurried to the window to look out. When she saw it was the doctor, she rushed from the bedroom to meet him downstairs.

"Thank God, you're here!" she exclaimed.

"I came as soon as I got word from Harry." Dr. Murray quickly grabbed his bag and climbed down from the carriage. He could see how distraught the normally dignified, elegant Elizabeth was, and knew Frank's condition had to be as serious as the ranch hand had said. "Harry will be along soon. He was on his way to see Sheriff Montgomery when I left."

Elizabeth led him inside to the bedroom.

Her usually vibrant, handsome husband looked so pale when she reentered the room that for an instant Elizabeth feared he'd died in the moments she'd been gone from his side.

"Is he—?" she asked, terrified.

Dr. Murray went to examine Frank and quickly reassured her, "No. He's still alive."

"Thank God."

"Why don't you wait in the parlor? I'll call you as soon as I'm done."

Elizabeth left the room and went downstairs to find Harry had returned and was talking quietly with Tom in the front hall.

"Sheriff Montgomery wasn't in his office, so I left word with his deputy about what happened," Harry explained as she joined them. "He said he'd send him right out when he got back."

"Thank you, Harry."

"If you need anything, let us know," Tom and Harry said, looking as if they wished there was something more they could do.

"I will."

After they left her time passed slowly for Elizabeth. Not for the first time in all the years she'd lived on the Circle D, she cursed the place. None of this would have happened if Frank had listened to her and moved back to Philadelphia as she'd wanted to do. Her family was there, and she and Frank would have been safe and happy in that civilized world. Now here she was, waiting in agony to hear if her husband was going to live or die—and all because someone had shot him down in cold blood.

Tears filled her eyes. Frank was a strong man, a powerful man. She loved him dearly, but she had never understood his passion for this ranch and this way of life. That was why she'd wanted Michael to go back East to college four years before. She'd wanted her son to know there was a bigger, more refined world out there beyond the Circle D and Hard Luck, Texas. Frank had been reluctant to let Michael go, but she had insisted.

Elizabeth realized she would have to send one of the men into town to wire Michael as soon as she talked with Dr. Murray. Michael had just completed his studies, along with his cousin Nick, and they were scheduled to embark on a trip to Europe to celebrate very shortly. She wanted to get word to him of the shooting before they sailed. She needed Michael here with her.

Nearly half an hour passed before Dr. Murray sought her out in the parlor. She got tiredly to her feet when the physician appeared in the doorway.

"Is Frank going to be all right?" Elizabeth asked nervously, seeing his serious expression.

Dr. Murray went to her. "I think you'd better sit down."

Horror filled Elizabeth. She sank down on the sofa, and he joined her there.

"Frank's not—?" she began, terrified.

"No," he quickly reassured her. "He's regained consciousness. He's going to live."

"Thank God." Tears of relief and joy welled up in her eyes.

"But there is something you need to know," the doctor went on solemnly.

"Yes?" Elizabeth was cautious, wondering why he was so grim after telling her such good news.

"The gunshot wound was serious, very serious. It's left him paralyzed from the waist down."

Elizabeth stared at the doctor in disbelief as she tried to grasp what he'd just revealed. "Frank is paralyzed?"

"Yes."

"But it's only temporary. He'll get better, won't he?"

"I'm sorry, Mrs. Donovan, but no. He's not going to get better. Your husband will never walk again." Dr. Murray hated being the bearer of such tragic news, but he didn't want to give her any false hope. He waited a moment in silence, seeing her shock and giving her a moment to come to grips with what she'd learned. "Frank has been asking for you. Are you up to seeing him?"

Elizabeth nodded and slowly walked with the doctor to the bedroom. She paused in the doorway to stare at her husband as he lay as pale as death on the bed.

"Frank," she softly said.

At the sound of her voice, Frank opened his eyes and turned his head slightly toward her. "Elizabeth—" It took all his strength just to say her name.

She ran to the bedside crying and pressed a tender kiss to his cheek.

"Send for Michael," he whispered hoarsely. "You must send for Michael."

Philadelphia

"So tomorrow is the big day," James Paden said with great pleasure as he went to the bar in his walnut-paneled study. "I think this deserves a drink in celebration."

He poured healthy servings of whiskey into three crystal tumblers, then handed one to his son Nick and one to his nephew Michael Donovan. He took the third glass for himself and lifted it in a toast.

"To you, Nick, and to you, Michael. Congratulations."

"Thank you, sir," they replied.

They all took a drink.

James smiled at the two young men who stood before him. He was proud of them and what they'd accomplished. They had graduated from the university and were ready to embark on their trip to the Continent.

James's gaze settled approvingly on Michael. He'd been worried when his nephew had first arrived in Philadelphia four years earlier. Michael had been a rough-and-tumble cowboy then, but no visible trace of his Western background remained now. Tall, darkly handsome, and perfectly well-groomed, Michael had matured into a polished gentleman and fit easily into sophisticated society. James knew that that had been his sister Elizabeth's hope when she'd sent him there to attend the university, and he was glad Michael had made the transformation so successfully.

"I'm sure your mother and father are very proud of you, Michael. It's just a shame that they couldn't join us here for the ceremony."

"It's a busy time on the ranch right now," Michael told him, fully understanding why his parents hadn't made the trip.

"You plan to go see them when you get back from Europe, don't you?"

"Yes. I'll go home for a visit then."

"Good. Now, Nick has been to Europe before, so he'll be more than happy to show you the sights," James said, glancing over at his son and smiling.

"I'm looking forward to it."

"We're going to enjoy every minute," Nick said confidently.

"I'm sure you will," his father agreed. "Michael, have you thought about what you want to do now that you are done with school? Do you want to return to ranching, or stay here with us?"

Before Michael could answer, Nick put in, "He does have certain interests here, you know."

"You do?" James looked at his nephew.

"Karen Whittington, for one, Father," Nick finished.

"Well, should you decide you want to stay on and work here in Philadelphia, there will always be a position open for you with Paden Shipping."

"Thank you." Michael was honored by his uncle's offer.

"As for Miss Whittington—you could do far worse," James went on thoughtfully. "Her family is quite affluent and very influential. Have you proposed to her yet?"

"No," Michael answered quickly. He found Karen an attractive woman, but their relationship hadn't progressed that far. He wasn't sure it ever would.

"Are you planning to see Karen again before we set sail?" Nick asked.

"Yes, I'm meeting her later tonight."

"I don't think she's happy that you're leaving."

"She hasn't said anything—"

"From what I know about Karen, I'm sure she would prefer you to stay right here in Philadelphia with her." Nick knew how spoiled the rich, beautiful blond debutante was, and he had cautioned his cousin about getting too involved with her. Karen had a reputation for being a very controlling young woman.

"What about all your women?" Michael countered. "Do they know you're leaving?"

Nick was one of the most sought-after bachelors in town. Many a mother had set her sights on him as potential husband material for her marriageable-age daughter. He had money and the Paden dark good looks, but he didn't see the logic in settling for just one woman, when he could have them all.

Nick chuckled at his cousin's question. "They know. In fact, I was wondering who was going to show up to see us off."

"Why don't you hire several carriages to transport all your admirers down to the station?"

All three men laughed good-naturedly.

A knock came at the study door, and the Padens' butler, Jonathan, came in.

"This telegram just arrived for Michael, sir," Jonathan announced.

Michael smiled as he took the telegram. He was certain it was from his parents, wishing him well on his trip. He tore open the envelope and quickly read the message.

Nick watched him as he read, and he noticed how serious Michael's expression became. "What's wrong?"

Michael looked up at him, his eyes dark with worry. Any thought of going to Europe had been instantly banished from his mind.

"I have to go home." There was no uncertainty in his voice.

"Why?"

"My father's been injured."

"What happened?" James asked worriedly.

"I don't know the details. Mother didn't say. She only said he's been paralyzed." Michael frowned, trying to imagine his strong, vibrant father crippled.

"What? Paralyzed?" James was shocked. "You've got to get back home at once."

"And I'll go with you," Nick offered, ready to help Michael in any way he could.

"But the trip to Europe—I can't ask you to give it up. I know how much you've been looking forward to going."

"You didn't ask me to give up the trip. I just offered. Besides, that's what family is for. I'm going to Texas with you. You might need me."

Michael smiled in appreciation of his cousin's support. "I'll check at the train depot right away and see how soon we can depart."

"How long will it take us to get there?"

"Depending on connections, it could take a week, maybe longer, to reach Hard Luck."

"Then we'd better get going."

"Do you need any money?" James offered.

"No, Uncle James, but thanks."

"Is there anything your Aunt Sarah and I can do to help?"

Michael looked up at him. "Just pray."

Chapter Two

The Bar T Ranch

"Race you back to the house!" Casey called out as she put her heels to her mount's sides.

Her horse bolted into action. They galloped off, leaving Pete Stuart, the foreman on the Bar T, standing in a cloud of dust.

"You're on!" Pete hollered. He swung up into his saddle and charged after her.

Casey was smiling as she leaned low over Raven's neck, moving as one with the animal. She enjoyed the feel of the wind in her face and the sense that they were almost flying. Pete had been bragging about how fast his new horse Lightning was, and she was determined to show him Raven was still the best on the Bar T.

They tore across the countryside, Pete and Lightning

trailing slightly behind. As the ranch came into view, Casey could tell he was gaining on her, but she wasn't about to give up. She urged Raven on, and they raced up to the stable in a cloud of dust, victorious.

Some of the ranch hands saw them coming and were cheering her on.

Casey reined in abruptly and was laughing in exhilaration when Pete caught up to her moments later.

"I told you Raven was the best!" she declared proudly.

"You may have won this time, but you had a head start," Pete countered.

"I won. That's all that matters," Casey insisted.

"Winning is everything to you, isn't it?"

"That's right," she said, still grinning at him as she dismounted and stroked her stallion's neck adoringly.

George, one of the hands, came to take Raven from her.

"Thanks." She handed the reins to him, then glanced up toward the house. She was surprised to see a horse tied up out front.

"Who's up at the house with Pa?" she asked.

"I don't know. I was busy working and didn't see anybody ride in," George answered as he led Raven away.

"I guess I'd better find out what's going on." It wasn't often they had company.

"You go on for now, but we're going to race again," Pete insisted, dismounting.

"Why would you want to lose to me twice?" Casey asked with good-humored arrogance as she started off toward the house.

Pete chuckled to himself as he watched Casey go. She was one helluva female. He knew the boss regretted not having a son, but Casey had proven herself time and again to be as good as any man when it came to riding and shooting. Pete respected her gumption and her abilities. He even respected her decision to dress like one of the hands in pants, shirts and boots when she was working on the ranch. She was a woman who knew her own mind. He was still smiling as he turned back to tend to Lightning. She won today, but he would have his rematch.

"Where were you early yesterday afternoon, Jack?" Sheriff Montgomery asked, eyeing the stocky, middle-aged rancher suspiciously as they stood face-to-face in the parlor of the Bar T ranch house. The bad blood between the Turners and the Donovans was common knowledge, and that put Jack Turner at the top of the list of people Montgomery needed to check out regarding Frank Donovan's shooting. Not that he had any proof Jack was involved. When he'd ridden out to the Circle D the day before to speak with the wounded rancher, Frank had had no idea who'd ambushed him.

"Where do you think I was? I was out working my stock," Jack replied sarcastically. "Shouldn't you be back in Hard Luck enforcing the law? What do you want with me?"

Montgomery ignored Jack's questions. "You got any witnesses who can vouch for you?"

"Ask my men. They can tell you." His gaze narrowed as he looked at the sheriff.

"I'll do just that," Montgomery told him as he started from the house to seek out the ranch hands.

"Wait a minute, Sheriff," Jack growled harshly, and he was gratified when the lawman stopped and looked back at him. "What's this all about?"

The sheriff looked him straight in the eye as he answered, "Somebody shot Frank Donovan yesterday."

"What?"

"You heard me. He was ambushed—shot in the back, robbed and left for dead."

Jack frowned. "I'm not denying I've got no use for Donovan, but I didn't shoot him."

"I'm just going to make sure of that."

"How is he?" Jack asked, following him.

"He's alive," was all Montgomery answered as they left the house.

"Sheriff Montgomery?" Casey was startled as she came face-to-face with him on the front porch.

"Miss Turner." He nodded to her but kept walking toward the corral where Pete and some of the other men were working.

Casey looked at her father as the sheriff moved off. "Pa? What is he doing here?"

Jack was disgusted as he quickly explained what he'd learned.

"And the sheriff thinks you did it?" she asked, both shocked and worried.

"Pete and the boys will tell him where I was. There's nothing to worry about."

"I hope not."

They waited together on the porch, watching as Sheriff Montgomery spoke at length with the men. When the sheriff started back toward the house, Pete came with him.

"Are you satisfied now, Sheriff?" Jack asked angrily.

"Your men covered for you, if that's what you're asking, Jack," he replied.

"We didn't have to cover for him," Pete said in his boss's defense. "We told you the truth. There's no reason to lie. Jack was with us all day yesterday."

Sheriff Montgomery mounted up and nodded to them. "I'll be seeing you."

Jack felt bile rise in his throat as he watched the lawman ride away. "Bastard."

"What did you say, Pa?"

"Nothing."

"Are you all right?" Casey asked, seeing that he had grown pale.

"I'm as fine as I can be, considering the sheriff just accused me of shooting Frank Donovan down in cold blood and robbing him."

"He knows you didn't do it now," Pete reassured him. "We told him."

"That's right, Pa. Everything's all right."

Jack moved slowly toward the stable. "Then let's get back to work."

John McQueen was furious as he stormed into the bunkhouse at his ranch, the Royal.

The men lounging there looked up, startled.

"Boss?"

"Get out," he ordered, his gaze focusing on the one man who lay asleep on his cot, an empty whiskey bottle on the floor beside him.

The men quickly disappeared outside, leaving him alone with Sid. They didn't know what Sid had done, but it had to be bad to get the boss this riled.

John stared down at the man who was passed out in a drunken stupor.

"Celebrating, were you?" he snarled as he picked up the small bucket of water sitting near the washstand and dumped the contents in the unconscious man's face.

Sid Midland sat up with a start, choking on the water and cussing wildly, only to find himself staring down the barrel of his boss's gun. Sid's bloodshot eyes widened in shock, for he knew how deadly and dangerous his boss could be.

"What the—"

"I don't pay you to miss, Sid!" he said in a low, threatening voice. He had hired the fellow because of his reputation as a gunman.

"Miss? What are you talking about?"

"Donovan is still alive!"

"No."

"Oh, yes." He stepped back and slowly holstered his weapon. "You told me he was dead. You told me—"

Sid interrupted him to protest, "I went down and robbed him just like you said. He wasn't moving!"

"He wasn't moving because he's paralyzed, but he isn't

dead. When I send you out to do a job for me, I expect you to do it right."

"You want me to go finish it?"

"No," John answered harshly. "You just lay low and keep your mouth shut. I'll handle it from here."

John stalked from the bunkhouse in complete disgust. He'd had a plan ready to set in motion. With Frank Donovan out of the way, it would have been simple for him to take over the Circle D. The newly widowed Elizabeth Donovan, alone and without any man to guide her, would have been eager to sell out. He would have been just as eager to offer his sympathy as he bought the ranch, which Frank had refused to sell to him when he'd made an offer several months before. Now, word had come from town that Frank was still alive, and everything had changed.

Silently John cursed Sid again as he began to rethink his plan for gaining control of the neighboring ranches. His goal was to be the biggest, most successful rancher in this part of Texas, and nothing was going to stop him.

As he considered his situation, John realized it was time to concentrate on the Bar T instead of the Circle D. He had had his eye on Casey Turner. She was different from any other female he'd ever met. Just the sight of her wearing those pants of hers left him hot with wanting. He had been taking his time with her, wooing her slowly, but now that his plan for the Circle D had been ruined, he would concentrate on Casey and her ranch.

The Turners' finances were so shaky, Casey might just marry him for his money. One way or the other, the Bar T—and Casey—would be his.

* * *

Michael stared out the window of the train car, wondering if it were possible for time to pass any more slowly. He and Nick had been traveling for three days now, and it had seemed an eternity to him.

"We'll get there," said Nick, who was sitting beside him.

"I know, it's just a matter of when," Michael said flatly.

Nick wanted to reassure him that everything would be all right, that he shouldn't worry, but he couldn't. There was no way for them to know what was happening with his father.

"Have you thought about what you're going to do once you get there? Is your mother going to need you to stay on at the ranch now that your father's so seriously injured?"

"It will all depend on my father. He'd never leave the Circle D of his own free will, but if he can't physically run things anymore—"

"It would fall to you."

"Yes."

"And will you stay?"

Nick had asked the question that had been haunting Michael ever since he'd received the telegram.

Michael frowned. "I don't know. Philadelphia has been home for a long time now. I'll just have to see what happens once we get to the ranch."

Both men fell silent as they tried to anticipate what they would face when they finally reached their destination. Nick hoped things weren't going to be as bad as they feared.

Chapter Three

Hard Luck, Texas

"So this is Hard Luck," Nick said as he got his first look at the town. Hot, dry and dusty, it was certainly a far cry from the sophistication of Philadelphia. He was accustomed to paved streets, brick buildings and greenery. It looked like he was about to learn a whole new way of life. He had a good idea how Hard Luck must have gotten its name, for some of the buildings definitely looked as if they'd seen better days.

Nick had come on this trip to help Michael. He wouldn't have had it any other way, but he had to smile at the realization that if things had gone as planned, they would have been standing on the deck of a ship, gazing out to sea as they sailed for Europe right now, not staring out a stagecoach window at this town he wasn't quite sure was civilized.

"Yes, this is it," Michael told him, watching out his side as they passed the general store, the hotel and the jail. Nothing seemed to have changed in the years he'd been away. The town still looked pretty much the same, although a little more run-down. It felt good to be there—to be home—but he felt a pang of regret that his homecoming wasn't for a happier reason.

The stagecoach slowed as it neared the stage depot. When it finally drew to a stop, Michael was the first to climb down. Now that they were so close to the Circle D, he was growing more anxious to get home.

"How long will it take to get out to the ranch?" Nick asked as he joined Michael in the street.

"About an hour by buckboard," he answered. "I'll rent one down at the stable so we can take our trunks with us."

"Let's go. It's been too long for you already. We need to get you home."

Leaving their trunks at the depot for the time being, they started off.

"Did you get him all fixed up?" Casey asked Fitz as she returned to the stable to get her buckboard. She'd come into town for supplies, and on the way in, one of the horses had thrown a shoe. She'd had to bide her time while Fitz took care of it for her.

"You're all set," Fitz told her, pointing to where he'd left the horse tied up. "You need any help?" Knowing

Casey's pride, he doubted she'd accept his aid, but he thought he'd offer.

"I can do it," Casey told him as she paid him for his work.

She got her horse and led him out in front to the buckboard to hitch him up again.

Michael and Nick made their way through Hard Luck, heading toward the stable.

"I think I'm going to need a change of clothes," Nick remarked with wry humor, noticing how some of the townsfolk were staring at them. The gentlemanly suits and ties they'd worn on the trip were common dress back East, but they certainly made the two young men stand out in Hard Luck.

Michael chuckled. "That makes two of us. Right now, everybody's wondering who the two Eastern dudes are."

"You don't recognize anybody?"

"No, not yet, but—"

"Michael? Is that you?"

Michael heard a man call out from behind them. He stopped and turned to see the tall, dignified, gray-haired pastor of their church, Reverend Harris, hurrying their way.

"Hello, Reverend," he greeted him.

They shook hands. Michael quickly introduced the pastor to Nick, and they exchanged greetings.

"It's good you're home." The minister looked back at Michael. His mood turned serious now that the pleasantries were over. "I know your mother will be relieved. She needs you here with her now—more than ever. I was just out at the Circle D, looking in on your parents yesterday afternoon."

"How is my father?"

Reverend Harris shook his head sadly. "It's painful to see him this way. He was such a vibrant man."

"How did it happen?" Michael asked. He had assumed his father's injuries had been sustained in an accident.

The reverend looked shocked that Michael was unaware of the shooting. "You don't know?"

"Know what?" Michael knew instantly that something was wrong, very wrong.

Reverend Harris realized there was no way to avoid telling Michael what had happened, so he told him everything he knew.

"My father was ambushed and robbed?" Michael repeated, stunned.

"Yes."

"Who did it?"

"No one knows. Sheriff Montgomery has been investigating, but he hasn't made an arrest yet."

"Who's this Montgomery? What happened to Sheriff Johnson?" When Michael had left Hard Luck, Sheriff Johnson had been the law in town for as long as he could remember.

"He moved on. Sheriff Montgomery has been on the job for about two years now."

"I think I'd better pay the sheriff a visit before I go home."

"If you need anything, anything at all, just send word."

"I will. Thanks, Reverend."

Michael looked at Nick after the minister left them.

"The stable's down at the end of the street," he directed, his mood even darker now. "Why don't you see about renting a buckboard for us while I talk to the sheriff? I'll meet you there."

"All right," Nick agreed.

Michael started to hurry off.

"Michael—"

He glanced back at his cousin.

"Why would anyone shoot Uncle Frank?" Nick realized his first impression of Hard Luck had probably been accurate. This place wasn't civilized.

"That's what I intend to find out." He looked grim and determined as he walked away.

Nick went on to the stable. The faster they got their trunks loaded up, the faster they could ride out to the ranch.

Michael strode straight into the sheriff's office. He walked in to find a dark-haired, mustachioed man sitting at the desk, the sheriff's badge pinned to his vest.

"Sheriff Montgomery?"

The lawman glanced up questioningly at the well-dressed stranger. "I'm Montgomery. What can I do for you?"

"I'm Michael Donovan. I just got into town on the stage."

The sheriff stood up to shake hands with him. "It's good to meet you. Your mother told me she'd sent for you."

The power of Michael's handshake and the hard look he saw in the young man's eyes told Sheriff Montgomery all he needed to know. Michael might be dressed like a gent, but he was Frank Donovan's son.

"I came as quickly as I could. What happened to my father? What do you know about the shooting?"

"Very little," Sheriff Montgomery told him regretfully.

"You don't have any idea who did it?"

"No. I checked out Jack Turner. I know he and your father have no love for one another, but old man Turner has a solid alibi for the time when your father was shot."

"How did it happen?"

"He was ambushed on Circle D land, shot in the back. He didn't see a thing. I checked the scene of the shooting, but I couldn't find any clues. There's nothing left for me to go on. Other than your pa's ongoing troubles with Turner, he didn't have any enemies we know of. He hadn't had any run-ins with anyone lately, and I haven't had any other reports of robberies happening this way."

It infuriated Michael to think someone could come this close to murdering his father and get away with it. "We've got to find the man who did this."

"Yes. We do," the lawman agreed. He was frustrated by his lack of progress in the case. "I'll let you know if I learn anything new or hear anything around town."

"I'd appreciate it."

"And you let me know if you come up with anything that will help me make an arrest."

"I will."

Michael turned and walked out of the office. His mood

was solemn as he made his way to the stable to meet Nick.

There was a youth harnessing a horse out in front of the stable when Nick walked up, and he assumed the boy worked there.

"Boy," Nick called out. "Could you tell me who I need to speak to, to rent a buckboard?"

Nick was puzzled when the youth ignored his request. He walked up to him to get his attention.

"Excuse me. I was told I could—" Nick stopped in mid-sentence as the "boy" turned to face him and he realized his mistake. "You're a . . ."

"What's the matter? Haven't you ever seen a girl wearing pants before?" Casey asked, grinning as she took off her hat, freeing the tumble of dark curls she'd stuffed up under it while she worked.

"Actually, no, I haven't," Nick answered, returning her smile. He realized she was quite an attractive female with her dark hair and flashing green eyes. True, her state of dress—vest, shirt, pants and boots—had shocked him for a moment, but he already was coming to appreciate the style as he let his gaze sweep over her.

"Well, come to think of it, I've never seen a man wearing a suit quite like yours before, either, so I guess we're even." She eyed him up and down just as openly as he'd observed her and had to admit he was handsome in a slick sort of way.

Nick's smile broadened at her quick wit. He liked her immediately. If all the girls in Hard Luck were like this one, he knew he was in for some interesting times. "I like the way you're dressed, and I'm sorry I mistook you for a boy. I do apologize."

"It's not the first time it's happened to me, and I appreciate your apology. My name's Casey Turner, by the way."

"And I'm Nick Paden."

"You're obviously real new in town."

"Yes, I just arrived on the stage. That's why I came here to the stable. I need to rent a buckboard."

"I can't help you with that. You need to talk to Fitz." Casey directed. "He's the owner. You'll find him inside."

"Thanks." He started on.

"Any time. And Paden—"

Nick turned and met her gaze.

"Welcome to Hard Luck," Casey said as she put her hat back on and climbed up into the buckboard. She took up the reins and drove off, giving him a nod and a smile as she went.

Nick watched Casey go, impressed by the expert way she handled the team of horses. He smiled to himself. He had known coming to Texas would be an adventure, and it had started already.

Nick made up his mind to ask Michael how many females in Hard Luck wore pants. This custom was certainly a far cry from what he was used to at home, and he thought he might just come to like it.

He went to seek out Fitz in the stable.

Casey drove to Lawson's General Store and tied up out front. She went inside to pick up the supplies she needed and was delighted to find her best friend, Anne, working behind the counter.

"I was hoping I'd get to see you today," Casey told her.

Anne's father, Gus Lawson, owned the store, and she often helped out there, as did her mother.

"I'm glad to see you, too," Anne said, coming out from behind the counter to give her a hug. "I've missed you."

"I've missed you, too."

"What have you been doing?"

"Working. There isn't much time for anything else these days."

"Is it true the talk we heard of the sheriff questioning your pa about the Donovan shooting?"

"Yes," Casey answered, her eyes flashing with anger at the memory of the lawman's unfounded accusation. "He came right out and asked Pa where he'd been at the time of the shooting. It's a good thing Pa was working with the hands that day or there's no telling what might have happened."

"Yes, it is," Anne agreed. "Did he come to town with you?"

"No, I came in by myself to pick up supplies. I had to stop at the stable, though, and while I was there, I met a very interesting gentleman."

"A gentleman? In Hard Luck?" Anne was surprised and curious. "Who was he?"

"His name was Nick Paden, and he was fresh off the stage from back East. You should have seen him. He was all dressed up and real handsome, too—for an Eastern dandy."

"I wonder who he came to see."

"He didn't say. He was more interested in the fact that I was wearing pants."

Anne smiled wryly at her. "He may be a gentleman on the outside, but he doesn't sound much different from any of the other men around here. I see how they all watch you whenever you're in town, and I've heard their talk."

"Well, I'm glad I give them something to talk about," Casey said jokingly as she took out her list.

"You're impossible," her friend teased.

"Pa tells me that all the time."

They laughed easily together and started to pick out the supplies she needed.

"Michael! You're back!" Fitz came out of the stable to greet him.

"Hello, Fitz." Michael shook hands with the heavyset stable owner.

"I'm sorry about your pa," Fitz sympathized. "Tell him I'm thinking of him."

"I will."

"You back home to stay?"

"I'm not sure yet."

"Well, it's good to see you. You need anything else, just let me know."

"I will. We'll get the buckboard back to you—probably tomorrow," Michael told him as they climbed up to the driver's bench. He took up the reins.

"That'll be fine. I know I can trust you."

They left the stable, stopping only at the telegraph office to wire Nick's father that they had arrived safely and then at the stage depot to load their trunks. That done, Michael was more than ready to head home.

Chapter Four

"Casey—so it was you," John McQueen said as he came inside Lawson's store. "I thought I saw you."

"Why, John—hello," Casey responded as she looked up from where she was standing talking with Anne to see the handsome rancher walking their way.

John greeted Anne. He found the blond, shapely Anne attractive, but Casey was the one he was really interested in. "This is a pleasant surprise, Casey. Whatever brought you in to Hard Luck today was good luck for me."

Casey laughed at him. "You are such a charmer, John McQueen."

"I try," he returned.

Anne couldn't believe Casey's luck. John was the most eligible bachelor in these parts and quite good-looking. He never flirted with *her* that way. She moved off to wait on another customer, giving them some time alone.

John was glad for the moment of privacy with Casey. He gave her his undivided attention and smiled down at her with his most ingratiating smile. "I wanted to tell you what a nice time I had with you at the box dinner."

"I had a good time, too, John. It isn't often I get to socialize that way."

"I'd like to see more of you," John told her. He kept his tone cordial, but his thoughts were on how much of her he really wanted to see. He loved that she wore those pants, but imagining her without them excited him even more.

"That would be nice."

"I'll try to come by the Bar T for a visit."

"I'm sure Pa would be glad to see you."

"What about you?"

"It's always good to see you, John," she assured him, completely unaware of the direction of his thoughts. She considered him only a neighbor.

When Anne returned to join them, John made his excuses and left.

Anne was smiling in delight over what had transpired. "My, my, my! Is John McQueen really courting you? How often have you been seeing him?"

"Anne—" Casey was embarrassed. "John's not courting me."

"You want to bet?"

"We just happened to eat together at the social at church, and he was telling me he had a nice time. That's all."

"He came in here *just* to talk with you, Casey Turner,"

Anne pointed out. "There are a lot of girls in Hard Luck who would give anything to have John seek them out that way."

"Then those other girls must live very pitiful, boring lives," Casey said, dismissing her friend's insinuation.

"Don't you like John?"

"John's nice enough."

"Only 'nice enough'?" her friend challenged. "In case you hadn't noticed, John McQueen is handsome."

"He's all right, but I've always liked dark-haired men best."

She groaned. "And John's got money!"

"Yes, he does. So?" Casey agreed.

"So?" Anne shook her head in disbelief. "Have you given any thought to the idea that the most handsome, most eligible, richest man in the area might be interested in you?"

"You are such a romantic. I don't have time to worry about men right now. But if you're so excited about them, then you can have John. Or, better yet, go find that man I met down at the stable. He definitely could give John a run for his money when it comes to good looks." Casey smiled at her. "Now, enough about men. I have to get my supplies loaded up and get back home."

"Oh, you!" Anne gave up and started to help her get what she needed.

"Pa was gunned down in cold blood, robbed and left for dead, and right now Sheriff Montgomery doesn't have any leads." Michael finished filling Nick in on what little additional information he'd gotten from the lawman. "I can't imagine why anyone would shoot Pa. He always carried some money on him, but never a lot. It's hard for me to believe robbery was the real motive."

"Whoever it is, we'll find him," Nick said fiercely.

"You're right. We will, no matter how long it takes."

The two men shared a knowing look. If there was one family trait Michael and Nick shared, it was their fierce determination. Once they made up their minds to do something, they did it.

"Right now, the bushwhacker thinks he's gotten away with it, but he's in for a big surprise," Michael said.

"And not a pleasant one."

"You're right about that," he agreed, his mood lightening a bit in anticipation of seeing justice done.

Nick managed a slight grin as he went on, "Speaking of surprises, I've found that things aren't always what they appear to be here in Hard Luck."

"Why? What happened to you?"

"When I first got to the stable, there was a boy working outside, harnessing a horse. I didn't see anyone else around, so I went to ask him about renting a buckboard."

"And?"

"Turns out the 'boy' was no boy. I know you warned me things were different here, but I had no idea Texas women wore pants. It was quite a revelation for me."

"A girl at the stable was wearing pants?" Michael frowned. "What did she look like?"

"For all that she was so unorthodox in her dress, she was quite pretty. She had dark, curly hair and—" Nick stopped as he saw Casey's buckboard tied up before the general store. "That looks like her buckboard." He pointed it out as they drove by.

Michael glanced toward the store just as two young women came outside carrying supplies. One was a pretty blonde wearing a dress, and the other was—

"That's her," Nick said.

It was just as Michael had suspected.

The girl in pants was Casey Turner.

Though Casey and Anne had both changed during the years he'd been away, Michael recognized them. Anne had matured into a very attractive young woman.

And then there was Casey.

She was the one female he would never forget, no matter how hard he tried.

"She said her name was Casey Turner," Nick told him, smiling.

"Yes," Michael answered curtly. "I know."

Michael hadn't planned to acknowledge Casey and Anne, or to even slow down. He had intended to keep on driving, but Anne spotted him and called out before he could get away.

"Michael? You're back!"

He had no choice but to rein in and speak with them. He quickly introduced Anne to Nick.

"Why, hello," Anne greeted him, seeing immediately what Casey had been talking about. He was one handsome man.

"It's nice to meet you, Anne," Nick said enthusiastically. He was growing even more impressed with the women of Hard Luck. Casey was darkly pretty in her unorthodox style of dress, while Anne was lovely, too, in a more classic, feminine way.

Michael looked over at Casey.

"Hello, Casey." His tone was less than friendly. "I understand you've already met my cousin."

"Yes, Mr. Paden and I ran into each other at the stable."

"Please, call me Nick," Nick said, smiling at her.

"And I'm Casey," she returned. "I told Anne about meeting you at the stable, Nick. We were trying to figure out who you had come here to visit. Now we know."

"When Michael got the news about his father's injury, I wanted to make the trip with him," Nick explained.

"I'm sorry about what happened to your father," Anne told Michael sincerely. "I hope he'll be better soon."

"Thanks."

"I'm sorry, too, Michael," Casey put in.

He only nodded at her in response.

"Give your father my best—your mother, too," Anne said.

"I will." Michael was more than ready to move on.

"And, Michael—" Casey called out, unable to resist as she eyed the fancy suit he was wearing.

He glanced warily her way.

"I like your clothes," she finished.

The look he gave her was meant to kill, and his jaw locked. He urged the team on without responding.

"Ladies." Nick didn't know what was going on. He tipped his hat to them as they drove away. He wondered at his cousin's reaction to Casey's remark about his clothes.

"Bye," Anne called out.

Nick waited a few minutes before broaching the subject.

"I get the feeling you're not too fond of Casey Turner," Nick ventured.

"That would be putting it mildly," Michael answered.

His tone was such that Nick knew better than to ask any more about her.

Casey stood with Anne as they watched the two men drive away.

"Michael certainly looks different now, doesn't he?" Anne observed.

"It's those fancy clothes he had on. He's been away so long, I wonder if he even remembers how to break a bronc or handle a gun."

"Of course, he does," Anne said. "Michael was always good with a gun, and he definitely was one of the best when it came to breaking horses. He hasn't forgotten."

"Well, you couldn't prove it by looking at him."

"I kind of like the way they were dressed," Anne remarked. "They looked so . . ."

"So *what?* Silly?" Casey teased, unwilling to give Michael any slack.

"No, they looked like honest-to-gosh, real gentlemen, just like you said Nick was when we were first talking about him. We don't see many real gentlemen around these parts very often."

"You're right about that, and there's a reason for it. It's probably because they're such dandies they don't last very long out here in the West."

"I hope Michael and his cousin stay on for a while. I'm sure Mrs. Donovan needs all the help she can get."

"I'm sure she does," Casey agreed. She could only imagine how hard it would be to try to run the Bar T without her father's help.

Casey and Anne finished loading the supplies, then Casey started home. She was anxious to let her pa know about Michael's return. Since her pa had been cleared of any involvement in the shooting by the sheriff, she wasn't too worried about any real trouble with the Donovans, but the ill will between the families had always been strong, and judging from Michael's reaction to her, it wasn't ever going to disappear.

"It's Michael!" Elizabeth cried when she heard the sound of a wagon approaching and brushed the curtain aside to look out the bedroom window. "Frank—he's here! And Nick's with him!"

Since the shooting, Frank had been too weak to leave the bed. Elizabeth had been staying by his side in case he needed anything.

Frank opened his eyes, and, for the first time since the shooting, he managed a smile.

"Michael's finally here?" he repeated.

"Yes. I'll go bring him up."

Elizabeth rushed from the bedroom.

Though Michael had been desperate to get home, now

that the moment of their reunion had finally come, he was dreading it. He knew he had to be strong for his parents' sake, but that didn't mean it was going to be easy.

"Nice place," Nick remarked, looking around at the prosperous spread. The house was a large two-story structure with a porch that wrapped around three sides. In the back, there were numerous outbuildings, the stable and a corral.

"Pa's worked hard over the years to build it up."

"Looks like Uncle Frank's done a fine job."

Michael reined in before the house just as his mother came outside. He quickly climbed down from the buckboard and went straight to her, embracing her fiercely.

"You're here! You're really here!" Elizabeth fought back tears as she gazed lovingly up at her son. It seemed an eternity had passed since she'd seen him last.

"Are you all right? How's Pa?"

"I'm fine," Elizabeth answered quickly, "but your father—"

"I heard the truth of what happened in town. I talked to Reverend Harris and the sheriff."

"Then you know about the shooting and his condition."

"Yes."

"He's not doing well." Her tone was solemn. She glanced toward the upstairs bedroom window, then back at Michael.

Michael could only nod. The news was not unexpected.

"Nick, it's good to see you again." She put on a gracious smile as she turned to welcome her nephew.

"It's good to see you, too, Aunt Elizabeth. I just wish the circumstances were different." Nick went to give her a supportive hug.

"So do I," she agreed quietly. "Let's go inside. Michael, your father is anxious to see you."

She led the way into the house and showed Nick to the parlor.

"Make yourself at home," Elizabeth bid.

Nick went into the parlor to wait, while Michael followed his mother upstairs.

Frank turned his head when the bedroom door opened and his wife and son walked in.

"You came—" he managed in a weak voice.

"You knew I would," Michael answered fiercely. Pain filled him at the sight of his father lying so pale and still on the bed. His father had always been a vigorous, powerful man. Michael had never seen him looking weak before.

Frank lifted his hand to him. Michael quickly moved to take it in a firm grip.

"What happened, Pa? Why would anyone do this to you?"

"I don't know, son."

They took comfort in each other's presence, and Michael noted that his father seemed to draw strength from him.

"Will you stay, Michael?" Frank asked. It had always been his hope that Michael would one day return to the Circle D.

"Yes. I'll stay."

"Good. We need you. I need you."

Michael silently offered up thanks that his father had survived the ambush. Though his injuries were traumatic and terrible, it would have been far worse if he had been killed.

Michael couldn't imagine life without his father. Frank Donovan had always been the guiding force in his life.

As Michael stood there holding his hand, he vowed silently from the deepest part of his soul that he would see justice done. He swore to himself that he would stay on at the Circle D for as long as it took to find the one responsible for ambushing his father.

Casey reined in before the house and jumped down from the buckboard. She noticed Ron Maguire's horse tied up at the hitching rail and wondered why the other rancher was there. She hurried inside, anxious to tell her father about Michael Donovan's return.

"Casey, you're back."

"Yes, Pa. Hello, Ron," she greeted him. "I have some news from town."

"Ron has news for us, too," Jack put in before she could go on. "He's moving on."

"You're leaving?" she asked, surprised. The Maguires had lived in the area for as long as she could remember.

"Yes. The last few years have been hard—real hard. There was some rustling going on, and then the drought hit. I didn't have the money to hold on any longer."

"Times have been hard for all of us," Jack agreed.

"Who did you sell out to?" Casey asked.

"John McQueen made me a fair offer, and I decided to take it."

"He's bought up a few of the ranches in the area, hasn't he?" Jack asked, feeling uneasy about the news. He'd never fully trusted McQueen. Something about the man bothered him, but he was never sure exactly what it was.

"Yes, the Royal is getting to be pretty big. I wish him luck. As hard as times are for ranching right now, he's going to need it—just like you are."

"Well, I hope things go better for you, Ron."

Ron shrugged. "I can't say for sure they will, but I can always hope."

"What happened in town, Casey?" her father asked.

"Michael Donovan is back. I saw him! He came in on the stage today."

"You had to figure Michael was going to show up, with Frank being shot and all," Ron said.

"I know," Jack said tersely. He was still angry about being accused of the shooting.

"Well, I'd better be going." Ron shook Jack's hand. "Good luck to you, Jack, and to you, Casey."

Jack tried to smile, but he was going to miss Ron. "You take care of yourself. Where are you headed?"

"Back to Missouri. We've got family there."

Jack walked his friend outside to see him off. He was feeling tense and decidedly uneasy when he came back inside.

"What do you think is going to happen, Pa?" Casey was

worried about the trouble with the Donovans and the news that Ron had been forced to sell out.

Jack didn't want Casey to know how concerned he really was about their situation. He managed a smile as he said, "I can tell you what's not going to happen. I'm not going to sit around here worrying about losing the Bar T. I'm going back to work and make sure we don't."

"I like the way you think." Casey smiled back at him. "Give me a minute to unload the supplies, and I'll be right with you."

Later that evening Michael, Elizabeth and Nick were having dinner in the dining room.

"What does the doctor say about Pa's condition?" Michael asked his mother. "Is there any hope he can make a full recovery?"

"No. None," she answered solemnly. She explained what the doctor had told her about the bullet wound and how it had severely damaged his spine. "Dr. Murray said he might be able to get in a wheelchair one day, but your pa absolutely refuses to even talk about it."

"What do you want to do?" Michael asked gently. "Do you want to stay on here at the Circle D?"

Elizabeth looked up at him, the turmoil of her emotions revealed in her tortured gaze.

"Right now I hate this ranch!" Her words were almost a snarl. "If I had my way, we'd sell out! Now!"

"Will Pa agree to that?"

"No. Never." The fire that had filled her a moment before was gone, extinguished as if it had never existed. "But

I don't know how I'm going to be able to keep things running by myself."

"I'm here," Michael reassured her.

"But for how long?"

"For as long as you need me. I'm not going anywhere."

"And I'm here to help, too," Nick added.

"Thank you." Relief swept through Elizabeth. She took comfort in knowing Michael and Nick would be with her—at least for the time being. Their presence gave her the strength she needed to face the uncertainty of their future.

"I'm going to find out who did this to Pa." Michael's tone was deadly serious. "It won't be easy, but the coward is out there somewhere. I'm not going to give up until he's behind bars."

Chapter Five

Michael awoke early the following morning. He got up and dressed in some of the old work clothes and boots he'd left behind when he'd gone back East. Going to stand at his bedroom window, he watched the sun rise over the Circle D. It was a beautiful sight, and a deep and powerful sense of belonging filled him.

Home.

He was home.

Turning away from the window, he caught sight of his reflection in the mirror over the dresser. He stared at himself, studying the serious, determined-looking cowboy who stared back at him. He found himself wondering if this was who he truly was. In the image, he saw no trace of the man who'd ridden into Hard Luck on the stage yesterday. He left the room, troubled by the thought.

After seeking out Tom at the bunkhouse, Michael returned to the main house to find Nick and his mother eating breakfast.

"I just spoke with Tom, and we're going to ride out to the place where Pa was ambushed so I can take a look around," Michael said as he joined them. "Do you want to ride along, Nick?"

"Yes. I'll go." Nick didn't know if he would be any help, but the ride would give him a chance to see more of the Circle D.

"You be careful out there," Elizabeth cautioned.

"We will be," Michael assured her. He had gotten his six-gun out of the gun case the night before and made sure it was cleaned and ready for action. He would be strapping it on again when they rode out. He planned to be ready in case of trouble.

"Are you good with a gun, Nick?" Elizabeth asked, knowing he'd led a sheltered life in Philadelphia

"No, but I'd like to learn, if Michael has time to teach me."

"I can do that. You're going to need a change of clothes if you're riding out with me," Michael said.

"You don't think I should wear my suit?" Nick asked with a grin.

"Not hardly. Not where we're going."

"Let me see what I can find for you," Elizabeth offered, excusing herself while they finished eating.

"I just hope I can find something there that will help us track down the gunman. There's only one neighbor Pa had any ongoing trouble with, but there's never been any bloodshed between us, and Turner had an alibi for the day."

"Turner?" Nick recognized the name. "As in Casey Turner, the girl in town?"

"She's his daughter," Michael answered flatly.

"That explains it."

"Explains what?"

"The way you reacted to her."

Michael was glad his mother returned just then with the clothes. He didn't want to get into a discussion about Casey.

Nick went upstairs to his room to change.

"Well, what do you think?" Nick asked when he came back down.

Michael and Elizabeth were both startled by the complete change in him. Nick no longer looked the dandy. In the denim pants, workshirt and boots, he could easily have passed for a regular ranch hand.

"You look like you belong here now," Michael told him.

"You think so?"

"Yep. If I didn't know better, I'd say you were born and raised in Texas."

Michael went to the gun case, got out another gun belt and handed it to Nick. "Here. I hope we don't need you to use it, but just in case."

Nick strapped the gun belt on as Michael buckled his, too, then got his hat.

"All you need is a Stetson," Elizabeth said to her nephew, and she handed him a hat.

"Thanks, Aunt Elizabeth." Nick put it on as they left the house.

Tom was waiting out front with horses for them.

"Who's this stranger? I haven't seen this cowboy around these parts before." Tom grinned at Nick, surprised and impressed by the change in him. Michael had brought his cousin out to the bunkhouse the night before to meet all the ranch hands.

"He's just some hand I found wandering around in town," Michael joked. "I hired him on."

"We can always use good help," Tom said, winking as they mounted up.

"We'll be back," Michael promised his mother.

The three men headed for the scene of the ambush.

"What exactly should I be looking for?" Nick asked.

"Anything that will help us find out who shot Pa."

"Is there any way we can be sure that it wasn't just a random act by someone passing through?"

"No. We can't be sure of anything right now, except that I'm not going to give up no matter how long it takes."

Nick studied the Texas countryside with interest as they rode on across the seemingly endless miles. Mesquite trees, Johnson grass and prickly pear cactus dominated the landscape, and in the distance a butte rose up against the horizon.

Tom finally spoke up, breaking the silence. "So, Nick, what do you think of the Circle D?"

"It's big." Nick was impressed by the size of the spread. "I think the Circle D is probably as big as a few of the states back in New England."

"I think you're right," Tom laughed.

"It is one of the largest ranches in this part of the state," Michael added proudly.

"Uncle Frank's done a wonderful job here. Why did you leave?" Nick asked, glancing at his cousin. He had noticed how Michael had begun to change the minute they'd arrived at the ranch. He had returned to his old ranching ways almost effortlessly.

"Mother wanted me to attend the university."

"I'm glad you did, otherwise we wouldn't have known each other as well as we do, but haven't you missed this life?"

Michael was thoughtful as he answered, "I did the first few months, you know that, but then I started to enjoy the life we were leading." He looked around at the open countryside. "I didn't realize how much I'd missed this—until now."

"Michael, some of the men have been wondering: Are you going to stay and take over running things for your pa, or are you planning to head back East again?" Tom asked in his usual forthright manner.

"I'm staying for now," was all he could answer.

"Good. They'll be glad to hear it. They've been uneasy because they didn't know what was going to happen. We didn't know if your mother was going to sell out or if she was going to try to keep things running by herself." Tom was relieved, too. With Michael's return, things were looking better for the Circle D.

They finally reached the site of the ambush. Tom showed them where Frank had been found, and they inspected the area carefully, searching for any clue. Their efforts proved futile, though. They turned up nothing.

Michael was frustrated when they finally gave up and started back to the house. They took a different route this time, riding along the river.

"Did Michael ever tell you how he used to go swimming down here?" Tom asked Nick, wanting to lighten their mood. He ignored the quick warning look Michael shot his way.

"It looks like a good place," Nick agreed. It was private, and the river was cool and clean and slow-running.

"It is a good place—unless someone catches you skinny-dipping," Tom joked.

"You got caught skinny-dipping?" Nick was grinning at Michael. "Who caught you?"

"Go on," Tom urged Michael. "Tell him."

"Casey Turner." Michael was annoyed with Tom for even bringing the subject up. It was one episode in his life he would like to forget.

"Our Casey?" Nick said, his grin broadening as he now understood more fully his cousin's reaction to the girl.

"Yes," he answered tersely.

"You've met Casey?" Tom asked.

"In town," Nick answered. "This story sounds interesting, Michael. I want to know more. What happened?"

"Tom, why don't you tell him, since you're enjoying yourself so much?" Michael said testily.

"Don't mind if I do," Tom went on. "Casey rode up on him while he was swimming. She stole his clothes before he could climb out of the river and stop her. She ran his horse off, too."

"She left you out here naked? No wonder you're not too fond of her." Nick laughed as he remembered Casey's remark about Michael's clothes. "What did you do? How did you get home?"

"It wasn't easy," Michael answered.

"Did you have to walk?"

"He was lucky," Tom explained. "His horse came back to him, but he still had to wait until dark to make the ride home. We were just getting ready to go out looking for him when he rode in."

"I bet everybody was really glad to see you," Nick added, laughing at the image that came to mind.

Michael groaned at his cousin's pitiful attempt at humor.

"They sure were," Tom agreed.

"How long ago did this happen?"

"About five years," Tom offered.

"I knew I liked Casey from the first moment I met her."

"You're a bad judge of character, Nick," Michael countered.

"No, I'm not. Casey Turner is some kind of woman."

"That's putting it mildly," Michael said.

"You have to admit, she's different from your ordinary female," Nick observed.

"There's no doubt about that."

"How did she get to be so wild?"

"Her mother died when she was real young. Her father raised her."

Nick nodded. "So, have you gone swimming here since then?"

"No," Michael answered. "Somehow this place has lost its appeal for me."

"That's a shame. It looks like a good swimming hole."

"Feel free to ride out here and go swimming anytime you want." Michael started to laugh. "Maybe Casey will ride by and find you skinny-dipping."

All three men were laughing as they rode on.

Michael realized it felt good to laugh a little after the tension of the last days. He was frustrated by his lack of success in searching the site of the shooting, but he wasn't ready to give up. He already knew what he was going to do the following day.

They returned to the barn and tended to their horses before going up to the house.

"Did you find anything?" Elizabeth asked when Michael and Nick came in. She'd been waiting anxiously for them.

"No. We checked the entire area, but we didn't find a thing. How much money do we have?" Michael asked.

"We're all right money-wise. Why?"

"Because I know what we need to do next. Tomorrow is Friday. A lot of the boys from the neighboring ranches will be in town for a little rest and relaxation. I want to ride in and spread the word that there is a reward for information leading to the arrest of the person responsible for the shooting."

"How big a reward?"

"A hundred and fifty dollars?" Michael suggested.

"That's fine. We can offer more if we have to."

"Let's start with the hundred and fifty and see what kind of response we get."

Elizabeth went to Michael and hugged him. "I am so glad you're here. I don't know what I'd do without you. If anybody can figure out a way to catch the bushwhacker, you will."

Michael returned his mother's embrace as he shared a determined look with Nick.

"I never thought I'd be back in Hard Luck so soon," Nick remarked as they rode into town late the following day.

"Missed it, did you?"

"The excitement here is hard to resist," he said wryly. "Where did you want to start?"

"I'm going to stop by the sheriff's office and tell him what I plan to do."

"Do you need me with you?"

"No. Why?"

"I was thinking that while you're doing that, I'll stop by the general store and see about buying some clothes."

"Go ahead. I'll meet you there after I talk to the sheriff. Then we can head to the Sundown saloon."

"How many saloons are there?"

"I don't know anymore. We'll find out tonight."

They parted company.

It had been a slow day at the general store. Anne's parents had gone home early, leaving her to close up. She had taken care of all her chores and was sitting behind the counter reading a dime novel as she waited for closing time. The novel was the latest by one of her favorite authors, Sheridan St. John. She loved St. John's stories. They were romantic and exciting. Nothing like her own dull, ordinary life. She was so enraptured with the fictional characters' adventures that she didn't hear Nick come into the store.

"Anne?"

"Oh—" Anne gasped, startled by the interruption. She looked up to find a tall, handsome cowboy standing at the counter. It took her a second to recognize Nick as the gentleman she'd met the other day. "Nick, it's you—" she began, a little flustered.

"Hello, Anne," he said, smiling at her. She was as pretty as he remembered, and he was suddenly very glad he'd come to town with Michael.

"You sure look different today."

"This is a change for me, that's for sure," he agreed. "What do you think? Am I cowboy material?"

"You had me fooled for a minute."

"Is that good or bad?"

"Good, of course."

He found he was pleased with her answer. "I know it's almost closing time, but—"

"No, we're still open. What can I do for you? I just got caught up reading this book and—"

"What are you reading?" Nick was curious.

"It's called *Arizona Captives*, and it's wonderful . . ." She stopped in mid-sentence and blushed when she realized how excited she sounded.

"It's a dime novel?"

"Yes. They're my favorites, and I think Sheridan St. John is the best writer ever."

"I'll have to read one one of these days."

"You've never read a dime novel?"

"No. I've been too busy studying at the university to have any time to read for pleasure, but it's probably time for me to start again."

"You'll enjoy them. Men read them all the time. My father likes these books a lot." Anne realized she was babbling a little, and quickly became more businesslike. "But you didn't come in here to talk about books. What do you need?"

"I need to get some work clothes for out at the ranch. It looks like I'm going to be staying on for a while."

She smiled at the news as she set the book aside. "The men's clothes are over here."

Anne showed him where the men's things were displayed and left him on his own to look around.

It didn't take Nick long to select several shirts and pairs of work pants. He also picked out a black Stetson hat to try on.

"What do you think?" he asked, approaching the counter wearing the Stetson.

Anne looked up from her book and nodded in approval. "I like that one on you. It looks real fine."

"Now that I have all the right clothes and this hat, I can pass for a genuine cowboy."

"Absolutely."

Working efficiently, she totaled up his purchase, and he handed her several bills.

"How are things going out at the Circle D?" Anne asked. "How's your uncle?"

"Uncle Frank is about the same. Michael's going to take over running the ranch for now."

"And what about you? I know you said you were staying—"

"Yes, I'm going to stay for a while in case Michael needs any more help. I've already learned a lot in the short time I've been here, but when it comes to ranch work, there's a lot more I need to know."

"Well, just don't forget how to be a gentleman."

He chuckled. "There's no danger of that."

"Good. Have you heard anything new from the sheriff about the shooting?"

"No. In fact, that's the real reason we came in to Hard Luck tonight. Michael's talking to Sheriff Montgomery right now. When he gets done there, we're going to all the saloons and spread the word that there's a hundred-and-fifty-dollar reward for information about who shot Uncle Frank."

"I hope it helps."

"So do we."

Michael came into the store as Anne finished wrapping Nick's purchases.

"Evening, Anne."

"Hello, Michael. Nick was just telling me about the reward you're offering. Good luck with it."

"Thanks. We could use a little luck right now."

"Sheriff Montgomery didn't know anything new?"

"Nothing. He agreed to put up some posters about our

reward offer, but it looks like if we're going to solve this, we're going to have to do it ourselves."

"Then let's get started." Nick picked up his package. "Thanks, Anne. It was good to see you again."

The two men left the store, intent on their mission.

Anne watched them go. Her gaze lingered on Nick as he fastened his package to the back of his saddle, then mounted up and rode off with Michael.

Anne sighed, mentally comparing the way he'd looked when he arrived in Hard Luck to how he looked today. She wondered what he was really like. She wished Nick could be like one of the romantic heroes in the novels she enjoyed, but she told herself those men were purely fictional. Men like Brand, the half-breed scout, and all the other heroes Sheridan St. John wrote about didn't really exist.

Anne checked the time and began to lock up the store. She could hardly wait to get home so she could finish reading her book.

When Michael and Nick entered the Sundown saloon, Michael was glad to see the place was crowded. The more people who heard what he had to say, the better. He wanted the word to spread as quickly as possible.

They went to stand at the bar.

"Well, well, well," Bill Clark, the bartender, said with a big welcoming smile. "I heard tell you were back in town, and now I know it wasn't just talk."

"How you doing, Bill?" Michael asked, returning his smile.

"I'm doing fine, but what about you?" he asked sympathetically.

"It's rough right now, but things will get better."

"They have to," Bill agreed.

"This is my cousin, Nick, by the way," Michael said, introducing them.

"Nice to meet you. What can I get you boys?"

"Whiskey," they both answered.

"Coming right up."

Rosalie L'Amour, as she called herself, owned and ran the Sundown saloon. A buxom, boisterous woman whose bright red hair was her trademark, she went to greet the newcomers.

"Evening, fellas," she said in her throaty voice. "How are you tonight?"

Michael and Nick turned to her.

"Rosalie, you remember Michael, don't you? Michael Donovan," Bill said. "And this is his cousin, Nick."

"Why, Michael—you've been gone a long time. Welcome home."

"Thank you."

"I wish you were here under better circumstances. How's your pa?"

He quickly told her, then added, "I wanted to spread the word here at the Sundown that my family has decided to offer a reward to help us catch the ones who did this."

"Good idea. Let's see if we can get everybody's attention." She turned to look out at the crowd. "Listen up!"

The piano player immediately stopped playing. Slowly

the noise level dropped until Rosalie was able to make herself heard.

"Michael Donovan's here and he's got something he wants to tell you," she announced. "Go ahead, Michael."

He faced the crowd. "I'm sure by now you've all heard what happened to my father. I'm here to let you know we're offering a reward for information that helps us catch whoever shot and robbed him."

"How much?" someone shouted out from the back of the room.

"A hundred and fifty dollars."

A murmur of surprise at the size of the reward went through the room.

"We're serious about this—real serious. If you know anything, anything at all, get in touch with us out at the Circle D or let Sheriff Montgomery know. Any help you can give us, we'd appreciate."

"Can I turn in old Murphy here and get the reward?" one drunk called out.

"It's got to be the guilty one." Rosalie laughed at the man.

"Thanks, Rosalie," Michael said, turning back to the bar to take a drink of whiskey.

"If I hear any talk, I'll let you know," she promised.

"You might want to watch for a gold money clip that has the Circle D brand on it. It was taken with the money when Pa was robbed."

"I'll keep an eye out."

John McQueen had been playing cards at a table in the

back of the room. When the hand was over, he got up to speak to Michael.

"It's been a long time," John said, shaking Michael's hand.

"That it has." Michael introduced the rancher to Nick.

"So the sheriff hasn't found anything yet?"

"Nothing. It's frustrating for us."

"Let me know if I can help out in any way."

"Thanks. I will."

Michael and Nick finished their drinks and left the Sundown to go to another saloon in town.

John went back to his card game, satisfied with what he'd learned.

Sid Midland was sitting across the table from him. "I take it they're not having any luck finding out who shot Frank Donovan."

"That's right," McQueen answered. "They're desperate."

"Pity," Sid said, trying not to smile.

Chapter Six

Philadelphia

Karen Whittington put aside all feelings of shame as her carriage pulled up before the Padens' town house. It had been weeks, and she had had no word from Michael. She was as angry as she was worried about what might have happened to him on his trip to Texas. Desperate to know how he was and when he was planning to return, she'd made up her mind to go straight to Nick's father for answers.

When the carriage stopped, the driver helped her down, and Karen hurried up the steps to knock on the front door.

"Miss Whittington—can I help you?" the maid asked, surprised to see the beautiful young woman standing there. She knew Michael had courted the lovely, arrogant blonde when he'd been in residence with them, but he and Nick had been in Texas for some time now.

"I need to speak with Mr. Paden," Karen replied in her most haughty tone.

"Come in. I'll let him know you're here," the maid said, holding the door wide to admit her.

Karen swept inside.

The maid directed her to have a seat in the parlor, then went to get James Paden. He appeared in the parlor doorway moments later.

"Karen, to what do I owe this honor?" James was a bit taken aback that the young woman would come so boldly to his home unchaperoned.

"I need your help."

"Of course, my dear. What can I do for you?" he said, taking a seat across from her.

"Have you heard anything from Nick or Michael? I've been so worried about them."

James knew exactly whom she was worried about, and it wasn't Nick. He smiled gently at her as he answered, "I did receive a telegram from Nick when they reached Hard Luck, letting me know they had arrived and would be heading out to Michael's ranch."

"So they got there safely." She was relieved to know that much, at least.

"Yes. It sounded as though things were as good as they could be, considering the circumstances."

"Did Nick give you any idea when they'd be coming back?"

"I'm afraid not. This is a most difficult time for Michael's family, so I'm sure they will be there for a while, helping out in any way they can."

Karen managed a sympathetic smile, but her frustration ran deep. It had been hard enough for her to accept that Michael had been leaving for Europe without her, but this sudden emergency at his family's ranch truly troubled her. What if he never came back? She was still upset that he had left town without even bothering to tell her good-bye in person. The short message he'd sent had been delivered to her by one of the Padens' servants. He'd written only that his father had been injured and he was needed at home and would be in touch with her later.

Karen had thought she meant something to Michael, but all this time had passed and she hadn't heard a word. Learning now that Mr. Paden knew more than she did, she felt a bit insulted.

"Is there any way to contact Michael?"

"The ranch is the Circle D, and it's outside of Hard Luck, Texas. You could write him a letter or send a wire to him there."

"Well, thank you for your time." Karen kept her tone cordial though she was seething inside.

She stood up, and James showed her out of the house.

Karen's driver was waiting, and he helped her back into the carriage. As they drove away, Karen was already planning what she would do next. She made up her mind that if she didn't hear personally from Michael in the next week, she was going to take matters into her own hands.

She was going to go to Texas.

A smile curved her lips as she imagined making the trip

to his ranch to surprise him. It would certainly be the most outrageous and daring thing she'd ever done, but she knew the prize of marrying Michael was worth the risk.

Jack glared at Allen Foster, the bespectacled, balding bank president, as he sat across the desk from him in his office.

"What do you mean my loan isn't in good standing, Foster?" Jack demanded. "I just made a payment."

"You owe the bank a lot more, Jack. I don't see how you're going to be able to pay it off. The way things are going for you, I may have to call in your loan."

"What are you talking about? You can't do that!"

"Yes, I can," Foster said with calm deliberation. "Any time there's a perceived risk—"

"The Bar T is not a risk. We may not be the biggest ranch around, but we've got the best water in the whole county. You know that!"

"That's all well and good, but if you're not bringing in enough money to pay off your debts, there's no saving you."

"Don't you worry, Foster. You'll get your damned money," Jack gritted out furiously.

"I'm counting on that, Jack. I can give you a month."

"A month?" Jack reacted without thought. He leaped to his feet and reached across the desk to grab the banker by his shirt front. "You low-down, pencil-pushing son of a—"

"All right, all right! Two months! But no more!" Foster

gasped, frightened by this sudden display of fury. He'd never known Jack to be so violent before.

Jack shoved him back down in his chair in disgust.

"You'll get your money, Foster," he snarled, and turned to leave the bank. Somehow, some way, he had to get the money to pay back the bank. The only problem was he had no idea how he was going do it.

Jack stopped and stood for a moment on the sidewalk, staring blindly about himself, trying to decide what to do. The thought of a strong shot of whiskey appealed, so he headed for the Sundown saloon. He had some deep thinking to do. There was so much at stake, and he had so little time.

"How did it go?" John McQueen asked Foster when he met with him at the bank an hour later.

"I don't know if your plan will work or not. Turner was more than a little angry when he left here."

"Keep the pressure on him. I'll take care of the rest."

Satisfied with the work Foster was doing, John left the bank. Keeping the banker secretly on his payroll was one of the smartest things he'd ever done. He was very pleased with himself as he went in search of Jack Turner.

It didn't take John long to find Jack at the bar in the Sundown.

"Afternoon, Jack," he greeted him casually as he went to stand beside him.

Jack slanted him a sidelong glance as he took another deep drink of his whiskey. "Hello, McQueen."

John ordered a whiskey, too. "Life been treating you good?"

"Can't complain," he answered tersely, just wishing the other man would go away.

"Sounds like you're luckier than most. What with Donovan being ambushed and Maguire having to sell out, times are pretty hard around here."

"Seems that way."

"I wonder what the world's coming to."

"I don't know, and I don't worry about it. I just try to keep the Bar T running."

"The Bar T is a fine ranch."

"That's true. I heard you bought out Maguire."

"Yes, I did. You ever think about selling?"

"No."

John had known Jack would be tough. "I heard talk that you might be having some money problems."

Jack looked at him sharply. "Where'd you hear that?"

"Word gets around," he replied easily. "If you ever change your mind about selling, I'll make you a fair offer for the place."

"It doesn't matter what kind of offer you make me. The Bar T isn't for sale." His instinctive mistrust of McQueen was growing even stronger.

"Well, think about it," John insisted.

"I don't have to think about it. I told you, the answer is no."

John was angry with the old fool, but he kept smiling. "If you change your mind, you know where you can find me."

"That isn't going to happen, McQueen."

Jack hadn't been ready to quit drinking and leave yet, but McQueen's presence drove him from the bar. He quickly downed the rest of his whiskey and walked out.

The ride home was a long one.

It was a beautiful day. The sun was shining, but Jack didn't notice. He was too deeply lost in thought. He had to find a way to save the ranch.

Pain ate at him, gnawing at his insides. He tried to ignore it. He reined in as he topped the low rise that overlooked the house and took a moment to study the scene below.

It was almost sundown. The Bar T looked peaceful in the deepening shadows, almost heavenly to him.

Jack told himself he'd withstood hard times before and he could do it again. After his wife Emily's untimely death when Casey had been a young girl, he had almost given up. But the Bar T had meant so much to Emily that he'd been inspired to work even harder, to make the ranch a success in her memory.

Jack remembered other bad times, of rustling and drought. He'd had run-ins with the Donovans, too, but through it all, he'd kept working, believing he would succeed. Now, for the first time, he was deeply worried. He had to find a way to get the cash he needed to pay off the bank, and he needed to do it fast.

Jack rode on up to the ranch house, his pace slow.

Casey saw him coming and came outside to meet him.

"How were things in town?" she asked as he dismounted.

He had been debating how much he should tell her, and he realized he couldn't hide it from her much longer. "We've got some trouble."

"Trouble? What kind of trouble?"

"Foster's pressuring me to pay off the bank loan."

"Have we got the money?" She could tell by his manner just how serious the situation was.

"No."

"What are we going to do?"

"I ran into McQueen in town. He offered to buy us out—"

"We aren't selling," she interrupted him.

"That's what I told him." Jack was grim.

"Good. We'll figure something out. I'll go over the books again and see if I can find some extra money somewhere." She'd been doing their book work for the last few years. She'd known their funds were tight, but she'd never dreamed the bank would call in their loan so unexpectedly.

Jack was glad Casey was confident. He just wished he was as certain as she was about it. Unfortunately, the only thing he was certain about was how bad he felt.

"Are you ready for dinner?"

"No, I'm tired. I think I'll go rest for a while and eat later."

"I'll take care of your horse," Casey offered. She took up the reins and led the horse off to the stable.

Jack watched her for a moment, then went inside. He'd expected the pain he'd tolerated on the ride back to ease once he'd gotten home, but it had only intensified.

He tried to make it to his bedroom to lie down.

The pain hit harder, tearing through him, ripping at his left side—his arm—his chest.

Jack had never known such agony.

He gritted his teeth against the stabbing pain as sweat beaded his brow. He fought for control, but swayed unsteadily on his feet and feared for the first time that he truly might be dying.

Worry about Casey and who would take care of her consumed him.

Without him, she would be all alone in the world.

"Casey—" He tried to call her name, but it came out only in a hoarse whisper.

Jack grabbed the back of the sofa to support himself. He was too weak, though.

Blackness overwhelmed him.

He collapsed, unconscious, to the floor.

Chapter Seven

"You're lucky you're alive," Dr. Murray told Jack as he stood over him where he lay in bed.

"It's that bad?"

"Yes. It's your heart."

Jack met the doctor's gaze unflinchingly. "I want the truth, Doc. Tell me—how long have I got?"

"I'd be God if I could answer that question. The truth is, Jack, with a condition like yours, there is no way of knowing. It could be tomorrow or it could be six months from now—"

Jack's physical pain was gone for now, but a different agony filled him. He'd never faced the truth of his own mortality before.

"Don't tell Casey any of this. What happened today has already been too much of a shock for her."

"She needs to know the truth."

"I'll tell her when the time is right," Jack insisted. "You've got to promise me—"

"All right. I'll respect your wishes—for now. Just get some rest. In a day or two, you can start moving around. See how your strength holds up."

"When can I get back to work?"

"Jack, your condition is serious," Dr. Murray said worriedly.

"I have a ranch to run."

"You can't very well run it if you drop dead, now can you? You have to give yourself time to regain some strength."

"All right," Jack agreed, just to shut the doctor up. He had some serious thinking to do, and he wanted him gone.

"I'll check back in on you in a few days."

"Thanks."

Dr. Murray went to speak with Casey, leaving Jack by himself.

Jack was deeply troubled. The doctor had made it plain he could go at any time, and he was worried about what would happen to Casey if he died. With the Bar T in such a bad way financially, there would be no one to take care of her.

Jack knew she'd be furious with him if she were aware of his thoughts. Casey believed she was the equal of any man. She believed she could take care of herself, and she wasn't shy about letting everyone know it.

Still, Jack wished Casey had a man in her life—a husband who could take over for him at the ranch. Regret filled Jack that he hadn't encouraged her to be more feminine, but she'd shown no interest in those things while growing up. She'd always preferred working with horses and stock than attending the socials in town.

Jack grew desperate as he thought of Casey trying to repay the bank on her own. His desperation turned to determination. He had to find a way to make sure she was protected and to save the Bar T. With no close relatives to step in and take charge, there was only one solution.

He had to find Casey a husband who had money—and he had to do it fast.

The doctor had said he might die tomorrow or he might die in six months. Jack knew he didn't have a minute to waste.

He thought of the men around town. Casey had had a few suitors, but she hadn't taken any of them seriously. Young Al Burke, who worked in the telegraph office, fancied her, but she had only tolerated his attentions.

Jack lay there, trying to think of a man who could love his daughter for the woman she was, one who was strong enough to keep up with her, and who had money.

Time was of the essence.

Jack knew that if he died before he got Casey married, she would be left penniless. He realized, too, that convincing her to marry was not going to be easy. He just hoped that once he explained that her marriage would save the ranch, she would go along with it.

All he had to do was find the right man.

A great weariness overcame Jack.

He closed his eyes.

"Your father is doing as well as can be expected, Casey, but his condition is serious," Dr. Murray told her quietly as he sat with her in the parlor. "It's his heart."

Casey was still in shock from what had happened. When she'd returned from the stable and found her father unconscious on the floor in the parlor, his coloring had been so ashen, she'd feared he was dead.

"He's going to live, isn't he?" she asked, voicing the question that was haunting her.

"Yes," he answered, keeping Jack's confidence.

"Thank God." Tears of relief welled up in her eyes. She couldn't imagine life without her father.

"Now, I've told him to take it easy for a while, and I want you to make sure he rests up."

"I will."

"Good. I'll come back in a few days to make sure he's doing all right."

She showed him out of the house. "Thank you, Dr. Murray."

As Dr. Murray got in his carriage and started back toward Hard Luck, he thought the town's name was all too apt. A lot of bad things had been happening to good people. First, Frank Donovan had been shot, and now Jack Turner with his bad heart . . . He'd heard, too, that Ron Maguire had sold out and left the area. Things were changing, and he wasn't sure they were changing for the better.

* * *

Casey went to her father's room to check on him. He was sleeping peacefully and there was some color in his face now. She breathed a sigh of relief as she settled into a chair beside the bed. She planned to spend the night there, just in case he awoke and needed her.

When Jack awoke early the following morning, he found Casey asleep in the chair beside the bed. He took a moment to study her as she slept on, admiring the soft curve of her cheek and her flawless complexion. Her hair was a tumble of untamed curls—untamed just like she was, he thought, and his smile was bittersweet.

Again the thought of finding a suitable husband for her returned, and his smile turned to a frown. None of the bachelors in town had enough money to save the ranch.

Jack started trying to think of other single men in the area who had money, and John McQueen came to mind. As quickly as he thought of him, he rejected the idea. McQueen might have money, but Jack had seen the way the man looked at Casey and there was no way he wanted him anywhere near his daughter.

There was the widower Charles Barnhart, who owned a spread on the far side of town. He had cash, but he was going on sixty, far too old for Casey.

Casey needed someone she could come to care for. Someone she could eventually—he hoped—come to love.

Growing more desperate by the minute, Jack realized the only other rancher around who had money was Frank

Donovan. His frown deepened as he was lost deep in thought.

Desperate times did call for desperate measures, and—

Michael Donovan was back in town.

Jack cursed silently. He was furious that he was reduced to even considering going to Frank for help.

Jack looked at Casey again.

Maybe it was time to make peace—for Casey's sake.

All anger left him as he gazed lovingly at his sleeping daughter. Nothing was more important to him than she was. If that meant he had to put aside the animosity he'd held toward Frank all these years, he'd do it.

For a moment, the very real fear struck Jack that Frank might reject his offer. Jack knew he had to somehow convince his old enemy that uniting the ranches was in their best interests—that it was the only way to save both ranches. If Donovan didn't agree to his plan, he would be forced to sell out—probably to McQueen. Given the chance, Jack suspected McQueen might try to cut off the water supply to the Circle D—the water supply the two ranches now shared.

Jack hoped that argument would convince Frank to go along with him.

He was dying. He didn't have any time to waste.

Chapter Eight

Jack grew more and more tense with each passing mile. After making his decision to seek out Frank Donovan, he'd had to wait a full day before he could muster enough strength to leave the house. Dealing with the weakness had angered him, and now, as he drove his buckboard toward the Circle D, even that short delay worried him.

Time was of the essence.

Casey had ridden out with the hands early that morning, so no one knew where he was going, and that was fine with Jack. He'd promised her that he would stay at the house and rest, so as long as he returned before she did, everything would be fine. This meeting with Frank had to be private, strictly between the two of them—for now.

Jack wasn't sure what kind of reception he would get at the Circle D. It wouldn't be a warm one, that was for sure, since the sheriff had thought he was the one who'd ambushed Frank. Still, as difficult as it was for him to swallow his pride and go there, Jack had no choice. The upcoming visit might be humiliating, but he didn't even consider turning back. Casey's future was too important to him.

When the Circle D ranch house finally came in sight, Jack girded himself for what was to come.

Frank was in his bed, braced up against the headboard, staring out his bedroom window at the countryside. It was a beautiful day. The sun was shining in a cloudless blue sky.

Frank longed to be off riding with his men. He wanted to be out working the stock, living the life he loved. Instead, he was trapped inside the house in a body that was broken and would never work again.

His mood alternated between anger and despair—anger that this had happened to him and no one knew who'd done it or why, and despair because the future stretched so bleakly before him. He tried to push his dark thoughts away. Logically, he knew there was no sense in dwelling on what he could not change. He had to find a way to deal with his life the way it was now. If he could have been certain Michael was going to stay on permanently at the ranch, he would have felt better about the future of the Circle D. As it was, the uncertainty haunted him.

A buckboard came into view in the distance, heading up the road to the house. Frank wondered who was coming to pay them a visit. Dr. Murray wasn't due back until the end of the week. When the buckboard drew nearer and Frank was finally able to make out the driver, he was shocked to find it was Jack Turner. Frank was instantly wary. He was sure Jack hadn't come out of concern for his health or to pay him a social call. Something was going on.

As Jack drove up in front of the house, Frank lost sight of him. He waited tensely to see what was going to happen. It wasn't long before a knock came at the door.

"Frank?" Elizabeth called out as she came into the room to speak with him.

"What is Turner doing here?" he demanded before she could say another word.

"You saw him drive up?" Elizabeth had been as surprised as her husband by the neighboring rancher's appearance. The enmity between them was long-standing.

"You're damned right I saw him. What does he want?"

"He wants to speak privately with you. I told him I'd have to see if you were up to seeing anybody this morning."

"Where's Michael?" He wanted his son with him when he faced Jack.

"He and Nick rode out earlier with the men. I don't expect him back any time soon."

Frank looked around himself in disgust. The last thing he wanted to do was appear weak before Jack Turner, but short of having one of the hands carry him downstairs to the study, he was trapped. The thought that anyone had to carry him anywhere filled him with rage, but there was nothing he could do about it. He'd stay put. Jack Turner could come to him.

"Help me get a shirt on."

Elizabeth quickly helped Frank take off his pajama top and don a shirt.

"All right. Bring him up."

She went down to the parlor where Jack was waiting.

"Frank is ready to see you now."

"Thank you, Elizabeth." Jack followed her up the stairs.

Elizabeth let him in, then told her husband, "If you need me, just call."

Jack stepped quietly into the bedroom.

She closed the door, leaving the two longtime adversaries alone.

Frank glared at Jack. "What the hell are you doing here, Turner? What do you want?" he demanded aggressively.

"I need to talk to you." Jack had known this wasn't going to be easy. The sight of the once strong and powerful Frank Donovan sitting unmoving in his bed reminded Jack of his own vulnerability and mortality.

"About what?"

"About the Bar T." A sudden wave of weakness washed over Jack. He hated to look weak before Donovan, but after his collapse the other day, he had no choice. He asked, "You mind if I sit down?"

"Go ahead," Frank told him, indicating a chair by the bed. He eyed him warily, not trusting him. Jack never did anything without a reason, and he wondered what he was up to.

"First—I'm sorry about what happened to you."

"You think I believe that?"

"Believe what you want, but it's true."

"Being sorry don't change a damned thing."

"I know, but, Frank, as much as we've been at odds over the years, I didn't have anything to do with the ambush. It wasn't me."

Frank believed him, but that didn't change the way he felt about the other man. He continued to glare at Jack. "So what's going on? I know you want something or you wouldn't be here."

"There's trouble coming," Jack began.

"Trouble?" Frank repeated sharply, wondering how things could get any worse for him than they were already.

"That's right. There's trouble ahead for both the Bar T and the Circle D, unless we can work something out—together."

"Us? Work together?" Frank looked at him as if he were mad.

"That's right," Jack repeated, hating the idea as much as Frank did. "You think I like being here? You think I wanted to come to you? I didn't, but I had no choice. Frank"—he looked his enemy straight in the eye—"I'm dying."

"What?" Frank was shocked.

"It's my heart. Dr. Murray says I don't have long to live." Jack had never said it out loud before. He drew a slow, ragged breath before continuing, "That's why I came to see you."

"What's your being sick got to do with me?"

"I need to make sure some things are taken care of before . . ."

"Just what do you want to take care of?"

"Casey. If I die and she loses the ranch—"

"Why would she lose the ranch?"

Reluctantly, Jack was forced to explain his financial situation to Frank.

"Foster said he'd give me two more months, but that's all. And I don't think I can raise that kind of money, so fast. Even if I could, how could I protect Casey? I have to make sure someone is looking out for her after I'm gone."

"Why don't you just sell the ranch?"

"No," he answered fiercely. "Never. McQueen's already made me an offer—"

"John McQueen?" Frank was instantly alert. The other rancher had made him an offer, too, some months back. He hadn't been about to sell out to anyone, but there was something about McQueen he didn't trust.

"That's right. Did you know he bought out Ron Maguire?"

"No. I hadn't heard that."

"He did, and now he's trying to buy the Bar T, but I don't want to sell to him. I don't want to sell to anyone. Casey loves the Bar T. The ranch is her whole life. That's why I came to you."

"What do you want from me?"

"Do you know what could happen if McQueen gets hold of the Bar T? He could cut off your water supply. How long can you last without water."

"He wouldn't do that."

"You want to bet? I've got a feeling he will—if he gets the chance. But I don't intend to give him that chance. That's why I came here—to you. I want to make a deal—a deal that will protect us both."

"You want me to buy you out?"

"No. Look at you. I may not have long to live, but you might as well be dead already," Jack pointed out harshly. "You can't run the Circle D the way you used to. How would you run both ranches?"

"Why, you—" Anger surged within Frank at Jack's brutal words.

"Shut up and listen to me. I have a plan that can save us both."

"I don't need you to save me from anything, Turner."

Jack had feared he would react this way—that the hatred and mistrust between them would never end. Now, it seemed they would both ultimately be destroyed by it.

"All right. You've just proved to me that you're as stupid as I always thought you were." Jack got to his feet to go. "I'll leave. Enjoy your life. Just remember—you were warned."

He started from the bedroom, his mood despairing as he faced the devastating truth of his future.

"I don't like threats," Frank ground out.

"I wasn't threatening you." Jack looked back at him. "I'm just telling you what I know. You've got Michael back with you now, but once I'm gone, Casey will be left all alone. I thought I had a plan that would protect our ranches, but since you're not interested—"

"Why do you care about my ranch?"

"I don't care about you or your ranch," Jack snarled bluntly. "I care about my daughter."

"What's your plan?" Frank interrupted him.

"You're willing to listen?"

"Start talking."

Jack faced him fully. "It's simple. All you have to do is convince Michael to marry Casey."

"What?" Frank stared at him in complete shock.

"You heard me. It's the only way. United, our ranches will prosper, otherwise . . ."

"Michael and Casey married? That's crazy."

"You think so?"

"I know so. There's a simpler way. If you're in such deep financial trouble, sell the Bar T to me."

"No. I told you before, I don't want to sell."

"No?" Frank couldn't believe Jack had turned him down.

"That's right," Jack went on. "I have to make sure Casey is protected."

"From what I understand, your daughter is perfectly capable of taking care of herself."

"I'm sure she thinks so, too, but you and I both know the ways of the world. She'll be one woman, all alone."

"How does Casey feel about your trying to marry her off this way?" Frank knew the outspoken young hellion wouldn't appreciate her father's interference.

"She doesn't know I'm here. This is strictly between you and me for now. I haven't even told her the truth about my health, and I'm not going to. She knows I've been ill, but she doesn't know how bad it really is."

"If she doesn't know, how can you expect her to go along with the marriage?"

"Casey will do anything to save the Bar T."

"Even marry Michael?"

Jack ignored his question. "What about Michael? Is he back here to stay? Does he care enough about you and the Circle D to—"

"Marry your daughter?" Frank remembered the run-in Michael had had with her down at the river. "Honestly, after what happened between them in the past, I don't think he's too fond of her."

"This isn't about the past," Jack said somberly, meeting Frank's gaze again. "It's about the future—the future of the Bar T and the Circle D. Think about what I've said. I don't have much time, and I can't say anything to Casey until I know what you're willing to do."

Frank said nothing more. He was lost in thought.

Jack turned and let himself out. He drove away slowly, still unsure of what the future held.

Chapter Nine

"You want me to do what?" Michael stared at his father in disbelief as he faced him in his bedroom later that afternoon.

"You heard me. You have to marry Casey Turner."

"You can't be serious."

"I've never been more serious in my life," Frank said somberly and explained everything Jack had told him.

"It makes more sense for you to buy the Bar T."

"Not to Jack. He's worried about his daughter."

"He should be," Michael remarked sarcastically. "Surely they've got a relative somewhere who would take her in."

"No, they've got no other family. When he dies, she'll be left on her own."

"Somehow, I think Casey will be able to take care of herself."

"Jack doesn't. He wants to make sure she's protected. With no close relatives to rely on, getting her married off before he dies is the only way."

"This is ridiculous. Tell him to find somebody else. I don't want anything to do with her." Michael couldn't believe what his father was asking of him.

"Michael—" his mother put in gently. She'd been sitting quietly in the room with them, listening to their exchange. "Your father wouldn't ask this of you unless he thought there was no other way. If John McQueen gains control of the Bar T and cuts off our water . . ."

Michael looked between his parents and suddenly realized how serious the situation was.

"I'll be back later," he told them.

He needed time to think. Without another word he strode from the bedroom.

Nick was waiting for him in the parlor, but Michael didn't stop to speak with him. He just called out that he'd see him later as he left the house. Getting his horse from the stable, he rode off, desperate for time alone.

Michael spurred his horse to a gallop. He raced mindlessly across the miles of Donovan land. When he finally reined in, he was on a hilltop that overlooked the boundary of the Circle D and the Bar T. He sat there, staring out across the countryside.

When he had come back home, he had not intended to stay forever. He'd believed his future was in the East.

Until now.

Finally in that moment, Michael acknowledged to himself that he loved this land. His love for the Circle D was real. It was a part of him that could not be denied.

As the reality of his feelings took hold, he accepted full responsibility for the ranch's survival. Success rested on his shoulders. He would make whatever sacrifice was necessary to keep the Circle D going.

He wondered again if there was any way to protect the ranch without agreeing to the marriage, but he already knew the answer. Jack Turner was a hard man, a proud man. Just the fact that he had come to the Circle D to speak with his father showed how desperate he was. Michael knew that if he refused to marry Casey, Jack would probably sell to McQueen just to spite them.

Marry Casey.

Michael thought of the wild young woman and frowned. He couldn't even begin to imagine what being married to her would be like. She was a wildcat—a troublemaker—an untamed female, and it was going to be up to him to tame her.

Man that he was, Michael accepted what he had to do.

To save the Circle D, he would go through with the marriage to Casey Turner.

Jack was exhausted as he ate dinner with Casey that evening. The trip to the Circle D had worn him out, and he was nervous as he awaited Frank's answer.

Jack was tempted not to say a word to Casey about his plan until he had heard something, but he knew that wasn't fair.

He had to warn her.

He had to tell her what he'd done.

Jack looked up at his daughter and girded himself for what was to come. He was certain her reaction wasn't going to be pretty. He was glad she was so busy wolfing down her food like a starving ranch hand that she was unaware of his scrutiny.

He took the time to study her. After a day of riding and roping, Casey was as dirty and unkempt as any of the men. When she washed her hair and took a bath, she did look a little like her mother—God rest his beloved Emily's soul. Right now, though, Casey bore little resemblance to the beautiful young woman he knew she had the potential to be.

"Casey," Jack began, for the time had come.

"Yeah, Pa?" She kept eating as she looked up at him.

"We need to talk. It's important."

Casey was instantly alert. "Are you feeling all right?"

"This isn't about me—It's about you."

"Me?"

"That's right. There's something you need to know—something I've done."

"I don't understand." She stopped eating to stare at him.

"I didn't figure you would." Jack was hedging, trying to avoid the explosion that was coming. "There may be some big changes in our future."

"You're not thinking of selling the ranch, are you?"

"No. No."

"Good. I can keep the place going. I know I can, and I've been thinking of ways to come up with the money in time to pay off the bank loan."

"That's exactly what I have to tell you. I've already figured out a way to do it."

"You have?"

"That's right, and if everything turns out the way I hope it will, the Bar T will be safe."

"What's your plan? Can I help?"

"Oh, yes. I will need your help. That's for sure." Jack drew a deep breath.

"What do you need me to do? Name it. I'm ready." Casey was eager to do whatever was necessary.

"While you were working today, I went to see Frank Donovan."

Casey stared at him as if he were crazy. "What? You promised me you were going to rest like the doctor ordered! Are you trying to kill yourself?"

"No."

"Then why would you go see Donovan?"

"Because making a deal with him is the only thing that's going to save us."

"What? You made a deal with Donovan?" She was shocked. "Things are that bad?"

"Yes. They are that bad," he told her in the gentlest voice he could use. "And if Donovan doesn't go along with my idea, we will lose everything."

"No, we won't! There's a lot I can do! I told you I was making plans," she insisted, blindly refusing to accept the inevitable. "We are not going to lose the Bar T! We can try to sell horses to the cavalry. They might be interested."

"Casey, listen to me," he interrupted her. "I know you work hard here. I know you love the Bar T, but we both know the ranch has gone through some rough times lately. We never had a lot of money to begin with. We never needed it. Somehow we always made do, but things have changed now. With the bank pressuring us for such a quick repayment, I had to do something drastic. The plan I've suggested to Frank Donovan will help both us and the Circle D."

"Why would you suddenly start trusting Frank Donovan after all these years?" she demanded in a worried tone.

"I had no choice." He paused and looked up at her. "I had to make sure you were going to be protected."

"What are you talking about?"

"I'm worried about your future. After I was ill the other day, I realized how terrible things would be for you if I wasn't here."

"I can take care of myself."

"Not if you're left homeless with no family."

"That's not going to happen."

"You're right. It's not going to happen, because I've made a deal with Donovan. If everything works out the way I hope it will, you'll be taken care of no matter what happens to me."

"What's going to happen to you?" She gave him a worried look, wondering if there was something more she should know about his health. When he'd gotten up and started moving around so soon, she'd thought he was doing all right.

Jack quickly covered his slip. "Nothing is going to happen to me, but I've started to worry about these things, just in case."

"Well, I wish you wouldn't."

"I have to, and that's why I met with Frank Donovan."

The moment had finally arrived.

There was no way to avoid it any longer. He had to tell her. Jack met his daughter's gaze straight on.

"I talked to Frank Donovan, and I told him I wanted Michael to marry you."

Marry Michael Donovan!

Casey was shocked to the depths of her soul.

"You didn't."

She wanted him to deny it.

She prayed he would deny it.

"I did. With the two of you married, the ranches will be united," he confirmed. "Frank is talking to Michael right now. We'll have his answer, one way or another, real soon."

"You offered me up to Michael Donovan? Just like a steer at market?" Casey demanded in outrage.

"I did what I had to do to protect you—and to save the Bar T. It was the only way."

"Surely there's something else we can do," she raged in utter humiliation.

Marry Michael Donovan?

"Casey—"

He spoke her name so solemnly that she grew silent and lifted her troubled gaze to his.

"There was no other way. Believe me, if there was I would have done it. A marriage between you and Michael is the only way to insure we won't lose the Bar T."

"We can't lose the ranch."

"We will, unless—"

"I marry Michael," she finished flatly.

The thought of marrying anyone bothered her, but the prospect of marrying Michael Donovan was almost frightening to Casey, and she didn't scare easily.

"Michael will never marry me. He hates me," she said with what little confidence she could muster. She remembered their encounter in town and knew that the animosity between them had not faded during his time away from Hard Luck. She swallowed nervously.

"I guess we'll find out soon enough. If Michael agrees to the marriage, I am going to make sure you retain title to the Bar T. That way I know you will always be protected."

"I don't need the Donovans to protect me," she scoffed, angry over being perceived as so defenseless. "I don't need anybody to protect me. I know how to use a gun."

"Casey, I understand how you feel about the Donovans. Granted, I've had no use for them for years, but there is one thing about Frank—he's smart. He knows a good deal when he hears one. If he wants control of the water on the Bar T, he'll find a way to convince Michael to marry you."

Convince Michael to marry you.

Her father's words hurt.

Casey was no romantic. She'd never harbored any dream of a romantic wedding, but she'd never imagined that the man she married would have to be "convinced" to go through with the ceremony, either. She had always thought she would be in love with the man she wed, but there was one thing she knew for sure. She didn't love Michael, and Michael harbored no love for her in his heart.

"How could you even think I'd marry Michael?" she asked, her emotions in turmoil. She thought of the way he'd looked when she'd seen him in town. He was a dandy now, a dude. He probably wasn't even going to stay on his father's ranch. He was probably going back East with his cousin just as soon as he could. He wouldn't marry her.

Pain filled Jack as he saw Casey's distress. He had to convince her that this would be for the best.

"Listen to me, child," he insisted. "There is nothing unusual about an arranged marriage. If the two of you do get wed, it will benefit you both. You love the Bar T, don't you?"

When she didn't answer, he repeated himself.

"Casey—you don't want to lose the ranch, do you?"

"No," she said tightly. A part of her accepted her fate, but there remained a glimmer of hope within her that Michael would refuse to go along with their fathers' plan. "How soon do you think we'll hear something from them?"

"Soon—very soon."

Casey said no more as she got up from the table. Unease gripped her. Her appetite was gone. She wanted nothing more than to be left alone with her thoughts.

Retiring to her room, she washed up and got ready for bed, but sleep eluded her. She lay there thinking of Michael, picturing him as he'd looked when she'd seen him in town and remembering the man he'd been before he'd gone back East.

Casey wondered where Michael was and what he was thinking at this moment. She wondered if he was as upset as she was. When she finally drifted off, her sleep was troubled.

Michael handed Nick the tumbler of bourbon he'd just poured him as they settled in the study late that evening.

"So you are serious about this." Nick couldn't believe what Michael had just revealed to him.

"Yes."

"You're really going to marry Casey Turner," Nick repeated.

"That's right." Michael took a deep drink of his liquor.

"What about Karen?"

Michael frowned as conflicting images of Casey and the beautiful, sophisticated Karen played in his mind. "What about her?"

"I thought you were serious about her, and I think she thought so, too."

"I'm sure Karen won't have any trouble finding someone to replace me." Michael had enjoyed her company. There had been a few times when he'd considered a deeper relationship with the debutante, but not anymore.

"This should prove to be very interesting," Nick said with a smile. He lifted his glass in a toast. "Here's to you and your future bride."

"Will you stay and be my best man?"

"I'd be honored. I wouldn't miss this wedding for the world."

Nick was tempted to ask his cousin if he thought Casey would wear her pants to their wedding, but he didn't. He actually found he was impressed by Michael's determination to do whatever was necessary to help his family.

Considering how Michael had reacted when he'd seen Casey in town when they'd first arrived in Hard Luck, Nick knew their relationship was going to be tumultuous and challenging.

He silently wished his cousin luck.

He had a feeling Michael was going to need it where Casey was concerned.

Jack didn't sleep all night. Restless and troubled, he lay awake for long hours alternately anticipating and dreading the day to come. Soon he would know what the future held for Casey and the Bar T.

In the solitary darkness, Jack silently offered up a prayer that his health wouldn't fail him until he'd seen that everything had been taken care of. When the eastern sky finally began to brighten with the coming dawn, he gave up trying to rest and got up. He knew it was going to be a long day as he waited for word from the Donovans.

It was late morning when Jack saw the rider coming in and recognized him as David Martinez, one of the men from the Circle D. He went outside to meet him.

"Morning," Jack greeted him.

"Mr. Donovan sent me over with this." The ranch hand

held out an envelope to him without dismounting. "I'm supposed to wait for your answer."

"All right." Jack quickly opened the letter and read it.

Jack,

Michael and I would like to meet with you this afternoon.

He has agreed to your terms.

Be here at one o'clock.

Frank

Jack looked up at David and nodded. "Tell your boss we'll be there."

"I'll let him know."

When he'd gone, Jack went to find Casey.

Chapter Ten

Casey never openly admitted to any weakness, but the sight of the Circle D ranch house sent a chill through her and left her wanting to run in the opposite direction.

She controlled the desire with an effort.

She had to be strong.

She couldn't run away.

The Bar T's very existence depended upon her.

"Are you sure Michael has agreed to go through with the marriage?" Casey asked her father as she sat next to him on the driver's bench of the buckboard.

"Frank Donovan wouldn't have arranged this meeting with us if he hadn't," Jack answered, casting her a sidelong glance.

Casey was dressed in her usual work clothes—pants, shirt and boots. He'd wanted her to put on a dress, but she'd refused. She'd told him Michael was just going to have to accept her for who she was. She had no intention of changing her ways to please him.

"Isn't there any other way we can save the ranch?" Casey already knew the answer, but she had to ask.

"No."

Casey drew a deep breath and unconsciously squared her shoulders as her father slowed the buckboard before the Donovan house.

"They're here," Elizabeth said as she looked out the parlor window and saw Jack and Cassandra Turner pulling up out front.

"Good," Frank said.

He was in the parlor for the first time since he'd been shot. Though it had been humiliating, he had allowed Michael and Nick to carry him downstairs. Frank hated being dependent on others, but he knew he was going to have to come to accept it. He knew, too, that just because his legs had stopped working didn't mean his brain had stopped. Mentally, he was as sharp as ever; he would have to be to deal with Jack Turner.

"Are you ready for this, Michael?" Elizabeth looked at her son. He was standing stiffly across the room from her.

"I have to be. I don't have a choice."

There was a hint of bitterness in his tone, but Elizabeth knew there was no helping it.

"Where's Nick?" she asked.

"He went down to the stable. He said he'd stay away until we were finished."

"All right." She smiled slightly. "Then let's greet our guests, shall we?"

Ever the lady, Elizabeth went to welcome her future daughter-in-law and her father. The thought amazed her, for in all her wildest imaginings about whom Michael might marry, she'd never, ever considered it would be Cassandra Turner.

"Good afternoon. Come on in," Elizabeth said as she opened the door and held it wide for them to enter.

"Thanks." Jack ushered the reluctant Casey inside.

"Hello, Cassandra," Elizabeth said, smiling cordially.

"Mrs. Donovan," Casey returned. It felt funny to be called by her real name. Her mother had been the only one who'd ever called her Cassandra.

Elizabeth discreetly looked Cassandra over as she moved past her. She tried not to be judgmental as she studied her pants and work shirt and scuffed boots. Though Elizabeth thought the girl looked entirely too mannish, she could see the potential in her. With the right touch, Cassandra could be lovely, and Elizabeth made up her mind to be the one who offered her that "right touch." She knew Cassandra had had no feminine influence in her life for quite a few years now, and she decided it was time. Quietly and happily resolved to transform Cassandra into the woman she was certain she could be, Elizabeth closed the door behind them.

"Frank and Michael are waiting for us in the parlor," she directed, guiding them down the hall.

Casey was as ready as she would ever be to face Michael. She lifted her head and proudly followed her father and Mrs. Donovan into the parlor.

"Hello, Casey—Jack," Frank said.

"Mr. Donovan," Casey greeted him and then looked around for Michael.

Her first sight of Michael standing by the mantel, his dark-eyed gaze upon her, sent a startling jolt of awareness through Casey. This man bore no resemblance to the dandy she'd seen in town. The Eastern gent in his fancy suit was gone, vanished as if he'd never existed, and in his place was a man who appeared to be every bit the successful rancher. Tall and broad-shouldered, dressed in traditional Western gear, Michael had an aura of confidence and command about him. As much as Casey hated to admit it, she supposed Michael was handsome—in a rugged sort of way.

"Hello, Michael," Casey managed, struggling to keep her tone nonchalant.

"Casey," he returned without emotion, looking her up and down.

Casey had had men look her over before, and it had never bothered her—until now.

This time was different.

For the first time, she was aware of her state of dress, and it troubled her. She gave a slight lift of her chin in defiance of her own reaction. She told herself it didn't matter what Michael thought of her. It only mattered that he marry her.

"Please, have a seat," Elizabeth invited.

Jack and Casey sat down on the sofa, while Elizabeth took a chair near her husband's.

Michael remained standing.

"I've spoken with Michael," Frank began, broaching the subject straight on.

"And I take it he agreed to my deal, or we wouldn't be here?" Jack finished. He looked to Michael for confirmation.

"That's right." Michael met his gaze straight on as he answered in a voice completely devoid of emotion, "I'll marry Casey."

A powerful sense of relief filled Jack. "Good. You won't be sorry."

"I hope not," Michael said. "But how does Casey feel about this arrangement?"

"I'll do whatever I have to, to protect the Bar T," she answered.

Michael thought she sounded as if she were offering herself up as a sacrifice. Not that he'd expected anything else from her. They had never gotten along, and there was no reason for them to start now. He just wondered how they were going to make a marriage work when neither of them wanted it.

"How soon can the wedding take place?" Jack asked.

"We'll need at least a month to plan everything," Elizabeth said firmly.

"A month? Why wait that long?" Jack wanted to get the bank loan paid off as quickly as he could so that worry would be behind him. "They can elope. They can go to the justice of the peace right now—tonight."

"No." Elizabeth was adamant. "If we're going to do this, we're going to do it right. It's going to be a church wedding. We have to speak with Reverend Harris and make arrangements."

"All right," Jack said, giving in. "One month it is."

"Good. That's settled." Frank was satisfied. "As soon as they take their vows, I'll arrange for the payment to the bank. Then we'll see about changing the title to the land and—"

"Wait," Jack interrupted. "There is one thing I insist on."

The Donovans looked at him warily.

"This wedding will unite the two ranches to the benefit of us all, but I want it understood from the beginning that Casey will retain title to the Bar T."

"What? You didn't say a word about that before," Frank said, shocked. "Why?"

"I'll tell you why, Frank Donovan." Jack might have made a deal with the man, but that didn't mean all those years of distrust were suddenly forgotten. "What's to stop your boy here from divorcing Casey just as soon as he gets the title to the Bar T? I know you only agreed to do this to get my land."

"We've made a deal," Frank told him. "I'm a man of my word. What about you? Once I save your ass by paying off your debts, what's to stop you and your daughter from cutting off my water just like you say McQueen would?"

"I've never cut you off before, why would I start now?" Jack demanded.

The two adversaries eyed each other skeptically.

"All right," Frank finally relented. "Let's shake on it."

For the first time, the two men shook hands in good faith as Elizabeth, Michael and Casey watched.

Casey wasn't sure what to feel as she looked on. It seemed as if her life had just been taken away from her. The only thing she had to cling to was the knowledge that she was saving the ranch—and after her father, the Bar T was the most important thing in her life.

Michael wondered how his life had come to this. Just a short time before, he'd been in Philadelphia, getting ready to travel to Europe.

And now—

Now he was going to marry Casey Turner.

Casey Turner?

For a fleeting instant, he almost wished he and Nick had sailed for Europe, but as quickly as the thought came, he grew angry with himself.

His father needed him.

There was nothing more important than family.

He would do what he had to do to make sure the Circle D continued to prosper.

"This will work out fine, you'll see." Elizabeth could sense the uneasiness in the room, and she tried to reassure everyone. She looked at Cassandra. "I guess the first thing we have to decide is where you and Michael are going to live after the wedding."

"Do we really have to live together?" Casey asked, glancing nervously toward Michael.

"You're getting married," Elizabeth pointed out.

"But this is an arranged marriage," she argued. "I thought I'd stay at home with my pa."

"And you'll need me here," Michael said to his mother, not the least bit put off by Casey's suggestion that they live apart.

"My marriage to your father was arranged," Elizabeth offered, although she doubted the knowledge would be much consolation to either of them.

"What?" Michael was startled by the news.

"Oh, yes. Your father and I barely knew each other when we got married, but it's worked out fine, hasn't it, Frank?" She smiled warmly at her husband.

"Yes, it has," Frank agreed.

"And, Michael, if we hadn't lived together after our marriage, how would you have gotten here?" she asked her son, her eyes twinkling in good humor.

"Mother—" Michael was uncomfortable with the direction of the conversation.

Casey, too, was all but squirming over their discussion. She hadn't come to grips yet with the knowledge that she'd be living with Michael, let alone making love with him. She shivered at the thought, then glanced his way to see his scowling expression. It was obvious he was just as put off by the idea as she was.

"You will be living together," Elizabeth went on, unfazed by their discomfort. "The question is, where? I'm sure you won't want to stay with us or with Jack."

"No," Michael answered before Casey could reply. "We've got time enough to build a house."

"But I have to be close to the Bar T," Casey insisted.

"And I want to be close to the Circle D," he returned.

"Why don't you build on the hill overlooking the river?" Frank suggested.

"Good idea. You'd be right there on the property line," Jack added. "That way you wouldn't be too far from either one of us."

"That's settled, then," Frank said, not waiting for any more discussion.

"And Foster?" Jack demanded.

"I told you. I'll pay off your loan after the wedding."

"You want everything signed, sealed and delivered first."

"That's right."

They eyed each other again. There was a tentative peace between them, but it was an uneasy one; old hatreds were hard to put aside.

"I guess that's all we have to discuss today," Frank said, satisfied with the way things had turned out.

Jack and Casey got up to leave.

"I do need to talk with you about the wedding plans," Elizabeth said to Cassandra as she showed them from the room. "Do you want to go with me to speak with Reverend Harris?"

Casey was nervous at the prospect, but agreed.

"Good. I'll send a note to Reverend Harris and ask when he can meet with us. I'll let you know as soon as I hear back from him."

"Fine."

They had just reached the front door when Michael came out of the parlor behind them.

"Casey—"

She stopped and looked back to see him coming toward her. Her father and Mrs. Donovan went outside to give them a moment of privacy.

"We need to talk," Michael said in a serious tone.

"Yes, we do."

"Can you meet me later?"

"Where?"

"At the river?"

"All right." She agreed to the rendezvous for she knew they had a few things to say to each other that could only be said in private.

Michael walked with her out to the buckboard. He started to help her up, but she shrugged off his touch.

"I don't need any help." Casey climbed easily up to sit next to her father.

Elizabeth saw the exchange between them and knew she had some work to do to turn Cassandra into a lady. It was going to be a challenge.

"We'll be in touch," Jack said as he took up the reins.

Elizabeth and Michael stood together watching as they drove away.

Chapter Eleven

It was late afternoon when Casey reached the rendezvous spot to find Michael already there, waiting for her.

When Michael saw her riding in, he went to meet her.

"Did you have any trouble getting away?" he asked as she reined in before him.

"No. I just told Pa the truth. There was no point in lying about it." She dismounted and tied up her horse. "He understood when I told him we needed to talk a few things out."

"That we do," he agreed.

"So talk," Casey urged, walking along with him to stand in the shade on the bank. The thought that in four short weeks Michael was going to be her husband was intimidating, and she needed to clear the air between them right now. She wanted to make sure they understood each other from the start.

"My mother's comments aside, you and I both know this upcoming 'marriage' of ours is strictly business," Michael began. "We're only going through with it because we have no other choice."

Michael was blunt, Casey gave him credit for that.

"That's true," she agreed. "And speaking of your mother's comments, there is one thing we definitely should get straight between us."

"What's that?"

"We may have to live together, but that's all we're going to do."

"You're saying you want a marriage in name only?" Michael looked at her skeptically. For some reason, her suggestion bothered him. Not that he had wanted to have an intimate relationship with her—far from it. He had never been fond of Casey, and he wanted very little to do with her. Her outright refusal to even consider that kind of relationship with him, though, was a slap in the face. It almost seemed like a challenge to him.

"Are you saying you don't?" she asked, suddenly nervous that he would be expecting more from her than she was willing to give.

"No," he answered quickly, wanting to strike that thought from her mind. "This kind of arrangement will be fine with me."

"Then we understand each other?"

"Perfectly."

"You want to shake on it, like our fathers did?"

"Why not?"

"I'm glad we got this settled between us."

Casey faced him and extended her hand, ready to seal the deal. She was relieved that Michael had proven so agreeable to her terms. When his hand engulfed hers, she was surprised at the warmth and strength of his touch. She shook his hand firmly, then tried to draw away, but Michael held on to her, refusing to release her.

"We may have settled this deal, but not everything is settled between us," he told her in a low voice.

"What are you talking about?" Her eyes widened as she looked up at him. She thought she'd heard a bit of a threat in his tone.

"I still owe you for our little run-in here."

"You wouldn't."

"Oh, yes, I would."

Before Casey could react, Michael made his move. He was a strong man and he picked her up with ease.

"What are you going to do?" she demanded as she found herself helplessly crushed against his chest, unable to move. Her heart began to race at this close physical contact, and she looked up at him, her eyes wide and uncertain.

For just an instant, Michael paused. The feel of her soft curves so tight against him was unsettling. He had never thought of Casey as having a womanly figure, but he'd just found out different. He hesitated, staring down at her for a moment, before the temptation to exact his revenge overpowered him. He tossed Casey bodily into the water.

She came up sputtering and coughing in outrage at being so manhandled.

"Why, you—!"

Michael stood on the bank laughing at her. "It's not so funny when you're on the receiving end, is it, my dear?"

Casey glared up at him as she stood in waist-deep water, dripping wet. "Are you happy now?"

"Very." He grinned in satisfaction. "Want me to help you climb out?"

"No. I want you to just leave me alone," she snarled, starting to wade out of the river. Never one to give up without a fight, she smiled as an idea came to her. She started to climb up the bank and then pretended to slip and lose her footing.

Michael had been watching her, and he reacted automatically, going to her aid when he thought she might fall.

His reaction was just what Casey had been hoping for.

This time she pretended to appreciate his help. She took the helping hand he offered, but instead of allowing him to pull her up, she yanked him forward with all her might, hoping to catch him off balance on the slippery bank.

Her plan worked.

Michael realized immediately he'd made a serious mistake in trusting her, but it was too late. He slipped and fell forward, landing with a splash right beside her in the water.

"Gotcha!" Casey was howling with delight and feeling quite proud of herself for having gotten even with Michael so quickly.

"Oh, yeah?"

Casey knew a sudden moment of uncertainty. She

turned and tried to flee, but the water slowed her escape.

Michael lunged at her and snared her around the waist. He dragged her backwards and dunked her.

Casey fought to free herself, flailing away at him, but her efforts proved futile. Michael Donovan was one strong man.

They were both laughing as Michael got to his feet, taking her with him. He held her tight, her back to his chest, and controlled her with ease.

"Take it easy, there. Calm down, little lady," he taunted, grinning at her pitiful attempts to escape him.

"Little lady?" she echoed. "I'm no lady!"

"Don't I know it," Michael returned, still laughing as he let her go.

"Oh, you—"

She spun around to face him, and in that moment as she stood there before him, Michael caught a glimpse of the woman she could be. Her hair had come loose and was a tumble of dark, wet curls around her face and shoulders, and her shirt clung to her like a second skin, revealing the outline of her full breasts beneath the sodden fabric.

Michael reacted as any normal, red-blooded male would when faced with such a situation. He enjoyed the view and reached out for her. Without saying another word, he dragged Casey into his arms and kissed her.

The touch of his lips on hers sent a jolt of sensual awareness through Casey, unlike anything she'd ever known before. She knew she should resist him, but right then, she wasn't really certain she wanted to move out of his arms.

Michael hadn't expected to enjoy Casey's kiss. The kiss had strictly been on impulse, but it was an impulse he was glad he'd given in to. Her response surprised him, and he deepened the embrace, tasting of her sweetness.

Casey shivered as his mouth moved over hers in a dominating caress that left her breathless.

And then reality returned.

It didn't matter that he had made her laugh—

It didn't matter that his kiss was exciting—

This was Michael Donovan!

The thought was like ice water thrown on her.

Casey jerked away from Michael and stomped up the riverbank, desperate to put some distance between them. She needed to be thinking straight when she dealt with him, and she definitely wasn't thinking straight while he was kissing her. She was mad at herself for having enjoyed being in his arms, even if only for a minute.

"Oooh—you stay away from me, Michael Donovan!" she ordered, scrubbing at her lips with the back of her wet shirt sleeve. "Kissing is not part of our deal!"

"You're right. It's not," he agreed easily as he, too, climbed out of the water. "Pardon me for being so thoughtless. You don't have to worry, though. For a minute there, I mistook you for a girl, but it won't happen again."

"Good! Hey, wait a minute." Casey knew she'd been insulted.

Michael ignored her and walked past her to get to his horse.

"I'll be in touch," he told her easily as he swung up into the saddle.

Casey was too upset even to look his way as he rode off. She couldn't decide if she was more angry at Michael or herself. She'd told Michael theirs was to be a marriage in name only, and then he'd gone and kissed her! She was going to have to make sure that it never happened again.

Upset and swearing under her breath, she mounted up and headed home. She wondered what the future held for her as Michael's wife. The thought sent a shiver through her.

Nick was down at the stable working with Tom when Michael rode in. The two men took one look at him and started chuckling.

"How did your meeting down at the river with Casey go?" Nick asked.

"Better than the last time he ran into her there," Tom said, grinning broadly. "At least this time she let him keep his clothes."

"You two are real funny," Michael told them as he dismounted and tended to his horse.

"What happened?" Nick wondered.

"I slipped."

"I wish I'd been there to see it," Tom added.

"How's Casey?" Nick asked. "Is she just as wet as you are?"

"She's wetter."

Tom and Nick laughed again as Michael headed up to the house. He was more than eager to get out of his wet clothes.

"Michael?" Elizabeth had seen him ride in earlier, and she called out to him when she heard him come in the house. "I need to talk to you when you get a moment."

She stepped into the main hall as he was hurrying up the steps, and her eyes widened in surprise at the sight of him.

"What happened?"

"I went for a swim."

"I thought you were meeting Casey."

"I did," he answered. "I'll be back down after I change."

"All right. I'll be in the parlor." Elizabeth was smiling to herself as she watched him go.

At least this time he'd come home with his clothes on.

Her smile broadened, but she knew better than to say anything to him.

Michael made short work of changing, then went back downstairs to seek out his mother.

"Is something wrong?" he asked.

"No, nothing is wrong. I wanted to give you this." She got up and went to him, holding out a small jewelry box.

"What is it?"

"Open it and see."

He did as she'd directed and found his grandmother's diamond engagement ring in the box.

"It's for Cassandra. I think it's only appropriate she should have it."

"But Casey is hardly the kind of female who would wear a ring like this."

"Michael, the two of you are engaged. She is going to be your wife. You need to start treating her that way."

"But marriages are usually between two people who love each other."

"Your father and I barely knew each other when we were married. Sometimes it takes a while for things to work out, but they will work out if you try hard enough. It isn't always easy—not even when you are in love."

"Being married to Casey is going to be a challenge, that's for sure."

"I'm not defending her rough ways, but she hasn't had the easiest life, what with her mother dying when she was so young."

"I know."

"Be a gentleman when you're around her. Try treating her like a lady. She's never known that kind of consideration and respect."

"But she's as tough as any of the hands." Even as he said it, he remembered the way she'd looked down at the river and the unexpected wonder of her kiss.

"She may wear pants, and she may be able to ride and rope with the best of the men, but deep down inside, Cassandra is still a young woman. Court her. Woo her."

"But—" he started to protest further.

She interrupted him. "When will you see her again?"

"I don't know."

"Well, the next time you do pay her a visit, think about taking her some flowers."

Michael listened to his mother's instructions, but he knew there was no point in trying to woo Casey. They had already agreed upon the kind of marriage they were going to have. He couldn't very well tell his mother that, though.

"Cassandra is going to be your bride, Michael," Elizabeth continued.

"I know, but she's always going to be a Turner."

Elizabeth fixed her son with a steady regard. "That's where you're wrong, Michael. Once you're married, Cassandra will be a Donovan."

Chapter Twelve

"Michael, you need to ride over to the Bar T and invite Cassandra to dinner tonight," Elizabeth told her son when she sought him out at the stable early the following morning.

After their talk the day before, Michael had had a feeling his mother was going to try to bring Casey and him together; it looked like she was wasting no time.

"Why?"

"Because we need to talk about your wedding plans, and, besides, the two of you need to get to know each other better."

"I know everything I want to know about Casey."

"Michael Donovan, I'm ashamed of you." She used her motherly tone of voice on him.

He hated it when she did that.

"All right," he gave in. "I'll just send one of the boys over—"

"I didn't say send one of the boys," she replied sternly. "It's important you go."

"But I've got work to do."

"Tom can take over for you."

Michael knew it was pointless to argue. "What time should I tell her to show up?"

Elizabeth gave him a stern look. "You can tell Cassandra that you'll pick her up at five."

"You want me to pick her up?"

"That's right. It wouldn't be appropriate for her to ride back home by herself after dark."

Michael was thinking to himself that if Casey ate fast, she could make it back to the Bar T before sundown, but he knew better than to say that to his mother.

"I'll get Nick, and we'll ride over there right now."

"Good." Elizabeth was pleased when he didn't argue further.

"All right, Pete. Turn him loose," Casey said, settling down in the saddle.

Pete had been holding the stallion's bridle. At her order, he released the animal and ran quickly to get out of harm's way.

Word of what was about to transpire had spread around the ranch, and some of the men had gathered at the corral to watch. The stallion was as stubborn, strong-willed and proud as Casey was. The ranch hands knew it was going to be an interesting contest.

As soon as Pete freed the stallion, the horse reared in violent protest of the weight on his back. He spun wildly around, trying to rid himself of the unwanted domination, but to no avail. The stallion bucked, then raced headlong about the corral, yet the rider stayed with him.

Cheers went up from those watching. They recognized fine horsemanship when they saw it.

Michael and Nick were riding up to the house when they heard the men cheering down by the corral. Curious, they rode over to see what was going on.

"Isn't that Casey?" Nick asked in amazement.

"I'm afraid so," Michael responded at the sight of his future bride on the back of the bucking stallion. He thought about his mother's advice to treat Casey like a lady, and wondered if his mother would have changed her opinion if she could have seen Casey now.

Michael and Nick dismounted and went to stand with the other men to watch.

Michael knew that few men could have stayed in the saddle for as long as she had, and he reluctantly admitted to himself that Casey was good—damned good.

Casey's battle with the stallion continued.

Neither the horse nor the rider was willing to surrender.

When the stallion made a particularly savage move, twisting violently and bucking, Casey was thrown. She landed hard in the dirt and lay unmoving for a minute.

"Is she all right?" Nick asked Michael, worried. He'd never seen anyone thrown like that before.

"I'd better check," Michael said, entering the corral.

"I don't need your help," Casey snapped as she slowly got up. Her expression was fierce with determination as she dusted herself off. She jammed her hat back on her head, stalked toward the stallion, ready to climb back in the saddle.

But Michael wasn't about to let her try again so soon. He reached the stallion before she did and took up the reins of the quivering steed.

"Why don't you let a real bronc buster show you how it's done?" he told her.

"You think you're going to ride him?" Casey scoffed, believing Michael was too soft after all his years back East.

"I know I can," he answered her challenge.

Michael thought he was ready as he swung up in the saddle, but he learned real fast that he wasn't. The horse was powerful in its refusal to surrender. It twisted violently and bucked in wild contortions in its effort to rid itself of the man on its back.

Casey was genuinely surprised that Michael stayed on the horse as long as he did. Ultimately, though, the stallion managed a ferocious bucking turn, and Michael lost his seat. She wasted no time chasing down the stallion and mounting up.

"This is how it's done, cowboy," she called as she prepared herself to continue her battle.

Michael couldn't believe she was so eager to try again. He returned to Nick's side to watch.

"Casey is one tough woman," Nick said in amazement.

"I know." And he did, judging from the way he felt from just being thrown one time.

The stallion tried every maneuver he could to throw Casey again, but to no avail. At long last, he quieted and came to stand in the middle of the corral, trembling from exhaustion.

Victorious, Casey kneed him to action and rode at a controlled pace past the onlookers.

The ranch hands cheered her success.

"I told you if anybody could break that stubborn piece of horseflesh it would be Casey," Pete bragged to the other hands.

"She is one helluva horsewoman," they agreed.

"They're right about that," Nick told Michael as they watched her pass by.

Casey smiled at Michael, gloating, "Now, that's how it's done."

"You only broke him because I wore him out for you," Michael countered with a grin.

Casey grinned back and finally reined in where Pete had come back into the corral to help her.

"I did it," Casey said with a confident smile as she dismounted and handed him the reins.

"Were you worried?" Pete teased.

"If I was, I'd never tell you."

They laughed in easy camaraderie.

"I had faith in you, Casey. This big boy didn't stand a chance against you."

"It wasn't easy, but he's worth it."

"What are you going to name him?"

Casey looked up at the beautiful, but stubborn stallion

and stroked his neck. "I think I'll call him Buck, because he sure knows how to do it."

"Good name," Pete agreed. "It suits him. What's your fiancé doing here?" Pete had been surprised when Jack had told him about Casey's upcoming marriage. He'd understood the need to join the two ranches, but he wondered at the wisdom of her marrying Michael.

"I guess I'm about to find out," she told him as she let herself out of the corral and went over to join with Michael and Nick as everybody else drifted back to work.

"This is a surprise," Casey greeted them, smiling at Nick in welcome.

"That was some fine riding, Casey," Nick complimented her. "I've never seen anyone actually break a horse before. You're very good."

"Thanks."

"Do you enjoy doing it?"

"When it's over," she laughed.

He laughed with her. "I can understand why. Have you ever run into a horse you couldn't break?"

"Not yet," she answered. "If you want to learn how, I can teach you."

"I'll think about it."

Michael listened to their conversation and almost felt a little envious of how at ease they were with each other. He grew irritated for even caring, and turned his thoughts to what his mother might think of Casey's activities that morning. Though his mother had advised him to treat Casey like a lady, Casey wasn't going to make that easy for him. She'd caused him nothing but trouble for as long as he'd known her, and he doubted that was going to change—even after she became his wife.

"What brings you to the Bar T? Did you really come over to help me break horses?" She looked at Michael. "I know you two weren't just passing by."

"I came to invite you to dinner tonight," he answered.

"Why would you do that?" she asked.

"Because it will give us a chance to discuss our wedding plans."

"Did your mother hear from Reverend Harris yet?"

"She's hoping he'll let her know something this afternoon, so she can tell you what time you'll be meeting with him when she sees you tonight."

"Let me go make sure it's all right with Pa for me to leave tonight. He's up at the house," she said. She was hesitant to get too far away from him these days. After his trip to the Circle D, she didn't trust him to take care of himself anymore. The memory of finding him unconscious on the floor still haunted her, so she'd gotten promises from the hands to check on him during the day to make sure he was all right. "You haven't met my pa yet, have you, Nick?"

"No, but I'm looking forward to it," he told her.

Casey led the way to the house, and Michael watched her for a moment as she walked away. Though she was wearing a man's work clothes, there was nothing masculine about the way she moved. He found himself watching the natural, easy sway of her hips. He reminded himself that this was Casey as he and Nick followed after her.

"Come on in," Casey invited as she went up the porch steps and into the house. "Pa," she called out.

Jack was in the back of the house, and he came out to see what she wanted.

"Why, Michael. This is a surprise. Welcome to the Bar T."

"Thanks."

"And who is this young man?"

"This is Nick, Michael's cousin from back East."

"Good to meet you. So, what brings you here today?" Jack asked as he showed them into the parlor.

"I wanted to invite Casey to dinner tonight," Michael answered.

"And I wanted to make sure it was all right with you before I told him I would go," she explained. She was almost hoping her father would insist she stay home with him. The last thing she wanted to do was spend any more time than necessary with Michael. It was going to be difficult enough once they were married, she didn't see any reason to rush things.

"Of course it is, darling," Jack said. "That will be fine."

"Good. I'll come back for you about five o'clock," Michael told her.

Casey frowned. "You don't have to come here. I'm perfectly capable of riding over to your place on my own."

"No," Michael insisted.

"But—" she started to argue with him.

"It will be dark by the time we finish with dinner, and it wouldn't be safe for you to be out by yourself."

"Safe? Nothing's going to happen to me," she scoffed.

"You're right. Nothing is going to happen to you, because I'll be with you. After what happened to my father, there's no point in taking any chances."

"Casey, Michael's right," Jack advised.

"Yes, Pa," she relented, annoyed but resigned to her fate. It looked as if she was destined to spend the entire evening with Michael.

"I'll see you around five," Michael said, more than ready to leave.

"She'll be waiting for you," Jack promised.

Casey stood with her father on the porch and watched the two men ride away.

"You know, since you're going to the Circle D for dinner, you're probably going to want to get cleaned up and wear a dress tonight," Jack advised.

"I had a feeling you were going to mention that, but I'll worry about it later. Right now, I've got more work to do," she told him as she escaped back down to the stable.

It was three o'clock before Casey returned to the house to start getting ready. Her father was gone, out with the men somewhere, and she was glad. She needed some alone time before she had to face Michael again.

After heating water, she bathed and washed her hair. As she stood before her small mirror combing out her hair, Casey wondered how she had come to this. She would be marrying Michael in a few short weeks. She kept hoping she would wake up soon and find out that this was all a bad dream—that her father hadn't really been sick and the ranch was not really in debt.

But that wasn't going to happen.

She knew it was time for her to accept what she couldn't change.

To save the Bar T, she was going to have to become Mrs. Michael Donovan.

Casey started listing the things about Michael that irritated her: He was arrogant, and he was annoying, and he was—

Then the memory of his kiss returned.

Casey told herself that there hadn't been anything particularly wonderful about Michael's kiss, but even as she denied his appeal, she couldn't forget the shiver that had gone through her when she'd been in his arms.

"I only shivered because I was wet," Casey told her mirror image.

Then she turned away and got dressed.

A short time later when Jack came back up to the house to look in on her, he found her dressed and ready to go, waiting in the parlor.

"You look mighty pretty," he complimented her.

"Thanks, Pa." She turned and smiled uneasily at him. "But I really wish I didn't have to do this. I can't imagine who in the world decided women should have to wear all these clothes. It had to be somebody who wanted to torture us."

Jack couldn't help laughing. "For all that you feel like you're being tortured, you do look lovely wearing a dress. Michael will be pleased."

"I just hope he doesn't expect me to start dressing like this all the time."

Before Jack could say anything more, they heard a

buckboard driving up. He took a quick look outside and saw Michael drawing to a stop in front.

The day had passed far too quickly for Michael, and the trip to pick up Casey had gone by even faster. He wasn't exactly dreading the evening to come, but he wasn't looking forward to it either. He just wasn't quite sure how to handle his intended bride.

For a moment after he'd thrown her in the water the other day, they'd actually laughed together, but the light mood hadn't lasted. Theirs would be a marriage of necessity, and they were going to have to make the best of it.

His mother had reminded him before he'd left the house that he should treat Casey like a lady tonight. He was bound and determined to do his best—as long as she cooperated and let him.

Michael climbed down from the buckboard and went up the steps to knock on the door.

"Come on in, Michael," Jack said as he opened the door for him.

"Is Casey ready?"

"Just about."

Michael stepped inside as Casey came out of the parlor. He couldn't remember the last time he'd seen her in a dress. The one she was wearing wasn't fashionable, but it was a definite improvement over her work clothes.

"Nice dress, Casey," he told her. He meant it as a compliment.

"Don't get used to it," she retorted.

Casey paused to give her father a kiss on the cheek, and then walked ahead of Michael out of the house.

"Good night, Jack," Michael said before following her to the buckboard.

Michael was glad that he was right there behind her, for just as Casey started to climb into the buckboard on her own, her skirt got in the way. She lost her balance and was falling backward when he put his hands at her waist to catch her.

Casey tensed at his touch. She was forced to lean on him as he lifted her easily the rest of the way up to the bench.

"Are you all right?" he asked as she sat down.

"I'm fine," she ground out, humiliated that she hadn't even been able to climb into the buckboard on her own wearing a skirt.

Michael climbed up beside her and took the reins. "Ready?"

"As I'll ever be," she said.

Casey lifted a hand to wave good-bye to her father as they drove away. She only wished they were returning home instead of leaving. The evening before her was going to be a long one.

Chapter Thirteen

"How come you're out here eating with us tonight?" Tom asked Nick as he joined the ranch hands at the table in the bunkhouse.

"Aunt Elizabeth thought it would be a good idea for Michael to have some time alone with Casey," Nick told them. "So I decided to come down here with you."

"I wonder how Michael's going to feel about being all alone with his little fiancée?" Harry grinned at the thought.

"Maybe we should go up to the house and eat there. Michael might need us," Tom suggested to the laughter of the other men.

"Why do you think he'll need our help?" Nick asked.

"You've seen Casey," one of the other hands spoke up. "She dresses like a man—and acts like one, too."

"What she wears doesn't matter," Nick said, feeling the

need to defend her. "I watched her break a horse over at the Bar T earlier today, and I was impressed. She's very talented."

"Womenfolk shouldn't be breaking horses," another man put in.

"Why not, if they're good at it?" Nick countered.

"It doesn't matter if she's good or not," the hand continued. "She's a girl. She should act like one, but Casey Turner don't. Why, there was one day not too long ago when she ran one of our men off the Bar T. He was hunting strays, and she chased him off. He was damned lucky she didn't shoot him."

"You wouldn't have thought anything of it if she'd been a man."

"But she ain't."

"That's right," Tom added. "Michael is going to have his hands full—having to take over for his pa and marry Casey, too. It will be interesting to see how they end up."

"Hey—I got an idea," Harry said. "Anybody want to make a wager on how long this marriage is gonna last?"

"I'll bet ten dollars they never get to the altar!" one hand called out, and laughter roared through the bunkhouse.

"Ten dollars says it'll last two weeks and then she'll be back with her pa," another joined in.

"What about you, Nick? You want to place a little wager?" Tom looked at him.

Nick's expression was thoughtful. "I'll bet fifty dollars Michael and Casey go through with the wedding and their marriage lasts."

"Fifty?" Tom repeated, impressed by Nick's daring. "You know something we don't know?"

"You're sounding real confident, city boy," Harry said.

"That's right. I am confident. I think you're underestimating Casey."

"We'll see."

The ranch hands all made their wagers. Only time would tell who won the pot.

Casey wondered if she could possibly be any more miserable. It had been bad enough that she'd gotten tangled up in her skirt and Michael had had to help her, but now, sitting so close to him, every time they hit a bump she was thrown against him. She was wondering if fate could think of any other way to torture her today. She hoped not.

"How is your father doing?" Casey asked, struggling to make conversation as they drove toward the Circle D.

"As well as can be expected," Michael answered. "He seems to be getting a little of his strength back."

"That's good. Have you heard anything new from Sheriff Montgomery?"

"Not a word, and we're even offering a reward for information. It's frustrating knowing that whoever it was who tried to kill Pa is still out there."

"Maybe the sheriff will come up with something soon."

"I hope so. What about your father? How is he feeling? He looked like he was doing better."

"He needs more rest now than he used to, but he's trying to get back to normal."

They fell silent again.

Michael was trying to figure out how to give Casey the engagement ring. He wasn't sure if he should just hand her the box when they got to the house or if he should try to do something romantic.

The moment he thought "romantic" he dismissed the idea.

This was Casey—not Karen.

Michael realized he'd never seriously thought about marriage before. The few times it had crossed his mind, he'd always imagined he would be marrying a beautiful woman who loved him as much as he loved her. He'd never considered his marriage would be an arrangement like his upcoming wedding to Casey. He wondered how they were ever going to make it work.

Casey was mentally assessing her situation as they turned up the main road to the house. She was wearing a dress and having dinner with the Donovans. The evening ahead looked pretty torturous to her. She resigned herself to the fact that there was no way out. She was doing what she had to do to save the Bar T.

"Well, here we are," Michael said as he stopped the buckboard in front of the house.

When Casey started to get up so she could climb down, he grabbed her arm to stop her.

"Wait a minute. I'll help you. I know you don't want me to, but I'd hate for you to land on your face in the dirt in front of my mother." He nodded toward the house, where Casey could see Elizabeth coming outside.

Michael leaped out of the buckboard and strode around to her side.

Casey was irritated at being considered helpless. She stood up, ready to get down on her own no matter what he said. But, Michael was there in front of her. He put his hands at her waist to help her. Their bodies made contact as he lifted her down, and she felt a jolt of awareness that startled her. Casey looked up at him from beneath lowered lashes to see if he'd been as affected as she had been, but he was already looking toward his mother. He obviously hadn't felt a thing. Casey couldn't decide if she was glad he'd reacted that way or disappointed.

"Why, Cassandra, you look lovely," Elizabeth was saying as Michael put a hand on her elbow and escorted her up the steps to the porch.

"Thank you, Mrs. Donovan."

"Please, call me Elizabeth."

"All right—Elizabeth," Casey repeated with a little smile.

"Dinner is almost ready. Come on into the dining room." She ushered her future daughter-in-law inside and down the hall.

As they stepped into the dining room, Casey noticed immediately that there were only two places set at the table.

"Isn't Michael going to eat with us?" she asked.

Elizabeth couldn't help chuckling at her observation. "You and Michael will be dining here together. I'm going to have dinner with Frank upstairs."

"Oh—" The evening ahead suddenly loomed even worse in Casey's estimation.

"This will give the two of you some time alone. You've hardly had time to talk since all this happened."

Casey wanted to tell her that she already knew everything she wanted to know about Michael, but she controlled the urge.

"What about Nick?" Casey asked, trying not to let her desperation sound in her voice.

"He's eating out at the bunkhouse tonight," Elizabeth explained. "So you'll be all by yourselves. Enjoy."

"Oh, we will," Michael said, grinning. He knew exactly what Casey was thinking, and he had to admit he was enjoying her discomfort.

"Before I leave you, Cassandra—I did want to let you know that Reverend Harris sent word he can meet with us tomorrow afternoon around two o'clock in his office at the church. Is that time all right with you?"

"That will be fine. I'll meet you there."

"I'm looking forward to it." Impulsively, Elizabeth gave her a quick hug. "Let me check on dinner for you." She went into the kitchen to see how the cook was doing.

Casey looked at Michael, not quite sure what to do next.

"Hungry?" he asked.

"I'm starving."

"Let's eat," he suggested, walking ahead of her to the table and pulling out a chair for her.

Casey knew what he was doing, but she wondered why he was doing it. He didn't have to treat her nicely or try to impress her. She had come for dinner. Nothing more.

"Thanks." She sat down, staring at the fine china, crystal glasses and silverware spread out on the linen tablecloth.

Michael sat across the table from her.

"Do you eat like this all the time?" she asked.

"Only on special occasions—like tonight." Remembering what his mother had told him about treating her like a lady, he went on, "This is our celebration."

"Of what?" Casey was at a loss as she looked at him across the table. She didn't know what was so special about this night. They were supposed to eat dinner. That hardly made the evening anything out of the ordinary. She wondered if Michael thought it was special just because she'd put on a dress for him.

The time had come.

Michael knew it.

He stood up and went to her.

"Casey—" He reached down and took her hand, drawing her up to stand before him. He was surprised by how soft her hand was, considering all the hard work she did at the Bar T; then he remembered how soft she'd been when he'd held her against him down at the river. "Will you do me the honor of becoming my wife?"

"You know—" Casey began, wondering why he was bothering to ask her when they had already settled on the marriage. She wondered, too, why his one simple touch had the power to send a rush of heat through her.

"Just answer the question," he said, trying to hide his irritation with her as he reached into his pocket.

"All right—yes."

"Good. Here," he said in a low voice, handing her the jewelry box.

"What's this?" She looked from the small box up to him and back.

"Open it and see."

Casey carefully opened the lid and stared down at the diamond ring resting there.

"Do you like it?"

"It's beautiful."

"It was my grandmother's."

"But I can't take this." She couldn't imagine wearing such an expensive ring, doing the work she did.

"You can and you will," Michael said firmly.

Without waiting for her to say anything more, he took the ring from the box and slipped it onto her finger. It fit perfectly. As Michael stood there holding her hand, their gazes met and locked. For a moment, it almost seemed as if they were enraptured.

And then reality returned.

Casey felt as if she'd been branded. She yanked her hand away from his.

Michael stepped back, putting a distance between them.

"There. We are now officially engaged," he announced.

Casey gazed down at the sparkling ring on her hand. She'd never had anything so lovely before. "Are you sure you trust me with this? I mean, if it was your grand-mother's—"

"It's yours now."

"Why are you doing this?" she asked, looking up at him suspiciously.

"Doing what?"

"Being nice to me."

"Because you're my fiancée, and you'll soon be my wife."

"But you've never been nice to me before."

"We've never been engaged before."

As he was speaking, Elizabeth and Alice, the cook, came into the dining room carrying their food.

"It's official now," Michael told his mother.

Elizabeth smiled as she saw Cassandra wearing the ring. "Good. And it fits?"

"Perfectly," Casey said, holding her hand out for Elizabeth to see.

"This is so wonderful," Elizabeth said with heartfelt emotion. She went to Casey and gave her a hug. Then she went to her son and kissed his cheek. "Everything is going to be fine. You'll see."

Silently Michael hoped she was right, but he had his doubts.

"You two enjoy your meal," Elizabeth said as she and Alice left them alone.

Michael and Casey settled in to enjoy the dinner. They were served tender beefsteak, potatoes and fresh hot bread. There was even a berry pie, and she savored every bite.

Casey began to think about the fact that in one short month, he'd be expecting her to turn out meals just like this one.

"I'm afraid I've got some bad news for you," she began tentatively.

Michael looked up surprised. He'd thought things were going reasonably well, considering the awkwardness of their circumstances. "What?"

"I know we're going to be living at our own place after we're married, but . . ."

He waited, unsure what to expect from her—which wasn't unusual.

"But I don't cook," she finished.

"What?"

"Becky, our foreman's wife, does the cooking at the Bar T, so you're going to have to take over the kitchen duties."

"I've got a ranch to run. I don't have time to do women's work."

"You've got a ranch to run?" Casey stared at him in irritation. "What do you think I'm going to be doing?"

"Taking cooking lessons from Alice, I hope." Michael said it deliberately to taunt her.

"No, I'm not," she said defiantly, their momentary truce at an end. "I'm going to be working on the ranch, just like I do now. Besides, you've been back East so long, you probably don't even know how to run things anymore. You're the one who should learn how to cook."

Her comment stung. "Just because I've been away for a few years, doesn't mean I've forgotten anything."

"We'll see."

"I thought once a woman married, she was supposed to love, honor, cherish and obey her husband."

"But it doesn't say anything in those vows about cooking, now does it?" she challenged.

Michael couldn't help himself. He laughed out loud. "You know, you're right. It doesn't. So I guess we're both going to starve to death, because I don't know how to cook either."

Casey found herself laughing along with him. "Have you got enough money to hire us a cook?"

"I'd better have, or we're going to get mighty hungry."

"Then I'd better enjoy a good meal while I've got the chance." Casey turned her attention to the food before her.

Later, when they'd finished eating and Michael was getting ready to take Casey home, Elizabeth joined them in the dining room to go over a few things about the wedding.

"Do you have a wedding dress? Your mother's perhaps?" Elizabeth asked. She was very aware of Cassandra's wardrobe limitations and wanted to help in any way she could.

Casey deliberately hadn't thought that far ahead. The thought of the actual wedding was too overwhelming. Just the fact that she had to marry Michael was hard enough to accept, but now she realized she had very little time to prepare herself—especially since the Donovans were insisting on a real ceremony instead of the elopement she'd hoped for.

"Actually, no—I don't."

Elizabeth didn't want to be pushy, but she knew Cassandra needed help. "Come with me, dear. I've got something I want to show you."

Michael remained behind as Casey followed his mother from the dining room and up the stairs.

Chapter Fourteen

"I was thinking about this the other day," Elizabeth said as she led Cassandra into the guest room and opened a trunk at the end of the bed. She lifted the carefully wrapped gown from the trunk and spread it out on the bed for Cassandra to see.

Casey stared down at the full-skirted white satin and lace gown which was trimmed in pearls.

"It's beautiful."

"You're welcome to wear it for your wedding, if you like," Elizabeth offered. "Do you want to try it on now, so we'll know if it fits?"

"You want me to wear it?"

"Yes. Let's see how it looks on you," she encouraged. "If it doesn't fit, we can visit the seamstress in town and see about getting you a dress made."

"But I don't have any money to buy a wedding dress."

"Don't worry," Elizabeth reassured her. "We'll work something out."

Once Elizabeth had closed the bedroom door, Casey slipped out of her dress. Elizabeth drew near to help her don the bridal gown. She lifted the heavy garment over Casey's head, then helped her arrange the skirts. Moving behind her, she buttoned the pearl buttons up the back, then stepped away to look at her.

Elizabeth thought the transformation was amazing. Cassandra had been pretty enough in her ordinary day gown, but wearing the wedding dress, even with her hair still unstyled, she was stunning.

"You're absolutely beautiful," Elizabeth told her. "Take a look at yourself."

She took Cassandra by the shoulders and turned her so she could see her image in the full-length mirror behind her.

"Oh—" Casey stared at her reflection in amazement.

The bodice of the wedding gown was modestly cut, but it was more revealing than anything she'd ever worn before. The gown was fitted to the waist, and the skirt flared out over her hips, showing off her feminine figure.

"Do you like it? It looks like it only needs a few minor alterations to fit you like a glove."

"You really trust me to wear it?" Casey was suddenly concerned about damaging the gown. This dress was far more expensive and delicate than anything she'd ever worn before.

"Of course," Elizabeth said. "Cassandra—I've never

had a daughter, but once you and Michael are married I will have a daughter-in-law."

"I never expected you to be nice to me, since I'm a Turner and all," Casey said honestly.

"Frank and your father have had their differences through the years, but it's time for us to start thinking about the future and not dwell on the past."

"I'm trying."

"I know this is difficult for you," Elizabeth sympathized. "You and Michael barely know one another, and what you do know about each other . . . well . . ."

"Exactly," Casey said seriously.

"If you ever need to talk to anyone, I'm here." Elizabeth's words were heartfelt.

"Thank you."

"It'll work out. Just give it some time," Elizabeth said encouragingly.

Michael decided to go to the bunkhouse once Casey and his mother had gone upstairs. He didn't see any reason to sit around in the parlor and wait for their return. Knowing women, he figured they would be a while.

"What are you doing here?" Nick asked, looking up from the table where he was playing poker with some of the men. "I thought you were having dinner with Casey."

"She went off with my mother, so I figured it was safe to come down here and see what you were up to."

"Want to join us?" Harry invited. "We'll be glad to lighten you of some of your money."

"I'll sit in for a hand or two, but I'm warning you, I don't intend to lose," Michael said, pulling up a chair.

Two games later, the men were glad to see Michael go. He'd won both pots.

It was growing dark when Michael started back up to the house. He noticed that the guest room was lighted, and as he looked that way, he caught a fleeting glimpse of Casey through the sheer curtains that covered the window. She was clad only in her chemise.

The vision stopped him.

That day he'd kissed her at the river, he'd had a hint of her true femininity, but he had never imagined she was this beautiful. He waited, watching to see if she would pass by the window again, but she didn't. And eventually the light went out.

Michael returned to the house to find Casey and his mother coming down the stairs. Casey was again wearing her day gown.

"We have a wedding dress," Elizabeth announced happily. "So, that much is taken care of."

"Good." He looked at Casey. "Are you happy with it?"

"The gown is lovely," she answered.

"Are you ready to head home?"

"Yes, it is getting late." She turned to Elizabeth. "Thank you for everything."

"It was my pleasure, my dear. I'll see you tomorrow at the church."

"I'll be there."

Michael escorted Casey out to the buckboard. This time she accepted his help up without protest. She'd almost proven earlier that pride did indeed go before a fall, and she'd learned her lesson. He climbed up beside her and they started off for the Bar T.

It was a pretty night. The sky was cloudless. A canopy of stars twinkled high overhead, and in the distance a sliver of a moon hung just above the horizon.

It could have been a romantic night—but not for Casey and Michael.

Casey held herself stiffly beside him, trying not to be thrown against him whenever they hit a bump, and Michael concentrated hard on not thinking about the way she'd looked when he'd seen her for just that instant in the window.

They had an agreement.

Theirs was to be a marriage in name only.

It was a business arrangement.

They both intended to stick to their deal.

In Philadelphia, Karen sat in the chair by her bedroom window, staring out at the night sky and thinking of Michael. She knew this must be a terrible time for him, with his father being so seriously injured and all, but she still longed for the day when he would return to her.

Karen was hurt and more than a little angry that Michael still hadn't contacted her. Since visiting Mr. Paden, she'd thought about wiring Michael, but had held back. Now, as the days passed and still no word came, the fear that he might decide to stay in Texas grew within her.

She wanted Michael.

He was handsome and he had money.

Karen had been almost certain he was going to propose

when he'd returned from his tour of the Continent, but all that had changed now.

She knew what she had to do.

She had to go to Texas.

She had to find him and remind him of what he was missing.

Karen was certain Michael would be glad to see her. Then, once she'd worked her womanly wiles on him, injured father or not, she'd be able to convince him to return to Philadelphia and they could begin living the life she had planned.

Her mind made up, Karen went to bed. In the morning, she would talk to her mother about her idea, and then make the necessary arrangements.

Michael stopped the buckboard before Casey's house and climbed down. He went around to the other side to help Casey. She put her hands on his shoulders to steady herself as he lifted her down, and they accidentally made full body contact as he set her on her feet. For a moment, they stood there unmoving in the moonlight, gazing at one another. Michael felt a sudden driving need to kiss her. Just as he was about to give in to the urge, Jack appeared on the front porch.

"Thanks for seeing Casey home," Jack called to Michael. "And you be careful going back."

"I will," Michael responded, frustration filling him as he stepped back from Casey.

"Good night," she said, quickly going to stand with her father.

"Good night," Michael said. "I'll be in touch."

Casey and Jack watched him drive off, then went inside.

"So, how was—" Jack began, and stopped when he noticed the ring on her finger. "Michael gave you that ring?"

"Yes. It's our engagement ring." She went to show it to him. "It was his grandmother's."

"I never expected him to do anything like this."

"Neither did I. I saw Mrs. Donovan tonight. She's been very nice to me."

"Has she heard anything from the minister yet?"

"Yes. Reverend Harris is going to talk with us tomorrow afternoon, so I told her I would meet them in town."

"Do you want me to ride in with you?"

"If you feel up to going, that's fine. If not, I can go alone. Either way, I thought I'd head in a little early, so I could give Anne the news about me and Michael."

"She'll probably be a little surprised." He smiled at her as he imagined her friend's reaction.

"That's putting it mildly." Casey knew Anne would be shocked by the very idea of a union between her and Michael. It was going to be an interesting conversation.

"Well, I'm glad things went all right at dinner. I was worrying about you. I know this can't be easy."

Casey impulsively hugged her father. "No, it's not easy, but I'll make the best of it. I have to."

With those words she left him to go to bed.

Now that he knew she was safely back home, Jack retired, too. He'd felt poorly all evening but had refused to lie down until she'd returned. He just hoped he felt better by morning, so he could accompany her into town to see the preacher.

"Good morning, Mrs. Lawson," Casey greeted Anne's mother in the general store the next day. "Is Anne here?"

"Why, Casey—it's good to see you. Yes, Anne's in the storeroom. Go on back," Marjorie Lawson told her.

"Thanks."

Casey made her way to the storeroom to find her friend sorting through a new shipment of canned goods.

"What are you doing back in town so soon? I didn't think I'd see you for at least another week or two," Anne said, spotting Casey as she came through the door.

"I wanted to see you," Casey began, sounding serious. "I have some important news, and I wanted you to hear it directly from me."

Anne stopped her work and frowned. "It's not your father, is it? He's not feeling worse, is he?"

"No," Casey hurried to reassure her. "He's doing all right. He seems to need a lot more rest now, but other than that I think he's fine."

"Good," Anne said with relief in her voice. "So, what is so important that you had to come all the way into town to see me?"

Casey wasn't sure about the best way to broach the subject, so she just blurted it out. "I'm getting married."

"You're what?" Anne stared at her friend in complete shock and utter amazement. Casey hadn't said a word to her about being in love. She knew John McQueen had been paying a lot of attention to her, but Casey had never seemed overly smitten with the man.

"I'm getting married. See?" She lifted her hand to show Anne the ring.

"The ring is lovely—but who is it? Who's your mystery man? Do I know him?"

"Oh, yes. You know him."

"Is it John McQueen? Did he propose?"

"No, it's not John."

"Then who?" Anne truly had no idea who Casey's future husband could be.

"It's Michael."

Anne was stunned into silence. She stared at Casey in disbelief for a long moment before speaking. "Michael Donovan?"

"The same."

Anne continued to stare at her friend, frowning as she tried to make sense of what she'd just heard. "You're kidding, right? You're not really serious about this."

"Yes, I am serious. It's true. Michael and I are going to be married in a month."

"But, Casey, how did this happen? And why? I know you don't love him. Why, you don't even like him!"

Her words struck a nerve. It was painful to hear the truth spoken so openly.

"You're right," Casey agreed. "But it had to be done."

"And Michael agreed to it?" That shocked Anne even more.

"Yes, he did."

"Casey—you've got to think about this some more,"

Anne advised, not wanting her friend to make a dreadful mistake. "Why would you agree to marry a man you hate?"

"I don't exactly hate him," she said, qualifying her sentiments.

"Well, you've certainly never been fond of Michael. Just the other day when you saw him here in town, you both acted like you couldn't stand the sight of each other—and now you're engaged?"

"It's a long story."

"So tell me. I've got to hear this," Anne insisted, curious to find out what could possibly have happened to bring these two together.

Casey started from the beginning, telling Anne everything about the financial woes of the Bar T and ending up with the arrangement she and Michael had come to.

"So he agreed to a marriage in name only?"

"Yes, and I'm glad. This is strictly business between us. If it wasn't for saving the Bar T, I wouldn't have agreed to go along with the plan, but Pa insisted there was no other way we could come up with the money fast enough."

Anne's expression was troubled. "Should I be happy for you? I always thought when one of us got married, it would be because we'd fallen in love."

Casey understood her closest friend's confusion. She felt the same way. "Yes, I want you to be happy for me. In fact, I want you to be my maid of honor at the wedding. That was why I came to see you today."

Anne finally managed to smile at her friend. "You want

me? Yes! I would love to be your maid of honor!" She hugged Casey impulsively. "Let's tell Mama! She'll be as surprised as I was, but I know she'll be thrilled with your news."

Chapter Fifteen

"Welcome, ladies," Reverend Harris greeted them at the door to his office. "Come in."

Casey and Elizabeth went in, and he peered behind them for a moment.

"Michael didn't accompany you?" he asked.

Casey was thinking *Thank God,* but Elizabeth answered for them both.

"No. He stayed behind to take care of his father. Frank is getting a little better, but we need to have someone there at the house with him all the time."

"I'm glad he's improving, and I'm glad we're here today to discuss your good news." Even as he said it, Reverend Harris was still getting over his surprise at this upcoming marriage. He knew how the Donovans and Turners felt about each other, and finding out that Michael and Casey were planning to wed had been a shock. True, he had prayed on numerous occasions for the two feuding families to find a way to make peace, but he had never thought it would happen this way. He supposed, smiling to himself as he directed the ladies to their seats, that it only went to show the power of prayer.

Casey and Elizabeth sat in the two chairs before his desk.

"Michael and Cassandra have become engaged, and they'd like to marry within the month if possible," Elizabeth began.

Half an hour later, all the arrangements were completed.

"So everything is settled, then," Reverend Harris concluded. "The wedding will take place three weeks from Saturday at two in the afternoon, with a reception following in the church hall."

"That's perfect, don't you agree, Cassandra?"

"Yes, thank you, Reverend," Casey answered. She wondered how good an actress she was, for she had been desperately trying to hide her unease over the realization that this marriage to Michael really was going to take place.

"And Michael will be happy with this arrangement?" the reverend asked.

"It's just what he'd hoped for," Elizabeth answered. "If there's anything else you need, let us know."

Reverend Harris saw them out, then returned to his desk to ponder the mystery of how the two feuding families had found peace.

It truly seemed a miracle.

* * *

"That went very well, don't you think?" Elizabeth asked Cassandra as they left the church.

"Yes. Everything is all set."

"Do you have time to go to Sissy Jones's with me? I brought the wedding dress along, and I thought this would be the perfect time to see about the alterations."

"All right."

They got into Elizabeth's carriage, and she drove to the seamstress's shop.

Elizabeth could sense Cassandra's confused emotions, and she understood this process couldn't be easy for her. "It's normal for you to be nervous about the wedding. I certainly was all those years ago." She smiled at the memory. "Is there any way I can help you?"

"I don't think so," Casey answered bluntly. "I've always been so busy on the ranch, I never thought much about getting married."

"So there's no other man in your life?" Elizabeth had worried that Casey might have been in love with someone else.

"No, no one. I knew I'd get married one day, but I never dreamed it would be to Michael. Knowing how he feels about me, I still find it hard to believe he agreed to go along with my father's plan."

"Michael loves the Circle D."

"He'd been away for so long, I didn't think he'd ever come back."

"I know. He got to see more of the world, but now he's decided this is the place where he wants to stay."

"Even if he has to marry me," Casey finished.

"I don't want you to look at your marriage that way," Elizabeth said gently. "Think about the ranches. You love the Bar T as much as Michael cares about our place. This union will make us the biggest, most successful spread around."

"I am glad about saving the ranch, but I wish I could have kept living on the Bar T with Pa," she said honestly. "I'm worried about his health, and I don't like the idea of him being alone. It was frightening that day I found him . . ."

"The ranch hands are there with him. They'll keep an eye on him after you're gone."

"I hope so."

"They will," Elizabeth assured her. "And you may be surprised. Maybe my son won't turn out to be so terrible after all."

Casey was a bit embarrassed. "I didn't mean Michael was terrible. It's just going to be awkward for us, that's all." She was glad his mother loved him, but no matter how she looked at it, being Mrs. Michael Donovan wasn't going to be easy.

They stopped in front of Sissy's shop.

"Cassandra, there is one thing I want to caution you about."

Casey looked at her expectantly.

"Sissy is my friend, but she has been known to carry a tale or two."

"So she likes to gossip?"

"That's putting it bluntly, but yes."

"Is there another seamstress we could go to?"

"No one as good as Sissy. She's the best in town—and she is a dear friend. All we have to do is be careful what we say around her. She will be surprised by our news, but so will everyone else when word gets out—and it won't take long once Sissy knows."

"Do we have to convince her this is a love match?"

"It couldn't hurt to try."

Casey wanted to tell her that it *would* hurt to try, but she didn't. "I'll think of something. Forewarned is forearmed."

"So you're thinking of this as a battle, are you?"

Casey gave her a smile. "Since we just left Reverend Harris, I'm trying to think of a way not to tell a lie."

"Good girl."

Casey carried the box with the wedding gown as they went to the front door.

Sissy had seen them pull up. She was surprised to see the Turner girl with Elizabeth, and wondered what they were doing together. She welcomed them warmly for Elizabeth was one of her best customers.

"Elizabeth! What a pleasure."

"Hello, Sissy. You know Cassandra, don't you?"

"Of course. Come inside." The middle-aged seamstress knew Casey from around town, and she also knew that, except at church, Casey usually wore pants. She eyed the girl's old, poorly fitting dress critically.

"We have a special request," Elizabeth began.

"What can I do for you?"

"Cassandra and Michael are going to be married soon and—"

"What?" Sissy was truly shocked, and she looked from Elizabeth to Casey and back, in disbelief.

"That's right, Michael and I are getting married," Casey affirmed with a calm she didn't feel. "And Elizabeth has graciously offered to let me wear her wedding gown for the ceremony."

"This is so . . ." the seamstress stuttered.

"Unexpected?" Elizabeth finished for her.

"Well, yes."

"I know. Michael and Cassandra surprised us, too," Elizabeth said. "But you know how young people are. I'm just glad they didn't elope. We just spoke with Reverend Harris, and all the arrangements for the wedding have been made."

"Congratulations, Casey," Sissy told her. "I'm very excited for you—and for you, Elizabeth. We're going to have a wedding!"

"Yes, we are," Elizabeth agreed.

"Let's get to work," the seamstress said, thinking that there was a lot of work to do with Casey.

An hour later, Sissy finished pinning the hem.

"There—that should do it." She rose from her kneeling position and stepped back to survey her handiwork.

"We're done?" Casey asked, standing on a step stool.

"Yes—I think that takes care of everything." Sissy looked at Elizabeth. "Does she need a few new dresses to go with this one?"

"Yes. Do you have the time?"

"For you, anything," Sissy told them.

"But—" Casey said immediately, wanting to remind Elizabeth about her financial situation.

"These will be my wedding present to you, Cassandra."

"Oh—"

"And, Sissy? She needs new underthings, too. Do you have something pretty we could look at?"

"I don't need—" Casey began, embarrassed to be talking about such things. She didn't care about her underwear. The marriage was to be in name only, but she realized her future mother-in-law didn't know that, and they were supposed to convince Sissy that this was a love match.

"It's all right, dear. Trust me."

"Let me show you what I have."

Almost another hour passed before they finally finished looking through the dainty piles of lace and embroidered fabric.

"Casey, can you come to town next week for one more fitting?" Sissy asked. "We want to make sure everything is perfect for your wedding."

"I can do that. Would you like to be here, too?" she asked Elizabeth.

Elizabeth was delighted that Cassandra had thought to include her. "I'd love to join you." She looked at Sissy. "We'll see you then."

Casey, who had entered the shop carrying the box with the wedding dress, left the shop carrying almost as much. Her future mother-in-law had purchased a number of undergarments for her and had ordered two additional gowns.

"I left my buckboard at the general store," Casey told her as they drove away.

"I'll drop you off there," Elizabeth said. "Was this the first time you've ever been to a dressmaker?"

"Yes. My mother used to make all our clothes. In fact, this dress was one of hers."

"How long has she been gone now? It's been a long time, hasn't it?"

"Oh, yes. She died when I was five."

"You were so young."

"I still miss her."

"She was your mother. You'll always miss her."

"I will?"

"Yes. I still miss my mother, and she's been gone for more than twenty years."

"I don't think people should ever die," Casey said with conviction.

"Neither do I, but there's not much we can do about it. It's part of life. We just have to come to accept it and make the best of things."

"It's not always easy."

"No, it's not. When I thought I was going to lose Frank, it was terrible." Elizabeth shuddered at the memory of that recent fear.

"Michael was telling me that the sheriff still doesn't know who shot Frank."

"No, but whoever did it is not going to get away with

it. We'll find the bushwhackers. It may take a while, but they'll pay for what they've done."

"Thank heaven he wasn't killed."

"I know, but it's hard for Frank to accept that he'll never walk again."

"Is there really nothing that can be done to help him?"

"No. Dr. Murray said he's done all he can."

"I'm sorry."

"Thank you, dear." Elizabeth gave her a heartfelt look. "I just hope things will get better with time."

They reached the general store, and Casey climbed down.

"Thank you for everything, Elizabeth."

"You're more than welcome. When will you see Michael again?"

"I don't know. He didn't say anything."

"I'm sure it will be soon. You be careful going home."

"I will."

Elizabeth drove away, and Casey went into the store to see Anne one last time before leaving town.

"How did it go?" Anne asked, eager for news.

"Reverend Harris was wonderful. Everything is set. The wedding will be at two o'clock in the afternoon three weeks from Saturday."

"You're really going to go through with this wedding?" Anne was worried about her friend. "You haven't changed your mind?"

"No, I haven't changed my mind, and I just got fitted for my wedding dress."

"In that case, you'd better let me know what you want

me to wear to the wedding since I'm going to be your maid of honor."

"I'll be wearing a dress, so I think you should wear my pants and boots. What do you think?"

"We'd certainly cause a lot of talk around town! It would definitely be a wedding to remember."

Chapter Sixteen

It was a blistering hot afternoon. Michael, Nick and six ranch hands had been working on the new house since sunup, and they were more than ready to take a break.

"At the rate we're going," Tom said, "the house might be ready for you to move in about this time next year."

"If it's not done by the wedding, I'm taking over the bunkhouse for me and Casey, and you boys will have to camp out up here," Michael responded.

"Casey would probably feel right at home in the bunkhouse," Harry remarked.

"Watch out, that's Michael's woman you're talking about," Tom warned him with a grin.

"So, once you and Casey are married, are you going to get her to settle down and start wearing skirts and have babies?" one of the men asked, chuckling at the thought of a domesticated Casey Turner.

"You'll see," Michael answered with a sly grin.

The men all laughed good-naturedly.

"If anybody can tame a wildcat like Casey, it'll be you, Michael," Harry told him.

"I guess we'd better get back to work. We don't have a whole lot of time left before the wedding, and I'd hate for you to have to spend your wedding night in our bunkhouse," Tom said.

"I appreciate your concern," Michael said.

"Yeah, it'd be rough for you, since all we got are bunks!"

Again the men laughed as they picked up their hammers and saws.

John McQueen rode into Hard Luck intent on enjoying himself in town. He hadn't had the chance to pay Rosalie a visit at the saloon in over a week, and it was time. He needed some relaxation, and she was just the woman who could give it to him.

"Whiskey, Bill," he ordered as he bellied up to the bar. It was still early, not yet five o'clock, and the saloon wasn't very crowded.

"How ya been, John?" the bartender asked.

"We've been working hard out at the Royal. How've things been going here?"

"Can't complain. It was just payday, so we've been busy," he said as he set McQueen's tumbler of whiskey before him.

"Thanks." John paid him, picked up the glass and took a deep drink. "Rosalie here?"

"She's upstairs, I think. You want me to get her, or you want to go on up?" Bill knew John McQueen was the only man Rosalie allowed in her room.

"I'll go find her." He drained the last of the liquor, then went up to Rosalie's private quarters.

Rosalie worked every night until long after closing time to keep things running smoothly in the saloon. The knock at her door roused her from a deep sleep.

"What do you want?" she called out sleepily, irritated at being awakened.

"I want you."

"Ooh, John." Rosalie's mood changed as soon as she recognized his voice and heard his reply. She got up and threw on a silken wrapper that covered her lush body but clung seductively to her curves. She paused only long enough to cast a quick glance in the mirror and smooth down her hair, then rinsed her mouth to rid it of the taste of last night's liquor and hurried to open the door. She'd missed him dreadfully all week. "John—I'm so glad you're here."

"I'm glad I'm here, too," John growled as he looked her up and down.

Her cheeks were flushed from sleep, and the tumble of her hair about her shoulders gave her a wanton look that sent heat straight to his loins. He didn't waste any more time with talk. He shut and locked the door behind him, then turned back to Rosalie and lifted her into his arms.

They fell together on the bed, hungry for each other. They shared kiss after flaming kiss as they eagerly caressed each other.

John was in no mood to waste time on foreplay.

He knew what he wanted, and he wanted it now.

After stripping away Rosalie's wrapper and gown, he finished freeing himself from the restraint of his own clothes and then buried himself in her body. She cried out to him in ecstasy as she accepted him fully.

John whispered no words of love. For him, this act was pure animal—pure lust.

Rosalie made love to John with all her heart, her body and her soul. She had loved him for years. He was the only man for her. She did everything in her power to please him, for she never wanted to risk losing him.

Their desire flamed to the heights. John reached the release he needed and then collapsed on top of her, momentarily sated.

"You stayed away from me too long this time, John," Rosalie whispered as she stroked the width of his chest.

"There were things I had to take care of out at the ranch." He didn't want to hear any more of her talk. He was there for sex, nothing more.

"Will you stay for a while?" she asked in a sensual purr.

"I'm not going anywhere," he growled, moving over her again.

"Good," she whispered against his lips.

It was much later that John's driving passion was temporarily slaked. He lay with Rosalie in his arms, just enjoying the feel of her silken body against him.

"What's been happening here in town? Have I missed anything?"

"I did heard some interesting news this morning," Rosalie began.

"What did you hear?" He was instantly alert. He'd wondered, with the reward being offered, if there had been any information about Frank Donovan's shooting.

"Well, it seems Michael Donovan's getting married."

"To some girl from back East?"

"No, that's the interesting part. Supposedly, he's marrying Casey Turner."

"What?" John had been idly fondling her, but he stopped, not believing what he'd just heard.

"From what I understand, they're going to be married in three weeks."

"But the Donovans hate the Turners."

"I know. That's why it's the talk around town. Nobody can figure out why they're doing this. It's not as if the two of them have been seeing each other for a long time; she can't be in a family way."

"That's right. The families have been feuding for years. Didn't the sheriff consider Jack Turner a suspect in the shooting of Frank Donovan?"

"Yes, but Turner didn't do it. He had an alibi. The sheriff still doesn't know who did it. That reward the Donovans offered hasn't brought in any good leads, but they know for sure it wasn't Turner. I don't know any more of the details. That's all the talk I've heard so far."

"This wedding between the two of them will ruin everything," he snarled under his breath.

"What, John?"

"I was hoping to buy the Bar T. I'd heard some rumors

that Jack was in financial trouble. I made him an offer for the ranch, but he said it wasn't for sale. I guess the Bar T wasn't, but his daughter was."

"What are you talking about?"

"Nothing."

"But—"

"Shut up and come here."

He grabbed Rosalie and pulled her roughly down to him. He was frustrated and in no mood to do any more talking. There was only one thing he wanted from her, and he wanted it now. She was nothing but a piece of meat to him.

Rosalie mistook John's lust for love. Sometimes he was violent with her, but she'd come to expect that from him. She gave him the pleasure he sought. She believed that one day soon he would propose and then she would have the life she'd always wanted. She would be John's wife.

Casey was quiet that evening as she sat at the dinner table with her father.

"Are you all right?" Jack asked.

"I was just thinking about everything that happened in town today. It's so hard to believe that in less than a month I'll be married and gone."

Jack still felt guilty, but he knew they'd made the best of a difficult situation. There had been no other way to save the ranch and protect Casey. He'd needed that much peace of mind to face his own uncertain future.

"I'm sorry I didn't feel well enough to go with you today. Did Michael go?"

"No. Only his mother."

"When are you going to see him again?"

"At the wedding will be soon enough for me."

"Don't you want to get to know him better?"

"I'm sure once we're married, I'll get to know Michael real well. I won't have much choice."

"I'm sorry things turned out this way."

"It isn't your fault, Pa. You didn't force me. I made the choice to marry Michael."

"Did Elizabeth say anything about how your house is coming along?"

"The only thing she said was that Michael and some of the men started working on it today."

"We'll take a ride over in the next day or two and see what they're doing. If it's going to be your house, you should probably be there as much as you can, to help arrange things the way you want them."

"All right. There was something else I was thinking about, too, Pa."

"What's that?"

"Elizabeth was telling me what a rough time her husband is having."

"I thought Frank was getting better." Jack was surprised by her statement.

"Oh, she said he is getting stronger, but no matter what, he's never going to walk again. Elizabeth said he's having a real hard time accepting it."

"What man wouldn't?"

"Exactly. That's what got me to thinking. I saw a picture somewhere of a chair with wheels attached to it, so people who couldn't walk could still get around. Do you think Dr. Murray would know how to get one of those?"

"I don't know. We can ask the next time we're in town."

"Or I could try to build one myself. I feel sorry for Elizabeth. If he could start getting around on his own a little, maybe he wouldn't feel like such a burden to everyone."

"Why don't you go talk to Pete? He's real good at fixing things. Maybe he can come up with an idea that would work."

"Thanks, Pa. I think I will."

Casey hurriedly finish eating, then went to look for Pete.

"Is something wrong?" the ranch hand asked when he came out of the bunkhouse to speak with her.

"Nothing's wrong, but if you've got time, I do need your help with something."

"Sure, Casey. What is it?" It wasn't often she asked for help doing anything, so Pete knew the request had to be important.

She quickly explained what she wanted to do, and when she finished she found Pete was smiling at her.

"You're smiling."

"Yeah, I was just thinking—a few months ago you wouldn't have given the Donovans the time of day, and now you're about to marry Michael and you want to help his father. Things are definitely changing around here."

"They sure are, and for the better, I hope."

"Let's see what we can come up with."

Pete led the way to the stable to rummage through their

cast-off items. They found two large wheels they thought might work for bearing most of the weight, but they still needed smaller ones for balance in front. They would also need a small platform in the front for Frank to rest his feet on.

"What chair did you plan to use?" he asked. "Whatever you pick, it's got to be a sturdy one. Frank Donovan is a big man."

"We've got one up at the house that should work. I don't think Pa will mind if I take it."

"Let's get it and see what we can put together."

"Do you think it will take us long?"

"We want to make sure we do this right, but with any luck, maybe we can be finished by tomorrow. How soon did you plan to give it to him?"

"I haven't thought that far ahead," she admitted. "I don't even know if he'll want to see me. The last time I was there, he stayed upstairs in his bedroom the whole time."

"Once he realizes what you've brought him, Frank Donovan will be real glad to see you. Let's get to work."

They went to get the chair from the house and brought it down to the stable. Then they set to work.

Casey silently prayed that they would be successful. She wanted to find a way to make life better for Elizabeth. Elizabeth had been so kind to her. Now she wanted to return the gesture. She prayed the chair would work.

Frank only mumbled to himself as she went outside to welcome them.

"Hello, Cassandra, Jack. What brings you to the Circle D?" Elizabeth asked.

"I have something for you," Casey began, smiling as she jumped down from the driver's bench and walked around to the back of the buckboard. "A present."

"Oh? What is it?" Elizabeth asked, curious. She couldn't imagine what Cassandra could be bringing her in a buckboard. Her first good look at the wheelchair stunned her. "Where did you get it?"

"We made it. Pete, our foreman, worked with me on it. I remembered what you told me about your husband not being able to get around anymore. Pete's real good at building things, so I talked to him, and we decided to make the wheelchair for you."

Elizabeth stared in awe as Cassandra climbed up in the back of the buckboard and pushed the chair toward her.

"It actually moves," she breathed. Tears burned in her eyes and deep emotion filled her.

"That's right. You can push it, or your husband can wheel it around by himself."

Jack came and lifted the chair down for them. Casey hopped down from the back of the buckboard.

"Shall we give it to him now?" Casey asked

"Oh, yes. This is wonderful, Cassandra—Jack. Thank you." Her words were heartfelt. "Let's go inside. Frank is downstairs in the parlor today."

Casey was a little nervous about seeing her future father-in-law. Frank Donovan had always been an intimidating man, and her encounter with him on the night she'd agreed to marry his son hadn't changed her opinion.

Elizabeth ushered Cassandra into the house, and Jack followed carrying the wheelchair.

"Frank—Cassandra's come to see you and she's brought you something," Elizabeth announced as they entered the parlor.

Frank looked over from his chair by the window.

"Mr. Donovan—" Casey began.

He gave her a stern look. "If you're marrying my son in a few weeks, it's time for you to start calling me Frank."

Jack appeared behind her and set the wheelchair down.

"What's that?" Frank demanded.

"A present. Cassandra made it for you," Elizabeth explained, taking charge.

"What the hell kind of present is that?"

Elizabeth pushed the chair forward so he could get a good look at it.

Frank glared at the chair, then looked up at Casey. "You made it?"

She nodded. "Our foreman helped me. Do you want to sit in it?"

"No," he snapped, not wanting to be seen as an invalid. As long as he sat still, he could pretend to himself that no one knew he was a useless shell of a man.

"Oh, well. Maybe you'll want to try it out later." Casey realized it was not easy for him to admit he needed it.

"Or maybe I won't!" Frank snarled.

Jack was irritated by Frank's reaction and immediately came to his daughter's defense.

"Frank, I always thought you were a stupid ass, and you've just proved it." He wanted to use worse language, but he controlled himself because Elizabeth was present. "My daughter worked hard to make you this gift. She was only trying to help."

Michael entered the house just then, to hear the very end of Jack's remarks.

"What's wrong?" Michael asked, coming into the parlor. He'd ridden in from the building site to get more supplies and had seen the buckboard out front.

"Nothing is wrong," Elizabeth said. "Cassandra brought your father a present, and now that you're here to help, everything is fine." She hadn't approved of her husband's reaction, but she'd understood it.

As Elizabeth spoke, Frank and Jack glared at each other.

"Where did you find this?" Michael asked Casey.

"She made it for me," Frank answered.

"You did?" He was impressed.

"I thought your pa might want to get around on his own."

"I'm sure he does," Michael said, looking at his father. "Casey, why don't you wait out on the porch with your father for a minute while I help him change seats?"

"That's a good idea," Elizabeth agreed, thankful that Michael had shown up and was taking charge. She'd been embarrassed by Frank's reaction to Cassandra's gift.

She led the way outside to give her husband the privacy he needed.

Michael rolled the wheelchair next to his father's chair. "I think you're going to like this."

"We'll see." Frank refused to allow himself to feel hopeful.

"Put your arms around my neck, and I'll shift you over," Michael directed.

Frank did as he was told. Michael lifted him into the waiting wheelchair and got him settled in.

"There," Michael said in satisfaction as he handed Frank the blanket he liked to keep tucked over his legs. "Give the chair a try. Let's see if you can get it moving."

Frank reached down and gave the two big wheels a push.

The chair moved.

"It works." He looked up at his son, his eyes brimming with emotion.

"That's right." Michael saw the look on his father's face and swallowed tightly against his own powerful reaction. It wasn't the same as seeing him get up and walk again, but at least his father could move on his own.

"There's somebody I need to thank." Frank was having a little trouble trying to figure out how to maneuver, but he finally managed to negotiate the parlor and wheel himself down the front hall. He had some difficulty opening the front door, but at last he got it open enough to call out to Casey. "Casey—"

Elizabeth, Jack and Casey had been standing in the

shade at the far end of the porch. At his call, they walked to meet him.

"Casey," Frank said, meeting her gaze. "Thank you."

His words were from the heart, and for the first time since he was shot, he smiled.

Casey returned his smile, delighted that he was pleased. "You're welcome. I hope it helps you."

"It already has," he answered tightly.

Michael had been standing back, watching all that transpired. He hadn't seen his father smile in weeks, and he was jarred by the strong emotions that this one smile roused in him.

"Casey," Michael began. "Thank you."

"I'm glad it works for him," Casey said.

"So am I." He was impressed by her thoughtfulness, and he truly was grateful, too.

Jack was satisfied with the way things had turned out. He looked at Casey. "You about ready to go?"

"Yes, Pa."

"Would you like to stay and visit for a while?" Elizabeth invited.

"Another time," Jack answered. He had a feeling Frank needed some time alone right now.

"All right." Elizabeth went to Cassandra and gave her a heartfelt hug. "This is the best gift we've ever received. Thank you."

Casey hugged her back. "You're welcome."

Michael walked with Casey down to the buckboard. He stood there with her as she climbed up on her own to take her seat.

"Can you meet me at the river later?" he asked her quietly. He wanted to have a chance to talk to her privately and to thank her.

She was surprised by his invitation and almost asked him if she'd be spared a dunking if she showed up at the river, but she could tell he was quite serious this time. "Yes. What time?"

"Is six good?"

"I'll be there."

"See you then."

Michael backed away from the buckboard as her father climbed up beside her and took up the reins.

Elizabeth stood beside Frank, and together they watched the Turners drive away. Michael came back up to join them on the porch, studying the wheelchair with interest.

"I had no idea Casey would do anything like this."

"I think Cassandra is a very special young woman."

"You're right," Frank agreed in a choked voice. "She is."

"Do you want me to push you back inside?" Michael offered.

Frank looked at his son, his eyes bright. "No. Just hold the door. I'm going to do this myself."

And he did.

"That was a good idea you had, Casey," Jack said quietly on the ride back to the Bar T. "Very good."

"I'm glad Frank liked it. I'll have to let Pete know how everything turned out."

"Did I hear you say you were going to see Michael later?"

"Yes. He wants me to meet him down by the river at six o'clock."

"Do you want someone to ride along with you?"

"No, I'll be all right."

"Are you sure?"

"He's my fiancé."

"I know."

"Are you worrying about my honor, Pa?" Casey grinned at him. "You didn't worry the other night when I went to dinner with him at the Circle D."

"That was dinner with his parents close by. This is the two of you meeting down by the river—alone."

"Well, there's nothing for you to worry about. Remember, this is Michael Donovan we're talking about. My honor is safe with him."

Jack looked at her adoringly. She was his whole world, and he wanted her to be happy. "I know, but you're still my daughter."

"I love you, Pa," Casey told him simply.

"I love you, too."

Tender emotion filled Jack. His love for her was all-encompassing. He only hoped that in the future she could find it in her heart to forgive him for not telling her the full truth about the state of his health.

Chapter Eighteen

"There's at least three more hours of daylight. Why did we quit early?" Nick asked Michael as they rode back to the ranch house later that afternoon.

"I'm meeting Casey at six, and I wanted to have time to get cleaned up."

"Where are you meeting her?"

"Our usual place," he said, giving Nick a sidelong glance.

"The river?"

"Exactly."

"You know, you could have gone down to the river and washed up there. It wouldn't have been anything new if she'd found you that way," Nick taunted with a grin.

"Thanks for the idea, but I think it's safer for me to take a bath at home."

"You're probably right."

They both laughed as they continued on toward home.

Casey rode out to the rendezvous spot and found Michael already there, waiting for her. He was sitting high up on the bank, watching her.

"Are you staying this far back from the water because you don't trust me?" she asked with a smile as she dismounted and tied up her horse.

"You could say that," Michael answered with an easy grin. Getting to his feet, he walked toward her. "I'm glad you came."

"I am, too."

Casey watched Michael coming her way, and for the first time she saw him as Michael Donovan, the man—not Michael Donovan, her adversary.

It made a difference.

Now she noticed how handsome he truly was with his chiseled features and dark good looks. She noticed, too, how he moved with a powerful, easy grace. His shoulders seemed wider, and as he stopped before her, she realized he towered over her. Casey lifted her gaze to his and found herself mesmerized by his dark-eyed regard. The look in his eyes was gentle and kind.

"Casey," Michael began, "you surprised me today, and that doesn't happen very often."

"Is that good or bad?" she asked cautiously, not quite sure what he was talking about.

"This time it was good," he explained. "Your gift to my father—I wanted to let you know what it meant to him."

"So he really likes it?"

"Oh, yes. He's very grateful to you. We all are."

Casey smiled and relaxed. "I'm just glad it worked."

"He's thrilled to be able to get around the house again."

"Good."

"I have to admit," Michael began almost apologetically, "I hadn't expected you to be so thoughtful."

"I felt sorry for your mother. She's been so nice to me, and when she told me what a bad time your father was having, I wanted to find a way to help."

"You did."

"I'm glad." Casey's smile turned wry. "But to tell you the truth, I was a little afraid you might be irritated with me."

"Why?"

"Well, building a wheelchair isn't exactly girl's work."

"Casey, it was a gift from your heart. That is all that mattered."

Michael looked down at her, ignoring the boyish way she was dressed, seeing only her bright eyes and sweet expression. He finally admitted to himself that she really was a pretty girl and that she might even be beautiful.

"Really?"

"Yes. Thank you," Michael said the last softly and seriously as his gaze dropped to her lips. He felt the need to kiss her, but he suppressed the desire. He firmly told himself he couldn't betray their arrangement, that there was no place for kisses in their deal.

"You're welcome." She smiled brightly again, unaware of his inner conflict.

"You want to sit and talk for a while?" he suggested.

"As long as we stay back away from the water, sure."

"Now who's the one who's not very trusting?"

They both laughed, and she followed him to a cool, shady spot on the riverbank. They sat down next to each other, but made sure not to get too close.

"It is pretty here," Casey remarked, looking out across the water.

"I used to like coming here a lot, until I had a run-in with a certain troublemaker," Michael said, grinning at her.

"You got your revenge. Aren't you satisfied?" she challenged.

"I have to admit I did enjoy getting even with you."

They both laughed at the memory.

It was then that Michael glanced down at her left hand. He expected to see his ring there.

"You're not wearing your engagement ring."

"Don't worry. I didn't lose it," she hurried to assure him. "I know how precious it is, and I was worried about damaging it. I figured it was safer to keep it on a chain."

Casey lifted the gold chain she was wearing out of her shirt to show him the ring.

"I guess you're right." Michael didn't know why it bothered him that she wasn't wearing his ring on her hand for everyone to see, but it did.

"So your pa is feeling a little better?" she asked.

"Yes."

"I wish I could say the same about mine."

"Why?" Michael knew he had to watch what he said to her about her father.

"When I left him, he didn't look very good. He was pale, but he wouldn't admit he was feeling bad."

"Maybe he was just tired from riding over with you to the Circle D today."

"I hope that's it. Pa's a proud man."

"I understand. My pa's the same way—proud and stubborn."

"Pride is one thing, but it doesn't make any sense when you put yourself in danger. Pa must have known he was feeling bad the day he collapsed. He should have said something to me. I could have gotten him to town to see Dr. Murray."

"He probably thought he could tough it out."

"I'm sure he did, and that kind of reasoning almost killed him. Next to my mother dying, that was the worst moment of my life—coming into the house and finding him lying on the floor. I thought he was dead." Casey shuddered at the memory.

Michael saw her distress and wanted to reassure her. "But he's fine now."

"I hope." She drew a deep breath. "What about you? That had to be horrible, getting the news that your pa had been shot when you were so far away."

"It was horrible. The trip back seemed to take forever. I was scared he was going to die before I could get here to see him."

"But you made it."

"Yes, thank God, I did, and he's still with us. I know

Pa's not happy, but maybe with time, he'll be able to accept what's happened and go on with his life."

"Can you accept it?"

"I have to. I can't change anything."

"What about your life back in Philadelphia?"

"I enjoyed the time I spent there. I learned a lot."

"Like how to dress like a dandy?" she teased.

"That was one of many lessons. My uncle was very glad when I started to dress like a gentleman. He wasn't overly fond of my usual boots and work pants."

"Do you miss being back East?"

"I miss some of it."

"What?" she asked, curious.

"The social life. There was a lot to do in Philadelphia."

Casey had been wondering if he'd left any special girlfriends behind. She knew he wasn't going to volunteer the information, so she just came out and asked, "What about girls?"

"What about them?" Michael looked over at her.

"Was there anyone special you were seeing?"

He hesitated, thinking of Karen. "There was one girl I was seeing regularly. Her name is Karen. We saw each other socially, but there was nothing more to it than that."

Casey found she was relieved at the news, and the emotion surprised her.

"What about you?" Michael asked. "Do you have another man in your life?"

"Only my pa," she answered, not giving a thought to John McQueen. "Michael, this must be very difficult for you. I mean, there you were, living the life of a gentleman, and now you're back in Hard Luck . . ." She almost finished with "being forced to marry me," but stopped herself in time.

"This is where I want to be," Michael said firmly.

His answer surprised her.

"It is?"

"Now that I've had time to think about it—yes." He looked out over the countryside. "I love this land. I tried to deny it. I did deny it for all those years I was away, but now I realize this is where I belong. It's a part of me."

Casey was glad to hear it. It had been difficult enough for her to deal with the idea of their arranged marriage, without thinking that Michael was going to hate everything about their life together after the wedding.

"I love it, too. I know some people don't approve of me doing so much work on the ranch, but I had to help Pa. Besides, it's what I want to do."

"You are good at it," he remarked.

His compliment caught her off guard. "Thanks."

"Nick is definitely impressed with you."

"He is?"

"That's right. If I hadn't claimed you, he might be next in line."

"Nick is very charming."

"That's for sure. He's quite the ladies' man. I bet the majority of the girls in Philadelphia are counting the days until he returns."

"Is Nick going to stay long?"

"He'll be here at least until our wedding. I've asked him to be my best man."

"Good," she said happily.

Michael was surprised that he felt a little jealous of her warmth toward his cousin.

"And I've asked Anne to be my maid of honor," Casey went on. "I guess we have our wedding party all set."

"It looks that way."

"What has Nick been doing?"

"He's been working on the house with me."

"How is it going?" She still found it hard to believe that in a few short weeks she was going to have her very own home—and would be sharing it with Michael.

"We've made a start," he said.

"When can I ride over and take a look around?"

"Any time you want. Why don't you come tomorrow?"

"I can do that. I'm anxious to see what you've done."

"I'm sure it could use a woman's touch."

"That's right. If I know men, you'll need all the help you can get with this, and it is going to be *our* house," she pointed out.

"Yes, it is, isn't it?"

Michael looked at Casey again as if seeing her for the first time.

Soon they would really be married.

They would be living together.

The enormity of it struck him.

This beautiful woman sitting with him beside the river was really going be his wife.

But in name only, he reminded himself.

Then his gaze dropped to her lips, and any thoughts of *in name only* were lost.

Unable to resist the temptation, he bent ever so slowly toward her in a very nonthreatening way, and then he kissed her.

It was a gentle kiss, a tender kiss.

Or at least it started out that way.

Michael hadn't meant for it to be more, but when he slipped his arms around her and drew her near, an arc of pure sensual awareness ignited between them. The power of it caught him unawares. He struggled to control his reaction to her, and he managed—until Casey gave a small sigh that sounded like a moan of pure pleasure.

Suddenly desperate for more, Michael deepened the kiss. His mouth slanted over hers. He parted her lips and tasted of her sweetness. Drawing her even closer, he enjoyed the feel of her soft body melding to his as they lay back on the sweet bed of grass.

At the first touch of his lips, Casey had warned herself that this was Michael. She'd told herself they had an agreement. But as his lips had continued to plunder hers, nothing mattered except the unexpected thrill of being in his embrace. And when he'd lain her back upon the soft bed of grass, she lifted her arms around his neck and drew him down even closer.

Her unspoken encouragement urged Michael on. Caught up in the delight of being near her, he boldly caressed the sweet curve of her breast.

Casey had never known such intimacy. Her breath caught in her throat. Desire shivered through her—and this time she knew she wasn't shivering from being wet, like the last time at the river. Michael's caresses aroused feelings in her that left her wanting—no, needing more. A deep and hungry ache grew within the womanly heart of her. Driven by that urge, she shifted her hips instinctively against him.

The movement of her hips against his was enticing. Primal desire urged Michael on. He pressed hot kisses to her throat as he freed the buttons on her shirt. His lips followed the path his hands explored, caressing the creamy tops of her breasts.

Delight trembled through Casey as Michael worked his magic upon her willing flesh. She had never been so intimate with a man before, and though she was nervous, she was also caught up in the splendor of his touch. It was pure ecstasy, being in his arms.

"Oh, Michael—" His name was a passionate whisper.

The sound of her voice jarred the last fragment of sanity that remained within Michael.

Somehow he summoned enough willpower to stop before things went any further.

Fearing if he didn't do it immediately he would never be able to, Michael shifted abruptly away from Casey. He sat far enough from her to make sure there was no physical contact between them. Tension was etched in every line of his body as he stared out across the river. He deliberately did not glance her way. He feared if he took one look at Casey, he would haul her back into his arms, and he couldn't risk that. He remained immobile, frozen in body and soul.

Casey was stunned—first by her own unexpected reaction to Michael's kiss and caress, and now by his complete and utter rejection of her.

A deep sense of shame filled her.

It had been foolish to think for even a moment that there was any real attraction between them. It was obvious from the way Michael was acting, looking so angry and disgusted, that he wanted absolutely nothing to do with her. She wasn't even sure how the whole thing had started, but she was sorry. They had actually been getting along for a moment, and now . . .

"I'm sorry," she muttered, getting nervously to her feet. She felt awkward and unsure of herself, and that was unusual for her.

"So am I," Michael answered tersely, still not looking her way. "It won't happen again."

Casey's humiliation ran deep. She took his words as a complete rejection of her. She didn't know how she could have been so weak-willed as to allow that kiss to happen, but she was going to have to make sure it never happened again.

From now on, Casey decided, she would keep her distance from him. She could not let him know that his embrace had thrilled her, when it was obvious he had no interest in her at all. He'd agreed to their marriage to get control of the water for the Circle D. Other than that, she meant nothing to him, and she never would.

Not knowing what else to do, Casey started to walk toward her horse.

"You're leaving?" Michael asked, still not looking her way.

"Yes."

"I'll see you tomorrow at the house."

Casey said no more. There was no point.

She mounted up and rode away. She did not look back.

Michael waited for some time before deciding to leave as well. He was proud that he had been able to stop himself, but he wondered at the unexpected passion that had erupted between them.

He and Casey had agreed their relationship would be in name only. They had both been satisfied with the idea that they would not be intimate with one another.

Yet her kiss had aroused him like no other woman's ever had.

Michael wasn't sure what to do. This was Casey he was dealing with.

She had always meant trouble for him—and it looked as if that wasn't going to change.

Chapter Nineteen

"How did your visit with Cassandra go?" Elizabeth asked Michael when he returned home.

Michael had known she would ask, so he'd practiced several different answers on the ride back to the house.

"Fine." He kept his tone light. "She was glad Pa liked the wheelchair."

"Despite her roughness, Cassandra is a very sweet young woman," Elizabeth began, singing her praises.

As she was speaking, Michael thought about just how sweet Casey was—her kiss—her touch—the feel of her in his arms.

"Yes—yes, she is sweet," he said, jerking his thoughts away from that all-too-dangerous memory.

"You do plan to spend more time with her, don't you?"

"Don't worry. We're seeing each other again tomorrow.

She said she'd come to the building site and take a look at how we're coming along."

Elizabeth smiled in open delight. "That's good, and don't forget what I told you about trying to court her and woo her. She is going to be your wife."

"I know, Ma," Michael answered, embarrassed by his mother's advice.

"I have to admit I did have some misgivings about this marriage, but I don't anymore."

"Why is that?" Michael asked.

"Cassandra has impressed me as being a very strong, bright young woman. The more I get to know her, the more I like her. She has suffered a lot in her life, losing her mother at such a young age. Now, with Jack not doing well, it looks like things are going to be even more difficult in the future. She's going to need you to be strong for her, Michael."

"I'll do my best." Michael thought about the strength it had taken for him to stop kissing Casey earlier. As aroused as he'd been and as willing as Casey had seemed to be, anything might have happened between them if he hadn't stopped. He was glad that he'd broken off their embrace, but he was still angry with himself for kissing her in the first place. He had no doubt she was furious with him right now, and he didn't blame her.

He had always prided himself on being a man of his word. He had to abide by their agreement.

"You're a good man, Michael. Cassandra is a lucky young woman to be getting you for a husband." Elizabeth stood up and went to her son to kiss his cheek.

"I hope she thinks so," he told his mother, managing only a half-smile.

"Give her time. Once she gets to know you, she'll love you," she stated with certainty.

Love me? Michael hated keeping a secret from his mother, but there was no way he could ever tell her the truth. He could see himself getting along with Casey, but he didn't think Casey would ever fall in love with him.

"What about you?" Elizabeth asked him point-blank. "How are you coming to feel about her?"

"I'm not sure." It was as honest an answer as he could give at that moment. He truly was confused by his own reactions to Casey.

"You shouldn't be, and that's good. It's much too soon. I'm glad you don't hold any animosity toward her and her father."

"No. It's just that Casey is very different from any other girl I've ever known."

"She certainly is. Who's the girl you were seeing back in Philadelphia?"

"Karen Whittington."

"How do you feel about her? Were the two of you serious about each other?"

Michael frowned at her question. It had been only a matter of weeks since he'd seen Karen, but it seemed much longer. At first, he had missed her occasionally, but now he seldom thought of her.

"Karen is a very beautiful woman. She's rich and sophisticated. We enjoyed each other's company."

"Are you in love with her?" Elizabeth was worried about

what Michael's answer would be, but she had to ask.

He hesitated for a moment as the memory of Casey's kiss played in his mind. He had never reacted so powerfully to Karen's embrace. "I'm not sure."

"If you were in love with her, you would know it," Elizabeth said with certainty.

"I would?"

"You would. If you loved her, you wouldn't be able to bear being apart from her, and you certainly wouldn't have agreed to marry Cassandra—not even to save the ranch. If you were in love with Karen, nothing would stop you from being with her."

Michael's expression turned serious as he considered what she'd just said to him.

"Don't worry, darling," Elizabeth went on. "Everything is going to work out fine."

"I hope you're right."

"I'm always right," she insisted. "I'm your mother."

Much later that night when Michael lay in his solitary bed, thoughts of Karen and Casey haunted him. Karen was everything a man could want in a wife. She was educated. She had beauty, wealth and social connections. Casey, on the other hand, knew little about social amenities and didn't seem the least bit interested in learning about them. She was pretty, but untamed. Kind, yet fearless.

Michael stared blindly up at the ceiling of his room, wondering about his future.

He had given his word, and he would keep it.

He would marry Casey.

And Karen?

He decided then and there that she was a part of his past. He wouldn't see her again. That part of his life was over.

When Casey returned home, she found her father had retired for the night. She checked to make sure he was resting comfortably, then sought her own bed.

She was tired, but sleep proved elusive. Her heart was torn by conflicting emotions. Michael's kisses had been her heaven—and her hell. She cursed her weakness in not moving away from him when he'd kissed her the first time.

Even as she told herself it was a weakness she would never give in to again, Casey knew the truth, and the truth was that she had actually enjoyed his embrace.

The realization was startling for her, and painful. She was certain Michael didn't feel the same way. It was obvious from the way he had acted that he wanted nothing to do with her.

A great sadness filled her. This was what her life was destined to be—she would be married to a man who didn't want her and who would never love her.

Resigned, she rolled over in bed and buried her face in her pillow. She tried to tell herself she didn't care, but she couldn't stop her tears. She had always prided herself on being strong, and it surprised her to find that Michael's unspoken rejection hurt so badly.

Casey could never let anyone know the truth of her feelings.

She would do what she had to do to save the Bar T. She told herself nothing else mattered.

"You doing all right, Pa?" Casey asked him the next morning at breakfast.

"I'm fine," he answered. He hated keeping the truth from her, but it was better this way. He didn't want to burden her.

"I'm going to ride over and see how the house Michael's building is coming along."

"You mean how 'your' house is coming along, don't you?" he asked, smiling.

"It's hard to think of it that way," she told him honestly. "Just like it's hard to believe we're going to be married so soon."

"It's for the best, darling."

"I know, but it's still scary."

"You? Scared of Michael Donovan? I never thought I'd see the day," he teased, hoping to lighten her mood.

"Oh, Pa." She smiled at him, for she recognized his ploy. "You never saw him in his fancy Eastern duds. Now, that was scary!"

"I guess that could be enough to frighten a soul," he agreed with a laugh. "That feels good."

"What does?"

"Laughing. We haven't had much to laugh about around here for a long time."

"No, we haven't."

"Things are looking up now. Everything's going to be all right."

"So, do you want to ride over and take a look at the house with me?"

"I can't today. I've got some work I have to get done with Pete." It was a lie, but Jack couldn't tell her that he didn't have the strength to go anywhere. "I'll go one day next week."

"All right. Well, I'm going now, but I'll be back."

Casey went to the stable to get her horse and then rode toward the building site. It was a beautiful day. The sky was clear and a brilliant blue, and the morning breeze was still cool.

Casey didn't notice how heavenly the weather was, though. She was too caught up in her thoughts about facing Michael again. She wished she hadn't agreed to visit the building site that day. In fact, she wished she didn't have to see Michael again until their wedding, but that wasn't going to happen. Very shortly, they would be face-to-face, so she had to prepare herself.

Casey had never thought about being an actress, but she hoped today she could put on a great performance. She was going to have to act as if nothing unusual had happened between them. Obviously, to Michael's way of thinking, nothing had happened, so she told herself it shouldn't be too hard to pretend around him.

As ready as she would ever be to see him again, Casey topped the low rise that afforded her a view of her new home. She reined in to look over the scene before her and was surprised to see how much progress the men had made in such a short time. She'd expected to see not much more than the frame, but the construction actually already looked like a house. It wasn't big. It was a single-story dwelling, but it would be big enough for the two of them, and it had a small porch across the front.

The men from the Circle D were already there and hard at work on the roof.

Casey urged her horse toward the house that would soon be her home.

"Here comes your future bride now," Nick told Michael as he slaved away beside him on the roof.

Michael looked up to see Casey riding in. He put down his hammer and climbed down the ladder to welcome her.

" 'Morning," Michael said, waiting as she dismounted and tied up her horse.

Casey noticed he hadn't said "good" morning.

"Hello, Michael," she said, then turned and smiled up at Nick, who was still working on the roof. "Hi, Nick!"

"Hi, Casey!" Nick responded. "What do you think of our handiwork?"

"It looks wonderful."

"I bet you didn't think I could do this kind of work, did you?" he asked.

"I'd never underestimate you, Nick," she answered with a smile. "Keep up the good work."

"For you, Casey, anything," Nick promised her.

Michael listened to their easy banter and grew annoyed. "Do you want to take a look around inside?"

"Yes," she agreed.

Turning her attention to Michael, Casey walked by his side toward the front door.

Several men were working inside the house. One of the hands called out, "Hey, Michael! You'd better practice carrying her over the threshold to make sure you do it right on your wedding day!"

"That's right, Michael. Let's see how good you are," another agreed.

"I'll wait until after the wedding." Michael didn't want to lay a hand on Casey today, much less carry her in his arms. He wanted to keep some distance between them. He planned to give her a guided tour and then send her on her way.

"Aw, c'mon, Michael! You're going to have a rehearsal for the wedding. Why not rehearse carrying her over the threshold?"

All the hands joined in, encouraging him to action, and Michael knew he was trapped.

"All right, all right."

Michael turned to Casey and saw the look of unease in her eyes. He was tempted to throw her over his shoulder and carry her inside that way, but instead, without waiting for her to argue or protest, he simply scooped her up in his arms. Holding her close to his chest, he strode purposefully into the house.

Casey had thought she was prepared to be in Michael's arms again, but being held against him that way set her pulse to racing. She actually found herself blushing as the ranch hands cheered them on. The thought that the next time he carried her that way they would be married almost unnerved her. When he finally set her on her feet inside their future home, Casey was surprised to find she felt almost bereft at being out of his arms.

The men shouted out their compliments to Michael on a job well done.

"I told you I didn't need any practice," he called back to them.

Casey moved away from Michael to look around. She'd known the house wasn't going to be very big, so the fact that it was small didn't bother her. Her home on the Bar T wasn't all that roomy. What did bother Casey, though, was the fact that there were only two rooms—one bedroom and one big room that would be a combination kitchen and sitting room.

Casey had assumed that they would each have a bedroom. She wondered how to handle the situation. Whatever discussion they had about it would have to be held between the two of them in private.

"So? What do you think?" Michael asked after watching her look around.

"It's going to be very nice."

At her answer, Michael called out, "It's all right, boys! She likes it!"

The hands were pleased at the news. Michael had warned them that she would be paying them a visit today, and some of them had worried the house wouldn't suit her.

"You've all done a fine job," Casey said as she and Michael went back outside.

Nick had climbed down from the roof and was waiting to talk to them.

"So you're pleased," Nick said. "That's good."

"You had doubts?" Casey asked, a teasing glint in her eye.

"There's no pleasing some females," Nick replied. "I'm glad you're not one of them."

"We should complete all the work here by late next week," Michael put in, changing the direction of their conversation. The easy camaraderie between Casey and Nick still bothered him.

"It's hard to believe the wedding is so close," she said.

"Yes, it is," Michael agreed. "We don't have a lot of time left to get things ready."

"If worse comes to worst, we can always move in with my pa for a while," Casey suggested.

"That's all right," Michael was quick to respond. "This is our home. We'll be living here."

Casey still liked the idea of staying with her father even if Michael didn't, but she had no choice in the matter. Once they were husband and wife, they would have to be together.

In that very house.

In the one bedroom.

Chapter Twenty

"Are you sure this is a good idea, dear?" Dorothea Whittington asked her daughter in a tortured voice as they suffered through yet another seemingly unending day of miserable travel.

"Of course it is. We're almost there. The driver said we'd arrive in Hard Luck by sundown."

"Thank God," Dorothea said melodramatically.

"Mother—" Karen gave her a censuring look. "We haven't come this far to give up now. You always taught me to persevere when I want something—and I want Michael Donovan."

Dorothea gave a strained sigh. "I know. I just wish he'd never had to return to Texas in the first place—and to a town called Hard Luck, at that." She rolled her eyes heavenward in an exaggerated show of distaste.

"Once we reach Hard Luck and I find Michael, I'll convince him to come back home with me right away. Don't worry, Mother," she said with confidence, "we won't be stuck in Texas very long."

"I hope you're right," she said.

"I am. Once I remind him of what he's been missing, I'm sure he'll come back to Philadelphia with us. Why, he was almost ready to propose when all this happened."

"Needless to say, I can hardly wait for the return trip. I'm sure it will be just as tedious, but I am definitely going to enjoy it more."

"I'm going to enjoy it more, too. Michael's going to be traveling with us," Karen said with a confident smile.

She couldn't wait to see him. It had been too long already. Though she was still upset with Michael for leaving without saying good-bye in person, once he apologized, she would forgive him, and everything would be wonderful between them—especially after she became Mrs. Michael Donovan.

Karen stared out the stagecoach window and completely understood why Michael had left Texas to go to Philadelphia. Texas was so . . . so uncivilized. They hadn't seen a building or any sign of humanity since they'd left the last depot, hours and miles ago. She wondered how anyone existed here. *She* certainly couldn't. Confident that Michael's love for her would draw him back to Philadelphia, she didn't worry in the least that she'd be forced to stay in Texas. Soon, very soon, they would be on their way back East—together.

It was late afternoon when the stagecoach rolled to a stop before the depot in Hard Luck.

"This is Hard Luck?" Dorothea said with disdain, looking out at the tiny Western town.

"Yes, ma'am," the stage driver said, opening the door for her.

"Oh, my." She took his offered hand reluctantly, for he was quite dirty, then descended from the rough-riding stagecoach.

Dorothea thanked him and stepped aside while he helped Karen down.

"Can you recommend any accommodations?" Dorothea asked him.

The driver frowned. He pushed his dusty hat back and scratched his head. "If you mean, can I recommend a hotel, well, sure. There's only one hotel in Hard Luck, little lady. It's the Hard Luck Hotel and it's right down the street there." He pointed the way. "I'll send your trunks there for you."

"Thank you," Dorothea said in her most prim tone as she and Karen moved off.

Dorothea tried her best not to gawk at Hard Luck, but it was difficult. It was a hot and dusty little town, and she wondered how it had even come into being. She couldn't imagine why anyone would want to settle down there. The stage depot was the only redeeming feature she could find, and that was only because it afforded her a way to escape the place.

"It's hard to believe that a gentleman like Michael comes from a town that is so . . . crude."

Karen understood her mother's reaction but wanted to

make the best of things. "Once I get to see Michael again, everything will be fine."

"Of course, dear," Dorothea said, holding her tongue for now. She hoped her daughter was right, for she certainly didn't want to spend an hour longer there than necessary.

They reached the hotel and went in.

"Afternoon, ladies," Ernest Williams, the hotel clerk, welcomed them as they approached the check-in desk.

"We need a room, please," Dorothea dictated.

"Yes, ma'am." Ernest quickly registered them, then escorted them upstairs to their room. "Where are you ladies from?"

"Philadelphia," Karen answered. "We're here to visit the Donovans."

"Oh, are you kin?"

"We soon will be," Karen responded, with confidence. "I'm Michael's fiancée."

"You are?" Ernest tried but couldn't quite hide his surprise. He'd heard the talk around town about the upcoming wedding between Michael and Casey, and he knew this woman's unexpected appearance was definitely going to cause trouble.

"You sound surprised," Dorothea said pointedly.

"Well, we hadn't heard Michael was engaged to anyone back East," he said, managing not to reveal anything. He didn't want to be the one who told them about Michael's upcoming marriage to another woman. He didn't want to be anywhere around when these two women found out about it.

"We hadn't publicly announced it yet, but Michael and I are going to be married," Karen said firmly.

"I'm real happy for you," Ernest said noncommittally.

"Is there a way to send a message to Michael at the ranch? Is there someone I can hire to contact him for me?"

"Yes, there surely is. The boys down at the stable are always willing to do odd jobs. I'll have one of them come see you."

"Thanks."

Ernest opened the door to their room for them. "I'm Ernest Williams. If you need anything, let me know."

"We will."

He left to find a messenger.

Dorothea and Karen went into the sparsely furnished room and looked around. There was a washstand, two single beds and a small dresser.

"It's clean," Karen pointed out. "And it's better than some of the places we've stayed in on this trip."

"That isn't saying much," Dorothea said as she sat down on one of the beds to test its softness. "But all this will have been worth it, once you're reunited with Michael."

Karen smiled brightly as she thought of her future as Michael's wife. "Yes, it will."

Ernest hurried down to the stable to talk to Fitz.

"I need someone to ride out to the Circle D," he told him.

"Let me get Rob for you," Fitz answered, searching the back of the stable for his helper. "What's going on that you gotta get in touch with the Donovans?"

Ernest liked to talk, and he quickly related what he'd learned.

"But Michael's marrying Casey," Fitz countered.

"I know that and you know that, but these ladies don't," Ernest replied with a sly grin. "This could get real interesting. It's been a while since we had any fun in Hard Luck."

"I wonder if Michael's going to think this is fun."

"We'll find out. This Karen Whittington is one fine-looking lady."

"I guess we'll be finding something out real soon, won't we?" Fitz remarked. "Rob! Ernest needs you."

Ernest returned to the hotel with Rob, and they went upstairs to the Whittingtons' room.

"This here is Rob. He'll be glad to deliver your message to the Circle D for you," Ernest told Karen and her mother.

They thanked him for his help, Ernest left them to settle in and returned to the front desk.

"I need you to deliver this letter to Michael Donovan at the Circle D ranch," Karen instructed Rob, holding out the envelope containing the note she'd written while waiting for Ernest to return.

"Yes, ma'am. I can do that."

"How long will it take you?"

"Not long. Less than an hour. Do you want me to wait for an answer?"

"No, that's not necessary."

Ernest had told her what the charge was and Karen

paid the messenger. When he'd gone, she closed the door and looked at her mother.

"I guess all we have to do now is wait."

"That may be what *you* are going to do, but frankly, I need a bath," Dorothea declared.

"Why don't we get cleaned up and then see if there's someplace nearby where we can get something to eat? By the time we finish eating, I'm sure Michael will be here."

Ernest wasted no time in spreading the news. His shift ended right after Rob rode out of town to deliver the message to the Circle D, and he went straight to the Sundown saloon to tell everybody what he'd learned.

"Bill, wait until you hear this," Ernest began as he took a deep drink of the beer the barkeep had served him.

Bill shook his head and grinned at him. He knew what a gossip Ernest could be, and he could hardly wait to hear the latest. "What is it now? It must be important, for you to get this excited."

"It is. Hard Luck hasn't had a scandal like this in years."

The bartender frowned. "What kind of scandal?"

"That's what I'm trying to tell you. Guess who showed up here in town today on the late stage."

"I have no idea."

"Two ladies—and I do mean ladies—and one of them claims to be none other than Michael Donovan's fiancée from back East," he finished with a flourish, relishing the news.

"She can't be his fiancée," Bill argued. "He's marrying Casey Turner."

"I know that and you know that, but Miss Karen Whittington of Philadelphia doesn't know it."

"She says she's his girl from back East?"

"Yes. She says she's his intended."

Bill agreed with Ernest's opinion of the matter. "You're right, Ernest. It does look like things could get exciting around here."

"What's this about Donovan?" John McQueen interrupted in an easy fashion as he joined them. He'd been playing poker in back, but he'd heard the two men mention Casey and Michael. As soon as the hand had played out, he left the game to speak with Ernest and Bill.

"Ernest here has some news," Bill led in.

Ernest told John McQueen the story.

"So, according to this young lady, she's engaged to Donovan?" John repeated thoughtfully.

"That's right. What do you think Casey is going to say about that when she finds out?"

"It'll be interesting, that's for sure."

"I sure don't want to be the one to tell her," Bill remarked. Everyone in town knew Casey, and they knew she had a temper.

"I almost feel sorry for Michael," Ernest said.

"I don't," John spoke up, thinking with great satisfaction that the man was going to get exactly what he deserved. John already knew what he was going to do, and inwardly he was smiling. Things were finally starting to go his way. "Bill, will you tell Rosalie for me that I had to leave, but that I'll see her later?"

"I'll tell her, but she ain't going to be happy about it," Bill answered.

John just shrugged and left the saloon. He didn't care what Rosalie thought. He had to find Casey. He had news she needed to hear right away.

John knew it was going to be late when he reached the Bar T, but he thought the news he was bringing would gain him admission. He certainly hoped Casey would appreciate his concern.

Chapter Twenty-one

Michael and Nick stayed late working on the new house. Time was running out, and there was still a lot to be done.

Whenever they took a break, Michael tried to school Nick in the art of using his six-gun, but with each passing lesson, Michael became more firmly convinced his cousin should probably carry a shotgun instead. Still, Nick insisted on keeping at it, so they practiced target shooting every day.

The two men were tired and dirty when they finally decided to quit work and head for home.

"I guess you're working so hard because you don't want to stay in the bunkhouse with Casey on your wedding night," Nick said.

"That's right."

"Sleeping in bunk beds wouldn't be very romantic, that's for sure."

"I wonder if Casey would want the top bunk or the bottom."

Both men laughed.

"To be safe, if it came to that, I'd advise you to both sleep on the bottom bunk," Nick told him.

Michael didn't even want to think about sleeping in the same bed with Casey, let alone imagine himself sharing a narrow bunk with her.

"You don't have to worry," he said, wanting to change the topic, "Casey and I are not going to be spending our honeymoon in the bunkhouse. At the rate we're going with the work here, I figure the house should be livable in another couple of days."

"I'll let the boys know. They'll be glad to find out they won't be evicted."

They reached the Circle D and stopped at the stable to tend to their horses before going to the house to get cleaned up for dinner.

Elizabeth had been anxiously awaiting Michael's return since the messenger from town had dropped off the letter. She was worried that it might contain bad news.

"Michael—Nick—I'm so glad you're here," she said, meeting them at the door.

Michael sensed her urgency and was immediately concerned. "What's wrong? Did something happen to Pa? Is he all right?"

"No, it's nothing like that," she answered as she ushered them inside. "It's just . . ."

"What?"

"You got a letter here," Frank announced as he

wheeled himself into the hallway, holding the missive.

"A letter? Who's it from?"

"We don't know. Rob brought it out from town a few hours ago. He said it was from a lady at the hotel."

Michael grew uneasy. He took the proffered envelope and went into the parlor to open it. His parents and Nick followed him, but waited in the doorway as he read the missive in silence.

My Dearest Michael,

I couldn't bear to be apart from you any longer. I've made the trip to Hard Luck with my mother to be with you. We are staying at the hotel here in town for now. As soon as I hear from you, we can come and stay with you on your ranch.

I am waiting eagerly to hear from you.

Love,
Karen

Michael stared down at the letter in silent disbelief.

Karen was in Hard Luck.

She had followed him to Texas.

He looked up from the letter to find his parents and Nick watching him with open curiosity.

"It's not bad news, is it?" his mother asked.

Michael grimaced inwardly. "That depends on what you call bad news and who you ask, I guess."

"Who's here?" Nick had a feeling he already knew the answer to his question, judging from the look on Michael's face.

"Karen. She's in town."

Nick nodded slightly. His suspicion was confirmed.

"Who is Karen?" Frank demanded, wondering what female could be causing so much trouble.

"Karen Whittington. She's the young woman I was seeing back in Philadelphia," Michael explained.

"Why did she follow you here?" Elizabeth asked, curious to know more about her.

"All she said in her note was that she missed me and wanted to see me."

"So she packed up and came here unannounced and uninvited?" Frank was amazed at the woman's audacity.

"Yes," he answered simply.

"That's something Karen would do," Nick said, knowing exactly what she was like. He knew, too, that Karen wasn't going to be happy when she discovered Michael was engaged to Casey.

"What are you going to do about her?" Elizabeth asked, already thinking about protecting Casey.

"It's too late to do anything tonight. I'll ride into town in the morning and see her."

"And you'll tell her about Casey. There's no point in her staying on when you're engaged to another woman."

"Don't worry," Michael promised his mother. "I'll tell Karen everything."

"I don't envy you that reunion," Nick said.

"You don't want to ride in with me?" Michael couldn't help smiling at his cousin's reluctance to face Karen's wrath.

"Thanks for the invitation, but I've got work to do on Casey's house."

"Coward."

"You're right about that."

"What's this Karen like?" Elizabeth asked. She found their remarks about her intriguing and wanted to know more.

"Her family is very wealthy and well-connected."

"Were you seeing her that often that she should feel it's appropriate for her to come here and track you down?"

"I had been seeing her, but there were no promises between us. When I got the news about the shooting, I sent word to her that I had to leave, and I honestly haven't thought much about her since."

Michael's mood remained tense that night. He didn't have much to say during dinner. His thoughts were on what the new day would bring. He considered letting Casey know what was going on, but decided against it. With any luck at all, he could straighten things out with Karen and send her on her way without Casey ever finding out the other woman had come to Hard Luck.

Not that it would matter.

Michael was certain Casey wouldn't care one way or the other about Karen coming to town, but he didn't want to put her in an embarrassing situation. Soon Casey would be his bride, and as his future wife, she deserved his respect.

John was smiling all the way out to the Bar T. He was feeling quite pleased with the way things were going, and by the time he got done talking to Casey, he was pretty sure life was going to be wonderful.

Michael Donovan had another fiancée.

And she had come to Hard Luck.

John was going to love telling Casey.

It was dark as he rode up to the ranch house. A light was shining from the window, and as soon as he'd reined in, Casey came out on the front porch.

"John? What are you doing here at this time of night?" She was surprised to see him so late, and uneasy, too, for her father had already gone to bed.

"I need to talk to you, Casey. It's important," he said as he dismounted and went to her.

John had a plan in mind. He believed that once he revealed the truth about Michael and his secret Eastern fiancée, Casey would throw herself into his own arms, seeking solace, and he'd be more than willing to provide all the comfort she needed. He was eagerly looking forward to that moment. Though he had been temporarily thwarted in his master plan, things were definitely looking up now. Casey was going to be his, after all.

"Of course, but let's sit here on the porch," she told him, indicating the wooden bench there. "It won't be all that comfortable for us, but Pa is already asleep and I don't want to wake him. He needs all the rest he can get."

John liked knowing Jack was asleep. It meant he and Casey were alone. Lecherous thoughts teased him, but he controlled them for the time being as he sat down next to her.

"How is he feeling? Better, I hope?"

Casey didn't bother to ask John how he'd heard of her father's illness. News—good and bad—traveled fast around Hard Luck. "Yes, he is better."

"Good. I was concerned."

"Thank you." She looked up at the handsome rancher, wondering what had been so important to bring him to see her at this time of night.

John glanced down at her hand and noticed she wasn't wearing Donovan's ring. His hopes soared for a moment, thinking she'd broken off the engagement to him already. "Aren't you engaged to Michael anymore?"

"Oh, yes. We're still engaged. I wear the ring on a chain to keep it safe."

"Oh." His previous thought that this trip might have been unnecessary was gone. "When I didn't see you wearing it, I thought you might have heard the news already."

Casey frowned. "News? What news?"

John was more ready than ever to tell her. "When I was in town today, I heard Ernest from the hotel talking—"

"About what?" Casey couldn't imagine what the man had to say that would cause John to ride all the way out to the Bar T tonight.

"According to Ernest, there are some new guests staying at the hotel—two women."

"So?"

"So, one of them—a woman named Karen Whittington—is Michael Donovan's fiancée from back East."

"What?" Casey didn't know what she'd expected him to say, but his announcement left her in complete and utter shock.

John's manner was serious as he related all the gossip he'd heard.

"But how could Michael promise to marry me if he was engaged to another woman?" A tumble of emotions assailed Casey—confusion and fury along with humiliation and, unexpectedly, pain.

"I don't know," John offered in his most sympathetic tone as he gazed down at her. He reached over and took her hand. "That's why I rode out here to see you. I thought you deserved to know the truth as soon as possible. Casey"—he said her name tenderly—"I'm sorry."

Stunned, Casey looked up at him. "John—"

"Is there anything I can do to help you?" he offered.

"No. I don't know," she responded, struggling to keep her runaway emotions under control.

John knew this was his opportunity and he drew her closer, slipping an arm around her shoulders. "You know how much I care about you, Casey. You know if you ever need me, I'm here for you."

Casey almost let herself relax against John. He was offering her comfort and protection and she longed for both, but as quickly as the urge came, she realized she would be no better than her lying, cheating, miserable excuse for a fiancé if she went into John's arms. She pulled back and stood up to move away.

John was thoroughly annoyed, but he told himself to be patient and bide his time. The news he'd given her was devastating; she would need time to adjust to Michael's betrayal.

"I'm sorry I had to be the one to tell you, but I didn't

want you to be caught unaware. You know how much I care about you, Casey," he repeated earnestly as he stood up beside her. "If you ever need anything, you only have to ask."

She nodded as she lifted her gaze to his. "Thank you, John."

He stared down at her in the moonlight. Casey was lovely—and soon, very soon, she would be his. He wanted her, but he would wait. In a gentle, nonthreatening move, he bent down and pressed a single kiss to her cheek.

"Good night, Casey."

John left her alone with her thoughts. He strode to his horse, mounted up and rode away. Things hadn't gone exactly as he'd hoped, but he'd started the fire, now he just had to wait for it to rage out of control. He was smiling as he rode off into the night.

Casey stood unmoving on the porch, staring after John until he had ridden out of sight. Only then did she sink back down on the bench. Her thoughts were racing as she tried to decide what to do.

Her first instinct was to get her gun and go after Michael.

She realized, though, that she wasn't willing to spend the rest of her life in jail or to be hanged over the likes of a miserable, no-good liar like Michael Donovan.

He wasn't worth it.

Casey wondered why John's news about Michael's secret fiancée hurt her so badly. She'd known from the beginning that their engagement was no love match, but this other woman . . . Michael must really love her. But if he loved Karen Whittington, why had he agreed to their marriage?

Casey had always prided herself on being strong, and when tears unexpectedly pricked her eyes, she grew even angrier at herself for her weakness.

Casey got up and walked away from the house.

She needed to be alone in the darkness.

She didn't want anyone to see her cry.

Chapter Twenty-two

It was late that night when Nick found Michael drinking alone in his father's study.

"Are you that worried about seeing Karen tomorrow?" Nick asked.

"I'm not looking forward to it," Michael ground out, taking a deep drink of whiskey. "Karen can be a very determined woman when she sets her mind to it."

"There's really nothing for you to worry about," Nick assured him. "Just tell Karen the truth and send her on her way. You're going to marry Casey. That's all Karen needs to know." Nick smiled at him. "You're man enough to handle her, I'm sure."

Michael chuckled. "I may be man enough to handle Karen, but what if Casey hears about this?"

"Then you'd better run for cover," Nick laughed. "Casey's a whole other story."

"That she is."

The tone of his voice changed so much that Nick frowned. "You do want to marry Casey, don't you?"

It was the first time that anyone had really asked him that. He looked thoughtful as images of his wildcat fiancée played in his thoughts.

He saw her breaking the bronc—

He saw her standing before him soaking wet after he'd dunked her in the river—

He saw her in his arms as they'd kissed—

He saw her as he'd carried her across the threshold of their new home—

Casey—

She had tormented him from the beginning—

She had stolen his clothes—

And now—

Had she stolen his heart?

Nick waited, puzzled by Michael's silence. Finally he asked him point-blank, "Do you want to go through with your marriage to Casey? Or do you want Karen? You'd better decide right now."

Then Nick quit the room, leaving Michael alone with his thoughts.

It was long past midnight when Michael finally made his way upstairs to bed. Despite all the liquor, he did not fall asleep right away. He lay in bed, thinking about the future and wondering about the wisdom of the decisions he'd made.

* * *

Casey stayed out of the house until she got her emotions under control. When she went inside to her bedroom, she lit the lamp on her dresser and caught a glimpse of herself in the mirror. She stood there unmoving, staring at her own reflection. The evidence of her crying was apparent in her swollen eyes and reddened cheeks, and she was thankful her father had been asleep and hadn't gotten a look at her tear-stained face.

She poured fresh water in the bowl at her washstand and scrubbed her face. She didn't want anyone to know she had shed tears over Michael Donovan.

After undressing, she donned her nightgown, put out the lamp and climbed into bed. She couldn't decide if she was eager for morning to come or if she was dreading it. Either way, she was going to confront Mr. Michael Donovan about his fiancée first thing tomorrow. She wanted answers to the questions that were tormenting her.

The hours passed slowly. There were times when Casey thought morning was never going to arrive. When dawn finally brightened the eastern sky, she got up and dressed. She left a note on the kitchen table for her father, telling him she was making a quick trip to see Michael and would be back soon. Then she strapped on her gun belt and strode from the house.

A few of the ranch hands saw her ride out, but none of them questioned her. They knew better than to mess with Casey when she had that look on her face.

Casey rode straight for the building site, believing Michael would be there working. When she found the house deserted, her first thought was that Michael must be off seeing Karen.

In frustration, she started off toward the Circle D ranch house. She would have preferred to have this discussion with him in a more private setting, but one way or the other, she was going to have it out with him this morning.

Nobody played her for a fool and got away with it.

Nobody.

"Hey, Michael!"

Michael was in the stable saddling his horse when he heard one of the men calling him. He went to the door and looked out.

"What is it?"

"You got company coming."

He looked down the road and immediately recognized Casey riding his way. He drew a ragged breath, trying to ignore the pain pounding in his head from his over-indulgence the night before. He went out to meet her.

"Good morning, Casey," he said. He tried to give her a smile, but the sun was hurting his eyes as he looked up at her in the saddle. He noticed she was wearing her side-arm today, and he was surprised. "Are you expecting trouble?" He gestured toward the gun.

"Trouble is already here, Donovan," she ground out, dismounting and facing him. "I had a visitor last night."

He wasn't sure what she was leading up to, but judging from her fury, he knew it would be bad. "Who?"

"John McQueen."

"What did McQueen want?"

"It seems John was in town yesterday and heard that your *fiancée* from Philadelphia had just arrived in town!"

"Casey, I—"

Before he could say more, she drew her gun and fired at the ground near his feet.

Michael jumped nervously as he faced the full brunt of her fury. "Casey, put that damned gun away before someone gets hurt!"

"I'm a very good shot," she answered coolly.

"Karen is not my fiancée!" he protested, staring at the gun in her hand.

"Liar!" She got off another round and found she enjoyed seeing him dance to her tune.

"Dammit, woman! I'm not lying to you!"

"Oh, yeah?" she snapped. "Then how come everybody in town thinks she is? Everybody in town knows all about her being engaged to you. I don't abide liars, Michael Donovan."

"And I don't lie, Casey Turner!"

They glared at each other for a moment in silence, unaware of the crowd that had gathered to watch the excitement.

"You are my fiancée, Casey. I've never proposed to Karen. Now cool off."

"Cool off?" she repeated in outrage. "You and your Eastern sweetie have just humiliated me before the entire town of Hard Luck!"

"I haven't humiliated you. In fact, I was just on my way in to town to meet with Karen and—"

"So you knew she was here!"

"Only because I got a letter from her late last night. She had one of the men from the stable deliver it to me."

"And you were going in to Hard Luck to see her and you weren't going to tell me about it?" Her rage grew.

"I was going to see Karen so I could tell her about *our* engagement."

"Sure you were," she sneered in disbelief.

"That's right. I was. Now"—he changed the tone of their exchange—"I want to know why McQueen felt it was his business to tell you about this."

"John was just being a friend to me. He didn't want me to be caught off guard by all your lies."

Michael grew even more angry. "I'm not going to tell you again, Casey. I haven't lied to you." He closed the distance between them to speak to her in a quieter tone so no one else could hear what he was saying. "What does it matter to you anyway? This marriage of ours is going to be in name only, so what do you care if I have a girlfriend back in Philadelphia?"

Casey stiffened as she stared up at him. "You're right, Donovan. I don't care."

In a smooth move, she holstered her gun and turned her back on him. Without another word, she mounted up and rode away.

Michael stared after her for a moment, then started back into the stable to get his own horse.

He had to pay Karen a visit.

When Michael turned around, he realized he'd had an audience the whole time.

"What are you looking at? Go to work!"

Just then, Elizabeth came hurrying around the side of the stable to see Cassandra disappearing down the road.

"Michael! I heard gunshots!" Elizabeth called out. "What happened?"

"Casey stopped by to take a little target practice."

"But—"

"I'll see you when I get back from town," Michael said, cutting her off as he swung up in the saddle. He'd done all the talking he wanted to do. He put his heels to his horse's sides.

Elizabeth looked around at the hands who'd gathered there, but they were already drifting away. Frustrated, she returned to the house.

"Karen, dear, I am so sorry," Dorothea told her in her most sincere tone. She knew how humiliated her daughter was that Michael hadn't come in to town to see her yet. "I never dreamed anything like this would happen."

"Neither did I," Karen bit out.

In her heart, Karen had expected Michael to rush to the hotel to see her just as soon as he got her note last night. But it hadn't happened. Now here it was already late in the morning, and still there had been no response from him.

"Let's go out to breakfast. We can't just sit here waiting forever for him to show up."

"Oh, yes I can," Karen said stubbornly. "You go ahead. I'm going to stay here a little longer."

Dorothea realized then that her daughter needed some time alone to deal with her troubled emotions. "All right, darling. I'll go over to the restaurant and have breakfast on my own. I hope the food will be better than what they served us for dinner last night. Do you want me to bring you something?"

"No. I'm not hungry."

"I'll see you in a little while."

Left by herself in the hotel room, Karen paced back and forth in growing agitation. She cursed Michael for not coming for her immediately, and then she cursed herself for caring.

How dare he treat her this way!

How dare he ignore her after she'd made this horrible trip just to see him!

After a few minutes, Karen went to stand at the window. She stared out at the miserable main street of the miserable town. Oh, how she missed Philadelphia! She longed to be back home in civilized society. If she could have arranged it, she would leave for Philadelphia that very moment. But she couldn't.

Karen made up her mind right then and there that if Michael hadn't shown up by noon, she was going to the stage depot to book their return trip. She didn't know where he was or what he was doing, but if he cared anything about her, he would have dropped everything and come to her. The hours were passing, and she was still waiting.

As Karen gazed despondently out the window, she saw a cowboy riding up to the hotel. Something about him held her attention, but she wasn't sure what it was.

When he dismounted and started inside, she finally realized the man was Michael.

Shock radiated through her.

The Michael she knew was a sophisticated gentleman. The man who'd just entered the hotel looked like nothing more than a lowly ranch hand.

Karen stood back from the window and turned to stare at the hotel room door. Any moment he would be there, knocking on it. Having just gotten a look at him, she wasn't sure if she was excited about seeing him again or dreading it.

Michael entered the Hard Luck Hotel to find Ernest at the front desk.

"Good morning, Michael."

"Ernest," he said tersely, not looking forward to the encounter to come.

"It's about time you got here," Ernest said.

"So I understand."

"Your lady is upstairs in Room 203."

"My lady?" Michael repeated.

"Yes, sir. Your fiancée, Miss Whittington."

Michael stifled an inner groan. Casey had been right. The news was all over town.

"Thanks, Ernest."

He wasn't going to waste time right then trying to set the clerk straight. It was more important to set Karen straight. He would take care of Ernest later.

Michael went up to Karen's room and knocked on the door.

Despite her disappointment, Karen was tempted to run to the door and throw it wide at the sound of his knock.

She controlled the impulse and asked calmly, "Yes? Who is it?"

"It's me, Karen. It's Michael."

"Michael! At last." Karen opened the door to him. "You're here—finally!"

Without waiting for him to say a word, she forgot all about caring how he was dressed or that he was so late in coming to her. Instead, she launched herself straight into his arms and kissed him passionately.

Michael was shocked by her kiss. He stood stock-still for a minute, then took Karen by the upper arms and pushed her away from him, ending the embrace.

"Karen, someone might come by."

"Oh—" She managed to blush a bit as she took his hand and drew him inside her room. She started to close the door behind them to give them privacy, but he stopped her.

"I wouldn't want anyone to question your reputation," Michael explained as he deliberately left the door open.

It made Karen angry that he didn't want to kiss her more. They'd been apart for what seemed like ages. She gave him a sweet smile instead of saying what she really felt.

She eyed his cowboy attire but didn't remark on it. The Michael standing before her bore little resemblance to the sophisticated man she'd known in Philadelphia. She realized with a start that Michael was even wearing a gun and holster! He looked almost primitive.

"To what do I owe this honor, Karen? Why are you here?" he asked, ready to get this over with.

"When you left Philadelphia so abruptly without coming to see me, I was upset. I thought you'd be returning right away, but when I didn't hear from you for so long, I got worried. I spoke with your uncle, and he told me where you'd gone. I thought you might need me here with you," Karen explained. "I've missed you, Michael, and I can't wait for us to get back home."

Michael had known that confronting her wouldn't be easy, but she was making it even more difficult than he'd imagined. "I'm sorry about the way things have turned out, Karen, but it looks like I won't be returning to Philadelphia."

"I know it won't be right away, but—"

"No. I won't be going back at all."

"You won't?" She stared at him, aghast. There she was, standing before him, ready to throw herself into his arms, and he was refusing her! Karen wanted to scream. "But—"

He quickly went on to explain, "My father was ambushed and seriously wounded."

"He was shot down?" She shuddered as the news emphasized her opinion of how uncivilized this place was.

"Yes."

"That's terrible. Who did it?"

"We still don't know."

"Dear God." In civilized Philadelphia, she was certain the assailants would have been caught right away. She wondered anew why anyone would want to live here.

"It's been a very hard time for my family."

"I'm sure it has, and that's why I came here. I knew you needed me," she said ingratiatingly.

Michael had to disabuse her of that notion right away. "There's nothing you can do, Karen. My father is paralyzed. He can't walk, so I have to stay and take over running the Circle D."

"No, you don't," she countered, dismissing his assertion out of hand. She believed he would listen to her because she was being logical, and her plan was, in her opinion, brilliant. "There are many fine doctors back East, and I'm sure they are far more qualified than any sawbones you may have here. All you have to do is sell the ranch and move your mother and father to Philadelphia with us. Your mother came from there. I'm sure she wouldn't object, and surely you could find a physician there who could help your father. If he is as bad off as you say he is, his only hope is better medical care."

"That's not going to happen, Karen."

"But—" She couldn't believe Michael didn't want to do what she suggested. It only made sense.

"My father wouldn't do it. The trip itself would probably kill him, and he has no desire to leave the Circle D. He loves the ranch."

"We could wait until he's stronger and then—"

"Karen." Michael realized the moment had come. He'd tried to be gentle, but it wasn't working. He was going to have to be blunt with her. "There's no point in going on about this. This isn't just about my father anymore. There's something else I have to tell you. Something you don't know."

"What?" She couldn't imagine what he was talking about.

"Karen, I won't be going back East with you, no matter what happens with my father. Since my return, I've become engaged."

Chapter Twenty-three

To say that Karen was shocked by the news of Michael's engagement was an understatement.

"You're engaged—to someone else?" she demanded, staring at him as if he'd suddenly grown two heads.

"Yes, to Casey Turner. We're getting married next week."

"Casey Turner?" She stared at him aghast. Never in all the time she'd known him had she heard him mention anyone named Casey Turner, and now— Now! He was going to marry her! Next week! "Who is she?"

"The woman I love." He wanted to convince Karen once and for all that there was no future for the two of them.

"What about us?"

"What about us, Karen? We saw each other socially,

but there was never anything more than that to our relationship."

"I thought we were going to be married when you returned from your trip to Europe with Nick," she insisted.

"I never told you I loved you, and I never proposed." Michael was blunt. "I'm sorry if you had the wrong impression about my feelings for you."

"But you've only been back here for a matter of weeks." In her mind she was trying to calculate if the other woman could be pregnant. "How can you be marrying her so quickly?"

"Casey and I have known each other for years. Seeing her again after all the time I've been away made me realize how much she means to me." Michael was determined that Karen should believe his marriage to Casey was a love match.

"And I mean nothing to you, Michael? After I made this trip out here just to see you, to let you know how much I care about you." Though she was furious, she forced herself to cry, hoping her tears would make a difference with him.

"I'm sorry, Karen."

Michael knew it was time to go. There was nothing more for him to say. He turned and left the room, shutting the door behind him.

Karen stared at the closed door for a moment, then her fury erupted. She grabbed the nearest thing—the pitcher from the washstand—and threw it as hard as she could. It crashed against the door and shattered.

Michael had just reached the steps when he heard the crash.

He kept on going.

Karen had never suffered a rejection before. Wealthy sophisticate that she was, she had always been the one who ended relationships. She couldn't let Michael just walk away from her. She wouldn't allow it! Karen was proud, and she had no intention of just giving up and going back home. Somehow she was going to find a way to make Michael hers.

"Karen, dear, I'm back," Dorothea began as she started to enter the room. She stopped when she saw the broken china on the floor. "Oh, my! What happened? Did you have an accident?"

"No. Michael was here."

"And?" Dorothea looked from the shattered china to her daughter.

"And he informed me that he's become engaged to another woman."

Dorothea understood how devastated Karen must be and immediately went to take her in her arms. "I'm so sorry, darling. We made this whole horrible trip for nothing."

"Michael may be engaged, but he's not married yet," Karen went on in a fiercely determined voice.

"What are you planning to do? Don't you think we should go home?"

"Oh, no. I didn't come all the way out here to just give up without a fight. There has to be some way I can see him again. Some way I can spend time with him."

"Well, you know, while I was eating in the restaurant, I did hear some of the townsfolk talking about a church social and dance this Saturday night. If you want a chance to show Michael what he's going to be missing, that would be your opportunity. But there is one thing I want you to think seriously about."

"What's that?"

"Do you really love Michael, or are you just acting out of anger? I know we came here to see him in the hope that the two of you would become engaged. You won't be opening yourself up to further embarrassment, will you?"

"Right now I'm not sure how I feel about Michael. I am furious with him for doing this to me, but love him? I don't know."

"I understand. I know you were set on marrying him, but everything has changed."

"Yes, it has. Michael also told me that he has to stay here in Texas and take over the day-to-day running of his father's ranch."

"Oh, then maybe it's fortunate all this happened. You certainly don't want to live here, do you?" Dorothea asked.

"No. I told him he should sell the ranch and move back to Philadelphia with his parents." Karen went on to tell Dorothea about his father's condition. "But Michael wouldn't even consider leaving."

"Let's see what Saturday brings."

"Do you think he'll attend?"

"The lady I spoke with at the restaurant seemed to think the whole town would show up. So we'll be there, too. Maybe when Michael sees you in a social setting, the way he's used to seeing you, it will remind him of how very wonderful you are and what he'll be missing."

"In the meantime, I want to find out all I can about his fiancée."

"What's her name?"

"Casey Turner."

"Casey? What an odd name for a woman," Dorothea remarked. "We can start asking around town—discreetly, of course. That way you'll be ready for anything that happens at the social."

"I'll be ready, all right. You'll see." She gave her mother a confident, superior smile.

"How did it go?" Nick asked when Michael arrived at the building site. He'd been watching and waiting for his cousin.

"About like I expected it would."

"That bad, huh?"

"Yes, but it's over. Now all I have to worry about is Casey."

"She was one angry woman when she rode away this morning."

"She sure was."

"It's a good thing she knows how to shoot, she could have done you a lot of damage if she'd missed—or aimed too high." Nick had been hoping to lighten Michael's mood, and he was glad when his cousin finally laughed.

"You're right about that. I'm just glad Karen didn't have a gun this morning."

"I bet." Nick was chuckling. "Think about it, though. You've got women fighting over you."

"Impressed, are you?"

"Absolutely. I've never had any women fighting over me."

"Trust me, it isn't as great as it sounds," Michael assured him. "Let's get to work."

"You know there is a church social this Saturday night," Elizabeth informed Michael and Nick over dinner that evening.

"Do you think Anne from the general store will be there?" Nick asked hopefully.

"Everybody will be there. It's quite the event. You will be taking Casey, won't you?" she asked, looking at her son. "It will give you the perfect opportunity to set things straight with her—and show everyone in town that there are no problems in your relationship."

Michael had told her everything that had happened with Karen. Elizabeth was coming to genuinely care for Cassandra, and she wanted to protect her from any ugly gossip.

"I haven't talked to Casey about it."

"Why don't you plan on going?" She said it in a way that would not allow him to refuse.

"What if Casey doesn't want to attend?"

"Cassandra and I have to go into town tomorrow for

her final dress fitting with Sissy. I'll speak to her about it then."

Michael could tell he was trapped. "Fine. Make the arrangements with her, and we'll go."

Casey had worked extra hard all day just to keep her mind off Michael. She was furious with herself for the way she'd reacted when John had told her Michael was engaged to another woman.

She'd actually been jealous!

Casey told herself she could not allow herself to care about Michael. He certainly didn't care about her.

It was late when she returned to the house, exhausted and ready for a quiet night.

"One of the boys from the Circle D brought this by for you," Jack said, handing her an envelope when she sat down at the dinner table with him. "He said it was from Elizabeth."

"Oh." Casey opened it and quickly read the note.

"What does she want?"

"I have to meet her in town tomorrow for the final fitting on the wedding dress."

"That's good. The wedding is getting close."

"And she wants me to attend the church social with Michael on Saturday night."

"That's not a bad idea," Jack encouraged, "especially after what you told me about the gossip in town."

Casey hadn't wanted to tell him any of it, but she had explained everything when she'd returned from the Circle D that morning. She'd realized everyone in town knew about Michael's "other" fiancée, so her father would undoubtedly hear about it sooner or later. The news would be better coming straight from her.

"All right. I'll tell her I'll go when I see her tomorrow."

Casey wasn't looking forward to spending time with Michael, but there was no way to avoid it. They were engaged, and soon they would show the whole town just how much "in love" they were. She grimaced inwardly at the thought and hoped the rest of the week went real slow. She was in no hurry to see her "beloved" fiancé again.

"There you are!" Sissy greeted Casey the following day. "Elizabeth is already here. Come on in."

They went back to the dressing room where Elizabeth was waiting for her.

"Hello, Cassandra, dear, how are you?" Elizabeth said warmly.

"Fine." She hesitated to say much more, for she didn't know how much Elizabeth knew about Karen Whittington.

"Michael told me about this whole awkward situation with the young lady from Philadelphia. I'm sorry if it upset you. I was just telling Sissy about the misunderstanding."

"It was awkward, but Michael straightened everything out."

"That's good," Sissy said. "You don't need that kind of excitement so close to your wedding day."

"No, we don't," Elizabeth agreed.

Sissy brought out the wedding dress.

Casey quickly shed her clothes.

Both Elizabeth and Sissy noticed she was wearing her old undergarments.

"Why aren't you wearing the pretty new things you got the last time you were here?" Sissy asked.

Casey blushed uneasily at her question. "They were so delicate-looking, I was afraid to wear them on a regular day."

"Nonsense, Cassandra. You start wearing them now. That's what we bought them for," Elizabeth said encouragingly.

With the seamstress's help, Casey slipped into the wedding gown.

Sissy arranged the skirts and adjusted the bodice, then stepped back to study her handiwork. Elizabeth stood with Sissy, and they both looked Casey over.

The white satin gown was perfect on her.

"What do you think?" Sissy asked Elizabeth.

"She looks positively radiant. You did a fine job."

"Thank you."

"Look at yourself in the mirror, Cassandra," Elizabeth urged.

Casey moved to the full-length mirror and stared at her reflection. "It's lovely."

"No, you're lovely," Elizabeth insisted.

"You are going to be the most beautiful bride Hard Luck has ever seen," Sissy complimented.

"I wouldn't say that." Casey had never been told she was beautiful before.

"We would," Elizabeth said.

"Now let's see how the other gowns I made for you fit. I think you're going to be pleased with them, too."

The first dress Casey tried on was a simple day gown. It required little in the way of alterations, and Sissy promised to have it ready before the wedding.

"This next one is special. It's going to look lovely on you," Sissy told Casey as she left the room for a minute.

Casey was expecting another day gown. She was awed when Sissy returned.

"What do you think?" Sissy asked, smiling in delight at Casey's surprised expression as she held up the lovely confection. "This will be perfect for the social Saturday night."

"Oh, yes, it will," Casey agreed, staring at the dark blue gown. She'd never owned anything as nice as this.

"We thought you might like it," Elizabeth said. "Try it on."

With their help, Casey donned the gown and, after Sissy had fastened the back, turned to the mirror. She almost didn't recognize herself. In the wedding gown, she had looked radiant and pretty. In this gown, Casey was shocked to think she almost looked seductive. The color complimented her, the silk clung to her curves, and the bodice, though modestly cut, revealed enough to let the world know she was a woman full-grown.

"I have a pearl necklace and earrings you can wear," Elizabeth said, studying her critically. The transformation was more complete than she'd dreamed possible. She'd always believed Cassandra was pretty, but now she knew her son's fiancée was beautiful. "We'll have to do something with your hair. Do you want me to come to your house and help you get ready Saturday afternoon?"

"Would you?" Casey looked at Elizabeth in delight, appreciating the offer of feminine guidance.

"Of course. This will be fun. We'll surprise Michael."

"He'll be surprised, all right," Casey agreed.

"Sissy, you've done a wonderful job. Thank you," Elizabeth told her.

"I loved every minute of it." Sissy had to admit the change in Casey was the most exciting she'd ever seen. Casey was lucky to be getting a mother-in-law who cared so much about her.

Sissy boxed up the gowns, and Casey put them in the buckboard she'd driven in to town that day. After thanking Elizabeth and saying good-bye, Casey drove to the general store, hoping that Anne might be working.

Chapter Twenty-four

Ernest was just coming on duty at the hotel when he noticed Casey driving her buckboard down the street. He'd had to clean up the mess Miss Whittington had made when she'd had her showdown with Michael Donovan, and he wondered if she knew what Michael's real fiancée looked like. He went into the hotel and hurried upstairs to knock on the Whittingtons' door.

"Yes, who is it?" Karen called out.

"It's Ernest."

She opened the door to see what the desk clerk wanted. "Yes?"

"I know this ain't none of my affair, but seeing as how you're interested in Donovan and all, I thought you might want to get a look at Casey Turner while you had the chance."

"She's here?" Karen was eager to see the woman who'd stolen Michael from her.

"She's outside, driving by right now if you want to take a look." Karen ran to the window, and her mother joined her there. They were all but hanging out, trying to see the woman outside.

"I don't see her," Karen complained.

"There's only a boy driving by in a buckboard," Dorothea told him.

Ernest snickered. "That's no boy, ladies. That's Casey Turner."

"Are you serious?" Dorothea asked, then turned to look out again at the driver of the passing buckboard.

"That's Casey?" Karen said in a shocked tone. The girl was wearing men's pants.

"That's her," Ernest affirmed.

"Thank you, Ernest," Dorothea said, signaling it was time for him to leave them.

"You're welcome, ladies."

When he'd gone, Karen looked at her mother, feeling quite smug. "I am going to have a wonderful time at the social this weekend. So Michael thinks he wants to marry a woman who looks and dresses like a boy. I'll show him what he's missing."

"Good girl!" her mother exclaimed.

"I was almost dreading the thought of going, but now I'm excited about it."

Karen couldn't wait for Saturday to arrive.

* * *

"Why, Casey! What a pleasant surprise," Mrs. Lawson said as Casey entered the general store. She and Anne were working together behind the counter.

"Hello, Mrs. Lawson. I had to come in to town for the final fitting on my wedding dress, so I thought I'd drop by and see you."

"This wedding is so exciting," Mrs. Lawson said.

"Yes, it is exciting," Casey agreed, but for different reasons. "Anne, are you going to the social Saturday night? Elizabeth thinks Michael and I should go together, so we'll be there."

"Oh, yes, we're going," Anne answered. Then she asked, "Casey, is Michael's cousin Nick going to attend?"

"I don't know. Do you want me to ask him to come?"

"I don't want to seem forward, but—yes!" Her eyes lit up at the thought of seeing the handsome Easterner again.

"I'll do my best. It'll be a good chance for you to get to know each other better. He's going to be Michael's best man, and you're my maid of honor."

"I can't wait."

"I've never known you to be so interested in a man before."

"Well, Nick is really different. He's a gentleman. I've never met anyone like him before, and I want to get to know him better."

"You have good taste in men, Anne. I like Nick, too."

"He reminds me of a hero out of one of the dime novels I read."

"You are such a romantic."

"I know," she sighed and smiled. "Some day my prince will come."

"Prince Nick?" Casey said thoughtfully.

"Oh, you!" Anne laughed at the thought. "But it would be nice, wouldn't it? To be swept off your feet by a handsome nobleman and live happily ever after."

"Yes," Casey said, hiding the sadness in her heart. "It would."

But it was never going to happen to her.

Saturday came far too quickly for Casey. The thought of seeing Michael again made her decidedly uneasy. Elizabeth had assured her that Michael had taken care of everything with the other woman, but even so, she wasn't sure how thrilled he was going to be to see her again. After all, the last time she'd shot at him.

Casey kept herself busy working around the ranch all morning. She returned to the house for the noon meal and to start getting ready. She knew it was going to take a while to go from being a cowgirl to becoming the lady Elizabeth hoped she could be. She just hoped she could do it.

After soaking in a hot tub, Casey scrubbed herself clean from head to toe. That done, she dried off and donned some of her new underthings.

Casey was actually a bit embarrassed as she put the silken garments on. She'd never worn anything like them before. She wrapped herself in her robe and sat down at her dressing table to brush out her hair.

The sound of a carriage approaching drew Casey to the

window. She looked out to see Elizabeth and Michael arriving separately. Michael came in the buckboard and Elizabeth in her carriage.

Within minutes, Elizabeth was knocking at her bedroom door.

"Hello, Cassandra, dear. How are you today? Are you all ready for tonight?" she asked as she was admitted to Casey's room. She was carrying a small valise.

"I'm as ready as I'll ever be, I guess," Casey answered, clutching her robe more tightly around her. She closed the door once Elizabeth was inside.

"I brought a few things that might work well with your dress. Let's get started, shall we?"

Casey was a bit nervous. She'd never had to worry about getting dressed up before. "Where do you want to start?"

"I think with your hair," Elizabeth said thoughtfully, eyeing her damp curls. "Why don't you sit down for me?"

Elizabeth loved a challenge. She was excited about helping Cassandra get ready today. She knew Michael still had misgivings about their coming marriage, and she wanted to show him what a beautiful woman Cassandra really was.

Elizabeth set to work.

Michael was sitting with Jack in the parlor, making small talk and waiting for the women to join them. Close to an hour had passed, and Michael was beginning to wonder if they were ever going to come out.

Jack noticed he seemed a bit impatient. "These are

women we're dealing with here, Michael. They're going to take a while."

"It would be good to get to town before the dance is over," Michael remarked dryly.

"You will," he assured him. "Michael?"

Michael glanced up.

"You know this hasn't been easy for my girl, getting married this way, and that whole scandal with your other woman—"

"Karen isn't my 'other' woman," Michael protested. "I had been seeing her socially in Philadelphia, but there were no promises made between us. I don't know where she got the idea to come to Hard Luck. I hadn't had any contact with her since I left."

"Be that as it may, everybody in town heard about her, and Casey was embarrassed by it all."

"Your daughter did make that point to me," Michael said, remembering all too clearly their encounter the other morning. "And I took care of it."

"That's good. With only a week left until your wedding, it's time the two of you got things settled between you."

Michael didn't know what there was to settle.

He and Casey were engaged.

They were going to be married in seven short days.

And tonight they were going to show the whole town just how devoted they were to each other to silence any remaining gossip, ignoring completely that the last time they'd been together, Casey had been shooting at him.

The men finally heard the bedroom door open and they both looked up as Elizabeth came to join them.

"Are you ready?"

"Yes, we are," Jack answered.

"Cassandra," Elizabeth called to her.

The door opened wider and a vision of loveliness came into the room.

Michael rose to his feet as Casey moved to stand before them. Never in his wildest dreams had he envisioned her being this beautiful. Casey was gorgeous. She looked every bit a lady. Her hair was styled up away from her face, giving her an elegant look. The gown, though demurely styled, was stunning on her, emphasizing her feminine figure. She wore pearl earrings and a single strand of pearls at her throat that complemented her creamy complexion. On her left hand, she wore the ring that marked her as his.

"Casey—you look lovely," Michael told her, unable to look away.

"Thanks," she replied in her usual casual manner.

" 'Thank you,' " Elizabeth cued her.

Casey grinned at her and repeated more demurely, "Thank you, Michael."

Her father hadn't said anything yet, and Casey looked at him to see his reaction. Her breath caught in her throat at the sight of him, standing there looking at her with tears in his eyes.

"Pa? What's wrong?"

"Oh, darling. I wish your mama could see you now. She would be so proud of you," he said, going to embrace her. "You're the image of your mother."

Casey struggled not to cry as she gave him a kiss on the cheek and whispered, "I love you, Pa."

"I love you, too, darling. I just wish I was feeling better so I could go along with you tonight. But you and Michael go on into town and have a good time."

"I wish I could go, too, but I need to get back home to Frank," Elizabeth said, still smiling over Cassandra's transformation. "I would love to be there to watch folks' reaction when they see you."

"Anne's going to be surprised," Casey agreed.

"Pleasantly surprised, I'm sure," Elizabeth replied.

"Are you ready to go?" Michael asked courteously. He suddenly felt the need to act the gentleman with her, so he went to offer his arm.

"I think so." She took Michael's arm and let him draw her toward the door. She would never admit it to anyone, but she was glad for his help. She was a little unsure of herself in these fancy clothes.

Together they left the house.

"We're taking the carriage," he informed her.

"Are you sure?" Casey knew it was his mother's.

"I insist," Elizabeth said as she stood with Jack on the porch.

"Thank you." Now she truly would feel like a lady, riding in the carriage instead of in the buckboard.

Michael helped her into the carriage, then climbed up beside her and took the reins.

"Have a good time," Jack bade them.

"We will," Michael answered, and he was surprised to find he meant it.

Jack and Elizabeth watched them drive away.

"They make a very handsome couple," Elizabeth said with great satisfaction.

"Yes, they do." Jack turned to look at her. "I hope they find a way to be happy together."

"So do I."

"Is Frank going to be able to attend the wedding?"

"He seems to be a little better, and he has been using the wheelchair. I'm hoping he'll be strong enough by next weekend to make the trip into town."

"I guess we could always ask Reverend Harris to hold the ceremony at your place."

"And I'm sure the reverend would do it, but I'd like the wedding to take place at church if at all possible. I'll let you know mid-week how Frank is doing."

"Will you be all right on the ride back in the buckboard?"

"It's still light out, so I'll be fine. You take care of yourself."

"I'm trying."

Jack helped Elizabeth into the buckboard, and she drove home, quite satisfied with the way things had turned out. She couldn't wait to tell Frank all about it.

Michael and Casey rode in silence for a few miles before she finally spoke up.

"I meant to tell you—I like your clothes," she said with a grin, looking him over.

He slanted her a quick glance and saw her devilish

smile. "Lady—" He was about to warn her that she was playing with fire.

"Lady?" Casey repeated, stunned. "You just called me lady—"

"That's right. Tonight you look like a lady, so try your best to act like one."

"Are you sure you want me to?"

"I'm sure."

"Well, I was trying to compliment you on your suit."

"Fine, just don't try to run away with it tonight," he chuckled.

"I don't quite think I'll get a chance at the church social."

"I hope not."

They both found themselves laughing at the outrageous picture that brought to mind.

At that moment as he laughed easily by her side, Casey looked up at Michael and realized all too painfully that she had come to care for him.

She hadn't meant to.

She'd fought her feelings for him every step of the way, but the sound of his laughter had touched her heart and melted the last of her resistance to the truth.

She loved him.

Yet she could never let him know, for he didn't want her love.

He only wanted her land.

Still, Casey knew that that very night she was living a fairy tale just like Anne had talked about. She was the princess who was going to the ball with the handsome prince, and she intended to allow herself to enjoy every moment of their time together. Reality would return far too soon. She wanted to pretend, for just a little while, that this upcoming marriage of theirs was truly a love match.

Chapter Twenty-five

John McQueen was in a good mood as he and some of his men rode into Hard Luck to attend the social. Tonight was the night he'd been waiting for. He hadn't been back into town since the night he had gone to see Casey. He was anxious to learn the outcome of his visit with her. He was certain Casey had broken off her engagement, and that made this the perfect night for him to make his move on her.

Tonight he would court Casey and woo her, and set the stage for making her—and the Bar T—his.

It was going to be a glorious evening.

Nick rode into town with the men from the ranch. He was looking forward to seeing Anne again and had even worn one of his suits to impress her. The other men had let him know what they thought of his getup, but he'd decided it was worth suffering their taunts to get Anne's attention.

"I wonder how Michael is doing with Casey," Harry remarked as they reached the edge of town. They all knew he'd ridden out early to pick her up at the Bar T.

"We'll be finding out real soon," Nick replied. "What time does the dance start?"

"Not until seven," Harry answered. "Do you want to stop at the Sundown for a drink since we're early?"

"Sounds good to me," Nick agreed.

"What do you boys think? Will they let Nick into the Sundown dressed this way?" Harry asked.

"They'll serve him," Tom replied. "Rosalie don't care how you're dressed. She just cares about the color of your money. If our dandy here is flashing his cash, he'll get waited on real fast."

"It's good to know I won't get run out of town because I'm dressed like a gentleman." Nick was smiling. He'd grown used to their ribbing and had proven to them that he could take it as well as dish it out.

"Of course, that don't mean any of us will be standing at the bar with you," Harry countered.

They were all laughing as they reined in before the Sundown. The men of the Circle D went inside to relax and have a drink.

Rosalie was already downstairs working the room.

"Good evening, boys. It's good to see you," she welcomed them. "You in town for the big dance tonight?"

"We sure are, Rosalie," Harry told her, "but we decided to pay you a visit first."

"Well, I appreciate your business," she said, then

looked at Nick. She remembered him from when he'd come in with Michael to offer the reward for information on Frank Donovan's shooting. "Did you ever get any response to the reward you and Michael offered?"

"Nothing ever came of it."

"That's too bad," she sympathized. "Frank used to come in here pretty regular. He's a good man."

"Yes, he is."

The men stayed at the saloon until it was time to head over to the hall for the dance.

Rosalie watched them go, and she actually felt a twinge of anger and jealousy. No doubt John would be at the dance tonight, but she was not accepted at such social functions. Of course, she was certain that once he finally got around to marrying her, all that would change. Once she was the wife of one of the most successful ranchers in the area, she would be accepted everywhere. She just wished he'd hurry up and propose.

"Are you ready to go?" Karen asked as she finished primping before the mirror over the dressing table and turned to look at her mother.

"Yes. Let's go see what this miserable excuse for a town considers a big social occasion."

"Well, how do I look?" Karen stood up and posed before her mother.

"Absolutely beautiful." Dorothea's gaze went over her daughter critically, taking in the rose-colored gown and the way she'd pinned her hair up in a complicated style. "I've always loved that color on you. Once Michael gets a look at you tonight, he won't give that boyish fiancée of his another thought."

"Good. That's my plan. By the time this evening is over, I intend to have him back in my arms."

"And then, thank heaven, we can start making plans to go home."

Anne was standing with her parents, watching the couples on the dance floor.

"I wonder when Casey is going to get here," Marjorie Lawson asked her daughter.

"Soon," Anne assured her.

"I don't envy Casey tonight," Marjorie sympathized. "Why, I can't believe that Philadelphia woman and her mother are still in town. If it had been me, I would have been so humiliated I would have left right after seeing Michael"

They had already noticed the two strangers mingling in the crowd.

"I would have, too, but I'll bet she thinks she still has a chance with him. Why else would she stay? She doesn't seem to be the kind of woman who would enjoy our kind of life."

"It should make for an interesting night."

"I'm not sure 'interesting' is the right word to describe what might happen."

"Let's just hope things go smoothly. I'd hate for there to be trouble. This will be the first time Michael and Casey have attended a social function as a couple, isn't it?"

"Yes, it is."

"Then let's say a little prayer for them."

"I already did, the minute I heard Karen Whittington was still in town."

Richard Perkins approached Anne for a dance, and she kept smiling as she allowed him to lead her out onto the dance floor. Richard was a nice enough man. Anne had known him all her life, and though he was gainfully employed as the telegraph operator in town, he just didn't excite her. In truth, even as she circled the dance floor in Richard's arms, she kept watching for Nick to arrive. She had her heart set on seeing him tonight, and she hoped he was making the trip into town from the Circle D to attend.

The hall was crowded when Michael and Casey reached town. They were forced to park the carriage a short distance away and walk over.

"Are you nervous?" Michael asked as he helped her descend.

"No," Casey answered quickly, then gave him a weak smile. "Actually—yes, a little."

"Don't be. Everything is going to be fine. You'll see."

"So I'm supposed to trust you?" Casey asked, wariness obvious in her voice.

"That's right. I'm your fiancé. If you can't trust me, who can you trust?" he countered.

"That's a scary thought."

"You'd better start getting used to it. This time next week, you'll be my wife."

"That's even scarier."

He chuckled and, always the gentleman, offered her his arm again.

Casey took it. She could feel his hard-muscled strength beneath the fine cloth of his jacket. She found it reassuring and clung to him as they started off toward the hall. They looked every bit the devoted, loving couple.

"Anne, may I have this dance?" John McQueen asked, approaching her.

"Why, thank you, John."

Anne allowed John to lead her out onto the dance floor.

"Are you having a good time tonight?" he asked, just making small talk. He'd been watching and waiting for Casey's arrival, and had decided to dance with Anne to find out if she knew when Casey would be showing up.

"Oh, yes, these dances are always enjoyable. It's fun to get to see everyone. It's not that often we get the chance to visit this way."

"Is Casey coming? I haven't seen her yet tonight."

"She'll be here. I talked to her just the other day, and she was looking forward to it."

Anne glanced toward the main door to the hall as she was speaking. Just at that moment Nick came in.

Excitement rushed through her at the sight of him looking so handsome and debonair.

Nick is here!

At last!

Anne wanted to break away from John and go straight to Nick, but she knew that might cause trouble since they were in the middle of a dance. She controlled her desire with an effort, continuing to smile up at John and make small talk.

Nick stood at the edge of the dance floor with Harry. He was looking around to see if Michael had shown up yet with Casey, but saw no sign of them. He did catch sight of Anne, dancing with another man. She looked as lovely as ever. He was tempted to cut in, but then he spotted Karen standing with her mother on the opposite side of the room.

After what Michael had told him about his ugly encounter with her, Nick had thought Karen and her mother would have packed up and taken the next stage out of Hard Luck heading back East. He was shocked that she was still in town, and he knew Michael would not be happy when he showed up and laid eyes on her.

It was at that moment Karen spied Nick. She quickly made her way through the crowd to him.

"Nick, darling," Karen greeted him, pressing a kiss on his cheek.

"Hello, Karen."

"Surprised to see me?" she asked archly.

"I'd heard from Michael that you were in town."

Karen gave a laugh as the music stopped. "I bet you did. Where is Michael? He is coming tonight, isn't he?"

"He should be showing up anytime now."

"Good. I can't wait to see him again," she purred. Another tune began, and she put Nick on the spot. "Dance with me?"

Ever the gentleman, Nick swept Karen out onto the dance floor.

Anne was delighted when the music finally ended. She kept her true emotions hidden as she thanked John for the dance, and immediately started looking for Nick. She spotted him just as the next dance began, looking on helplessly while he took the sophisticated, elegant woman from back East into his arms and out onto the dance floor.

Disappointment filled Anne. She started to make her way to the refreshment table to get a cup of punch. She hadn't gone far when she heard a murmur going through the crowd.

"Can you believe it?" one older woman was saying.

"No. What happened?"

"I don't know, but it's wonderful—"

"Maybe she did it to keep Michael from straying. I mean, if he's got women chasing him here from all the way back East—"

Anne realized they were talking about Casey and Michael, and that they must have just arrived. Heads were turning toward the main entrance, so she looked that way, too.

And there they were.

Michael was standing just inside the main door with Casey on his arm. Anne was mesmerized by the change in her friend. She had always known Casey was a natural beauty, but she'd never realized how lovely she truly was until now.

Tonight Casey looked every bit the lady. From her perfectly coiffed hair to her necklace and earrings and gown, Casey was stunning. And Michael looked proud to be standing by her side.

Anne went to join them.

"It's about time you got here," Anne scolded with a teasing smile. "You look marvelous!"

"Thanks," Michael answered, grinning at her.

"Not you! You!" she laughed as she gave Casey a hug.

"You really think so?" Casey was more than a bit nervous about making this grand entrance.

"I know so," Anne told her. "Come on. My mother and father are over by the refreshment table. I want to show you off."

Anne led them to her parents.

Nick had also seen Michael and Casey come in. He had always known Casey was attractive, but he'd never realized she could be this gorgeous. He forced himself not to smile as he thought of the eruption that was about to happen once Karen got a glimpse of her.

"Michael just got here," Nick told Karen as he continued to dance her about the floor.

"Where?" Karen twisted about, wanting to get a look at him.

Nick felt her stiffen in his arms the moment she spotted him.

"Who's that woman with him?" she asked, puzzled.

"That's Casey."

"No. That's not Casey. I've seen Casey. That can't be her. Casey Turner looks like a boy."

"You're wrong, Karen," Nick insisted. "That's Casey. And she definitely doesn't look like a boy tonight, does she?"

"But . . ."

"But what?" he asked

It wasn't often that it happened, but Karen found herself unnerved for a moment. The difference in Casey's appearance was astounding. Now she knew she had some truly serious competition for Michael's affections. Winning him back wasn't going to be as easy as she'd thought . . . but she was Karen Whittington of the Philadelphia Whittingtons.

"Nothing," she said, smiling up at Nick as if nothing unusual had happened. She changed the topic. "So tell me, how are you enjoying your time here in Hard Luck?"

"It's been interesting," Nick answered. "I just wish our reason for coming here in the first place had been different."

"Your uncle's getting better, though, isn't he?" She still held on to the hope that Michael would be returning back East.

"He's paralyzed, Karen. He's never going to walk again."

"I told Michael to bring him back to Philadelphia so some of our fine doctors could examine him, but he refused."

"Uncle Frank won't leave the Circle D. He loves it here."

"But that's so stupid," she said hotly.

Nick glared down at her. "Not to Uncle Frank, it's not."

The music ended and he put her from him.

"Thank you, Karen. If you'll excuse me—"

Casey stood at Michael's side talking with Anne.

"Is Nick here?" Casey asked her.

"Oh, yes. He's here," Anne answered. "In fact, he's right over there."

Casey glanced in the direction she'd indicated and saw Nick dancing with a woman she'd never seen before. "Who's she?"

"That's Karen Whittington," Michael put in. He realized there was no avoiding the topic.

"The woman who—"

"Yes. Karen is the woman I was seeing in Philadelphia," he answered, annoyed. "I'd expected her to be gone by now. I hadn't realized she was staying on."

"I think Karen likes to surprise you," Casey said, an unexpected surge of possessiveness coming over her. She knew there was only one reason Karen would have stayed, and that was to try to steal Michael away from her.

"It looks that way," Michael said.

"Do you like her surprises?" Casey asked, still feeling a bit unsure of herself.

"No," he answered as he looked down at her. He smiled, wanting to set her mind at ease. "Would you care to dance?"

"I'd love to," she answered.

"If you'll excuse us, Anne?"

"Of course, but you owe me a dance later, Michael," Anne teased.

"If my fiancée lets me."

"I might let you dance with Anne, but only Anne," Casey told him as he took her out onto the dance floor and swept her into his arms.

Chapter Twenty-six

The moment proved magical for Casey.

She'd never danced with Michael before. As he led her around the room, she found herself caught up in the pure bliss of the moment. She was in his arms, moving in rhythm with him to a beautiful melody. Michael's strength and his smooth, practiced lead made her feel delicate and protected. Casey had never felt so feminine in her life.

She lifted her gaze to find Michael staring down at her, and she actually blushed.

"You're blushing," he observed with a rakish grin. "I've never seen you blush before."

"I don't think I ever have."

"Why now?"

She frowned a bit. "I'm not sure, but I think I like dancing with you."

"You think?"

"Well, you're very good at it, and somehow it feels right."

It feels right.

At her words, Michael fell silent for a moment. He concentrated on the dance, allowing himself to appreciate having her in his arms. They were moving together as one to the music, and he realized, almost as an epiphany, that it really did feel right.

"You're beautiful, Casey," Michael told her in a soft, seductive voice.

"I am?" She looked up at him, startled. Her gaze met his, and she saw an intensity in his dark-eyed regard.

"Yes, you are."

His confirmation sent a completely unexpected shiver of desire coursing through her. She nervously wet her lips and forced a small smile.

Michael suddenly knew a driving need to kiss her. He wanted to pull her close and taste of her sweetness right then and there in front of everybody, but he couldn't. Instead he kept dancing and tried to think of a way to get her alone, outside under the stars.

John was talking with Allen Foster from the bank when Allen saw Michael come in with Casey on his arm.

"Take a look at that," Allen said in casual conversation, nodding their way. "It's hard to believe it's the same woman."

John turned and went still as he stared at the smiling couple. Allen was right. The woman on Michael's arm was gorgeous. John had always figured if Casey cleaned herself up, she would be good-looking, but he'd had no idea the change in her would be this dramatic. His shock was followed by instant anger.

"I can't believe she showed up with him," John snarled.

"I know. I heard the talk, too. Isn't the woman from Philadelphia still here?"

"Yes." John looked around the hall and caught sight of Karen standing on the opposite side of the dance floor. "I believe that's her right over there."

"She's pretty."

"I think I'll go ask her to dance." John had expected Casey to break her engagement to Michael. Obviously, that hadn't happened. He didn't know what was going on, but he intended to find out.

Karen was furious as she watched Michael and Casey. She couldn't believe the other woman had cleaned up so well. She had come to the dance tonight expecting Casey Turner to look little better than she had when she'd seen her driving the buckboard. She was shocked by the change in her and by the fact that Michael and Casey actually looked happy together.

Fury and jealousy ate at Karen.

She had to do something, and fast.

"Would you care to dance?" John McQueen invited as he appeared by her side.

Karen had been so intent on her tumultuous feelings that she hadn't noticed his approach. She looked up at the handsome, blond-haired man and flashed him her most devastating smile. "Why, I'd love to dance with you. Thank you."

"You're new in town, aren't you?" John asked as he led her out onto the dance floor.

"That's right. I'm a friend of Michael's from Philadelphia. My name's Karen Whittington." She followed his lead and discovered quickly that he was a very good dancer.

"It's nice to meet you. I'm John McQueen. I'm a friend of Michael's, too."

"Are you a rancher?"

"Yes, I own the Royal ranch. It's north of town."

"Is it truly royal?" she asked flirtatiously.

"My goal is to make it the biggest, most successful ranch in this part of Texas," he told her with confidence.

"How close are you?"

"Close—real close."

"You must be very proud of what you've accomplished," she said, playing up to him.

"I am, but enough about ranching. What about you? Are you enjoying your visit to Hard Luck?"

"It's been interesting. I've never been this far west before."

"How much longer will you be in town?"

"My mother made the trip with me, and we haven't decided yet when we'll be going back."

"So you're not staying on permanently."

"No. I came to see how Michael was doing. His father's situation is so tragic."

"Yes, it is, and the last I heard, they still don't know who shot him."

"Do the Donovans have a lot of enemies?"

"No more than anybody else in these parts, I guess. I suppose one day they might find out who did it, but right now there's nothing for anyone to go on."

As John led Karen in the dance, he deliberately kept moving toward Michael and Casey. He wanted to be near them when the tune ended. He planned to ask Casey for the next dance and turn Karen loose on Michael. He had seen how Karen was watching Michael. She might be calling herself Michael's "friend" now, but John was certain there were hard feelings.

John's plan worked perfectly. The music stopped, and he and Karen found themselves standing close to the other couple.

"Good evening, Michael—Casey," John said, giving them a smile. He was feeling proud of his acting abilities.

"John," Michael returned, and then looked at Karen. "Hello, Karen. Let me introduce you to my fiancée. This is Casey."

Karen smiled tightly at Casey. "It's nice to meet you."

Casey didn't believe a word she said, but she returned the smile. "I've heard a lot about you, Karen. Hello, John."

"Evening, Casey. I was hoping to have this next dance with you, if Michael doesn't mind," he invited as the music started up again.

Before Casey could say anything, Karen took advantage of John's ploy.

"Michael? Will you dance with me?"

Michael had no desire whatsoever to dance with Karen. The farther he stayed away from her, the better, as far as he was concerned, but he'd been put on the spot. There was no graceful way out of the awkward situation.

"Of course, Karen."

Karen didn't need any further encouragement. She went straight into his arms as if she belonged there.

Casey saw how comfortable Karen seemed with Michael. She watched them together even as John danced her about the floor.

"So you managed to work everything out with Michael?" he asked. "I was worried about you after our conversation the other night. I didn't know how things were going to go for you."

"Everything is fine. Michael was never engaged to Karen. She lied about their relationship. Michael and I straightened it out."

Inwardly John was seething. Once again it seemed his plans had been ruined.

"There's only a week left until your wedding," he said. "Are you really sure you want to go through with it, after all that's happened?"

"Oh, yes. I'm sure," she replied. She knew it was up to her to convince the world that her marriage to Michael was a love match, and she would start with John.

"With all the bad blood between your families all these years and then this unexpected trouble with Karen, I never would have thought you two would end up together," he remarked.

"I know. It hasn't been easy, but Michael and I are happy, and that's all that matters."

"Are you happy, Casey? Really?" John pressed the issue. "Are you certain Michael's not just using you? Casey—I care about you and I don't want you to be hurt."

"I appreciate your concern, John, but it's really none of your business." She deliberately made her tone a bit cool. She had no interest in him romantically, and it was time he realized it. "Michael and I love each other. I know it seemed to happen quickly, but we've known each other so long that once we recognized the truth of our feelings, it was all quite simple." The fact that she'd actually declared she loved Michael startled Casey, for she'd never said it out loud before.

John had hoped to rile Casey. He had wanted to get her furious enough to break off with Michael, but he realized now in a fit of barely controlled rage that it wasn't going to happen. He had been foiled again.

"What do you plan to do about Karen?" he asked.

"Nothing. She'll be gone soon. She means nothing to Michael."

"It doesn't look that way to me," he said, nodding in the direction of the other couple.

Casey looked their way to see Karen leading Michael by the hand from the dance floor toward the main door.

Jealousy seared through Casey. She didn't know what the other woman was up to, but she wasn't going to get away with it.

Casey was tempted to go after them that very minute, but she didn't want to draw attention to the situation. As soon as the dance ended, she was going to take action.

Michael Donovan was hers.

Karen was going to learn that lesson tonight—once and for all.

Nick made his way over to Anne.

"How are you this evening?" he asked cordially.

"Fine, now that you're here," Anne said with a smile. "And I love your suit."

"Some of the boys from the Circle D might argue that point with you."

"That's why I said it. I figured they were probably giving you a hard time," she laughed.

"They did, but I don't care what they think. There was only one woman I was trying to impress tonight."

"That's a wonderful line. I bet you use it on all the girls, and I bet they believe you."

Nick was accustomed to women falling at his feet when he turned on the charm. He'd never met anyone like Anne before, and he found himself chuckling. "You're right. I have used that line before, and it does usually work. There is one thing you need to know, though."

"What's that?" Anne's eyes were twinkling with good humor.

"I've never meant it before." He found it was the truth. Anne was different from any other woman he'd ever met.

Her eyes widened at his remark. She lifted her gaze to his. "Is that another line?"

"No," he said quietly. "Shall we dance?"

"Yes."

Anne almost felt like a princess in a fairy tale, like a heroine in one of her favorite novels, as Nick drew her out onto the dance floor. The rest of the world faded away as he whirled her about the room. There was only Nick and the music and the joy of being held in his arms.

The warning voice in her mind cautioned her that Nick belonged back East—that he would be leaving after Casey's wedding and she would never see him again.

But for right now, for this moment, Anne didn't care.

She let herself be swept up in the thrill of a fantasy come true.

A handsome prince had come to save her from her dull existence.

"Karen, whatever it is you wanted to talk about, we could have discussed inside," Michael said once they'd left the hall. He was ready to go back in. He had nothing more to say to her and wanted to be with Casey.

"No, Michael. What I have to say is private—just between us. I will not let our relationship be fodder for the town gossips," Karen insisted.

"We have no relationship, Karen. I'm engaged to Casey, and I'm going to be married next week. There's nothing between you and me."

"But Michael—" She looked up at him, her eyes aglow with the predatory excitement that filled her. "You can't mean that." She lowered her voice as she stepped closer to rub up against him. "I want you, Michael. I always have. That's why I made the trip all the way out here to see you.

I missed you. I wanted to help you. I wanted to be with you."

She lifted one hand to caress his cheek, wanting to draw him down for a kiss, but he caught her wrist and stopped her ploy.

"Stop it, Karen. Casey and I are getting married."

"But you aren't married yet. That can all change," she insisted in an even more sultry voice. "I can please you in ways your little cowgirl can't even imagine. Let me show you."

"This 'little cowgirl' is about ready to forget she's being a lady tonight!" Casey snarled, interrupting them.

Her first reaction to the sight of Karen and Michael seemingly embracing, had infuriated her. Then she'd overheard a part of their conversation and knew Karen was the aggressor.

"What are you doing here?" Karen looked at Casey in disgust, but stayed physically close to Michael.

"I came outside to see what you were doing with *my* fiancé. The dance is inside, you know."

"Casey, I can handle this." Michael could tell she was angry, and he knew what she was capable of.

"Michael and I were just talking," Karen insisted innocently, smiling at her with smug superiority.

"Good, and I'm joining your conversation," Casey declared, coming to stand at Michael's side.

"Our conversation is private."

Karen sounded so arrogant that Casey lost her ladylike veneer. She'd dealt with rough-and-tumble ranch hands all her life and wasn't the least bit afraid of Karen.

"There's something you need to know, bitch."

Karen gasped. "Michael! Are you going to let her talk to me that way?"

Casey didn't wait for Michael to answer. "Michael is mine," she stated firmly, stepping closer to physically intimidate Karen. "We're engaged. You haven't figured that out yet, so I guess you must be real stupid. Look! Here's my engagement ring!"

Casey held her hand up in Karen's face so she could see the diamond ring that marked her as Michael's.

"Michael gave this ring to me. Nobody invited you here. You're not welcome here. So I think it's time you took a hint and went back to Philadelphia where you belong. I'm sure there's a man somewhere in a city that big who will appreciate the fact that you can please him in such 'exciting' ways. Go find him. Michael's mine."

"But, Michael—" Karen looked up at him, shocked.

"Good-bye, Karen." He slipped an arm around Casey.

Karen was devastated by this, his final and complete rejection. She rushed away into the night, fleeing toward the hotel. Never in her wildest imaginings had she considered the possibility that Michael would really choose Casey over her. It was complete and utter humiliation.

Michael stood with Casey watching Karen hurry off. When Casey would have moved away from him, he tightened his grip and drew her with him into the shadows.

"Casey—"

"What?" She looked up at him, her expression guarded and a bit defensive.

"I didn't know you cared."

"I care about the ranch," she retorted, feeling suddenly very vulnerable before him. He was warm and strong and so devastatingly handsome, and he had just sent Karen on her way forever.

"Are you sure you're doing this just for the ranch?" he asked, his voice gentling as he drew her even closer.

Casey didn't respond as Michael bent down and claimed her lips in a passionate kiss.

Chapter Twenty-seven

Casey stood still for a moment as Michael kissed her, and then, unable to help herself, she looped her arms around his neck and drew him down to her. At her encouragement, Michael deepened the kiss, wrapping his arms around her and bringing her fully against him.

"Casey?" John called her name. He'd seen her leave the hall to look for Michael and Karen the moment their dance had ended. He'd followed after her to find out what was going on, under the pretense of concern for her.

At the sound of John's call, Casey and Michael broke apart. They stood there for a moment in the moonlight, staring at each other, overpowered by what had just transpired between them.

John found them and came up to speak to them.

"I take it you're all right," John said. He had witnessed their heated embrace.

"Casey's fine," Michael answered curtly, irritated that John had interrupted them.

John ignored Michael and looked at Casey. "Casey?"

"Everything is wonderful. Karen definitely won't be causing us any more trouble."

"Good." The fury burning within John was powerful. He didn't know what he had expected to find when he'd followed them outside, but it hadn't been the two of them in a clinch. He'd hoped for a nasty confrontation with Karen, but it hadn't happened. He could do nothing more for the time being than play his role of concerned friend. "I'm glad everything worked out."

"Let's go back in to the dance," Michael said, taking Casey's arm. He wanted to get away from McQueen. He didn't like the man meddling in their affairs and paying so much attention to her.

They started back inside, leaving John behind to follow.

But he didn't.

His anger was too red-hot.

John stood there staring after Casey and Michael, hating them for thwarting his grandiose scheme. Somehow, he vowed to himself, he would get even.

Right now, though, he needed a drink—bad.

John headed for the Sundown.

"Did you see Karen and Michael go outside? And then Casey follow them?" Anne was saying to Nick as they stood by the refreshment table sipping punch.

"It's going to be interesting to see what happens."

"Aren't you worried? Do you think we should go check on them?"

"No. Michael is perfectly capable of handling this himself."

"But I don't want Casey to be hurt," she said, worried about her friend.

Nick appreciated her kindness and concern, but wanted to calm her. "Karen is a smart, sophisticated woman, but she's no match for Casey."

"You really think so?"

"If Michael had wanted Karen, he would never have agreed to marry Casey."

"So they'll be fine?"

"Do you want to check and make sure?"

"Would you go with me?"

They put their cups aside, and Nick led her through the crowd. They reached the door just as Michael and Casey returned.

"Where's Karen?" Nick asked.

"With any luck, she's back at the hotel, packing her bags and getting ready to head back to Philadelphia right now," Casey said with confidence.

"What happened?" Anne asked.

"Casey helped me convince Karen that we really are getting married next week," Michael answered.

"Good. Now, as long as neither one of you decides to back out, there will definitely be a wedding."

"I'm not backing out," Michael said without hesitation, his gaze lingering on Casey.

She looked up at him and smiled softly, remembering his kiss. "Neither am I."

Nick and Anne watched the exchange and knew something had definitely changed between them, and it was all for the better.

Across the hall, Dorothea had been watching all that was going on. She'd seen Karen and Michael go outside, to be followed shortly by Casey. When Michael and Casey returned together and there was no sign of Karen, she knew things were not good. As quickly as she could, she left the dance and hurried back to the hotel to check on Karen. She hoped that they would be on a stage coach bound for home tomorrow. That thought and that thought alone made her smile as she went to face what she knew was a painful moment for her daughter.

Rosalie saw John come into the saloon and go straight to stand at the bar. She excused herself from the men she'd been talking with and went to wait on him.

"Evening, darlin'," she said in a husky voice. "The usual?"

"Yeah—and bring the bottle."

"You intend to have some fun tonight?" she asked flirtatiously as she poured him a straight whiskey and set it before him with the bottle alongside.

He only snorted derisively in answer to her question as

he downed the whiskey in one swallow, then poured himself another.

Rosalie had seen his darker moods before, and she knew better than to press him to talk when he was like this. She went about her business, keeping an eye on John in case he needed anything else. She hoped before the night was over to entice him upstairs, but she knew she had to let him drink for a while before she even suggested it.

John's frustration and anger did not abate as he continued to drink. He was a man who was not used to being denied. He always got what he wanted.

He took another deep swallow of liquor as he thought about Casey.

How dare she treat him this way?

How dare she pick Donovan over him?

His plans were ruined.

Women!

He hated them.

His thoughts grew blacker.

John lifted his gaze and found himself staring in the mirror behind the bar. In the reflection, he watched Rosalie move around the room and flirt with the other men. Tonight, even she had the power to enrage him.

John splashed more whiskey in his glass.

Rosalie returned to John's side some time later.

"Feeling any better?" she asked, giving him a smile.

"What do you think?" he snarled.

She was a bit surprised that he hadn't mellowed yet.

"Do you want me to make you feel better? We can go upstairs right now."

John stared at her for a moment. He hated her for being such an enticing woman, and he hated himself for his weakness in desiring her. "Let's go."

His curt answer wasn't what she expected, but she wanted him so badly that she didn't think there was really anything wrong. He seemed upset, but she knew just how to pleasure him. She'd make him forget whatever it was that was troubling him.

John grabbed the bottle, then took her by the arm, directing her almost forcefully toward the staircase.

Bill, the bartender, was watching, and he didn't like what he saw. He knew Rosalie loved John McQueen, but he personally had no use for the man. "Miss Rosalie—you gonna be all right?"

"I'm fine. You take care of things down here for me."

"I will."

Rosalie turned her full attention back to John as they started up the steps.

"John—you're hurting me," she told him quietly, trying to pull away without making a scene.

"That's not all I'm going to do to you."

She heard what sounded like a threat in his tone, but told herself he had no reason to be angry with her, so there was nothing to worry about.

John didn't release her until they were at her bedroom door. He let her go and waited as she opened it. She went in ahead of him and started to light the lamp on the bedside table.

"Don't," he ordered.

"Why?"

He shut the door and locked it.

"I want it dark in here." He wanted her to be nameless and faceless as he thrust within her.

"I like the way you think," Rosalie said, thinking he was being romantic.

That notion quickly changed when John came to stand by her. He put his bottle of liquor on the nightstand, then roughly pushed her down on the bed and fell upon her.

"John—what is it? What's wrong?" She was shocked by his actions.

He kissed her to silence her, but it wasn't a passionate kiss. It was a kiss meant to punish. After freeing himself from his pants, he pushed her skirts aside and stripped her undergarment from her. He mounted her.

Rosalie stiffened. She tried to resist, but there was no stopping him.

John thrust inside her, wanting to hurt her. He enjoyed her pain. For right now, there in the darkness, she was Casey—and he was punishing her.

Until that moment, Rosalie had believed they loved one another. Occasionally, John had been a little rough with her, but nothing like this. She almost felt as if she were being raped. She tried to twist away from him, to push him off her. He proved too strong, though. He kept her pinned to the bed, dominating her as he sought his release.

When at last he achieved the ecstasy he sought, John shuddered violently. He thrust all the more savagely into the depths of her body. Then he collapsed on top of her, panting from the exertion.

Rosalie couldn't believe what had just happened.

"Get off of me!" she demanded in disgust, pushing at his shoulders to try to dislodge him. She felt violated.

John was in no mood to listen to her. He raised himself over her and backhanded her across the face. "Shut up, woman. Nobody tells me what to do!"

He grabbed his bottle of whiskey and slugged down another long drink.

Rosalie was beyond shock. Her cheek was hurting from his blow, and she tasted blood. She was actually frightened by the change in him. She found herself wishing she kept a gun in the nightstand so she could defend herself. She was helpless before him, and she didn't like being helpless. Her only hope, she realized, was that he would drink himself into a stupor so she could slip away from him.

John put the bottle back on the nightstand and began thrusting deep within Rosalie again. He needed mindlessness. He needed a release for his pent-up lust for Casey.

Desperate to escape from him, Rosalie knew what she had to do. She reached out and grabbed the whiskey bottle off the nightstand, then with all the power she could muster, she hit him over the head with it. The bottle shattered, but her assault had the effect she'd hoped it would. John collapsed, unconscious upon her. In complete disgust, Rosalie shoved him off of herself and got up. Whiskey was everywhere, as well as broken glass, but she was free of him.

After lighting the lamp, she checked to make sure he was still breathing. Satisfied that he would wake up with only a headache, she got cleaned up and then dressed. She checked her cheek in the mirror and applied some makeup to the spot where John had hit her. Then she hurried downstairs. The farther away from him she got, the better.

Nick walked Anne home after the dance. When they reached her house and started up the path, Anne gazed up at the night sky. It was a clear night, and a canopy of stars twinkled high overhead.

"Are your nights this pretty in Philadelphia?" she asked with a sigh.

"No—and neither are the women," Nick answered, gazing down at her in the starlight.

"You always have the right line ready, don't you?" Anne asked with a grin.

"That wasn't a line," he told her seriously. "That was the truth."

"I'm supposed to believe you?" Her eyes widened.

"Yes," he said softly as he took her in his arms. "I don't lie."

Nick kissed her.

A sigh escaped Anne at the touch of his lips on hers. Nick's kiss was everything she'd fantasized it would be. It was gentle and cherishing and exciting all at the same time.

Nick had kissed many a girl in his day. He liked Anne and had had a nice time with her tonight. He had planned to kiss her good night and ride back to the ranch. He had not expected to be caught up in the wonder of Anne's kiss.

It was a simple kiss.

A gentle kiss.

But the power of it startled Nick.

He drew back, staring down at her in the darkness and seeing the same look of wonder on her face. He didn't say a word. He just kissed her again, wanting to make certain that he wasn't imagining anything, testing himself.

The second kiss passed the test with flying colors.

Nick drew Anne close as his lips moved over hers hungrily, devouringly.

For a moment, Anne was caught up in the wonder of his embrace. His kiss was pure heaven, and she wanted nothing more than to be in his arms, but she knew the truth. Nick would soon be traveling back East to the life he loved. She was only a diversion for him while he was in Hard Luck with Michael.

Summoning all her inner strength, Anne denied herself the pleasure of Nick's kiss and moved away from him.

"Good night, Nick," she said quietly. Then before he could speak or try to kiss her again and render her momentary show of strength useless, she hurried inside and closed the door.

Nick stood there staring after Anne. He couldn't remember the last time a woman had simply said "good night" to him and left him that way. He smiled as he stared at the closed door. He wanted to go after Anne and kiss her again, and his reaction surprised him.

Anne was a very special woman.

Nick turned and walked away.

Inside the house, Anne stood leaning against the door, trembling. Nick's kiss had excited her as no other man's ever had. She wondered how she was going to bear it when he left Hard Luck and went back to Philadelphia. She wondered, too, if there was any way she could make him stay.

Michael and Casey drove slowly on the trip home from the dance.

"Did you have a good time?" Michael asked as they drew up before the Bar T ranch house.

"Yes, I did. What about you?"

He climbed down and walked around to her side of the carriage to help her down. "There was one thing I didn't enjoy."

"Karen?"

"No."

His response surprised her as he reached up and put his hands at her waist to lift her out of the carriage.

"It was John. I didn't like him interrupting our kiss," he answered as he lifted her down. He didn't release her, but held her close and captured her lips in a sweet-soft exchange. Michael ended the kiss, then stepped back and walked by her side up to the porch. He remained on the walk as she mounted the steps. "Good night, Casey."

"Good night, Michael."

She remained on the porch watching him drive away.

In one more week, he would never have to leave her again.

Casey smiled as she went inside.

Chapter Twenty-eight

It was her wedding day.

Casey couldn't believe the week had passed so quickly. Now here she was at Anne's house getting ready for the ceremony that would take place in a little over two hours.

"Are you all right?" Anne asked, noticing how quiet she'd become.

"I'm fine," she lied. The truth was, she was more nervous than she'd ever been in her whole life, but she couldn't admit it, not even to Anne.

"You are going to be the prettiest bride Hard Luck has ever seen," Anne assured her.

"I don't know about that."

"I do. Your dress is gorgeous. You looked pretty at the dance last week, but today, in this gown, you're going to be positively radiant."

"Thanks, Anne."

"For what? Telling you the truth?"

They shared a hug.

"We'd better get going. You can't be late to your own wedding."

"I'm glad Michael's father was feeling strong enough to make the trip into town so we could be married in church."

"Everything is going to go perfectly. You'll see."

"What if Michael doesn't show up?" Casey joked, although the possibility had crossed her mind occasionally since they'd come to their agreement.

"He will. He'd be crazy not to, with a bride like you waiting for him at the end of the aisle. Now let's get you ready."

Michael and his family had come into Hard Luck a day early and taken rooms at the hotel. Elizabeth had wanted to make sure Frank was rested enough to attend the ceremony. It had been difficult for him to allow himself to be lifted out of the carriage there in town, but he'd suffered through the humiliation stoically. If people wanted to stare at him, so be it. He was determined to get on with his life.

Frank had made arrangements to meet with Allen Foster that morning. The banker had come to him in the hotel room, and Frank had paid off all of Jack's debts.

Elizabeth and Frank were waiting now for Michael and Nick to join them, and then they would all go over to the church together. Michael and Nick were right on schedule, and she let them into the room for a moment.

"You look so handsome," Elizabeth told her son as she gazed up at him adoringly. He was wearing his best suit, as was Nick. "Cassandra is a very lucky girl to be getting you for a husband."

"That she is, son," his father agreed.

"Are you ready to go to church?" Michael asked. He knew it would take them a little longer than usual with his father in the wheelchair.

"Yes, we're ready. I can't wait to see Cassandra in her dress. She is going to look so lovely."

"There's nothing prettier than a bride," Frank said. "Your mother looked gorgeous on our wedding day."

Elizabeth actually blushed. "Why, thank you, dear."

"It's true," he told her seriously, remembering.

"Everything is all set at your house, isn't it?" Elizabeth looked at Michael. She was still worried that something might go wrong on their wedding day.

"It's all ready," Michael assured her. They had run a little behind finishing up the house. He'd worked from sunup to sundown all week to make sure it was done. "We moved the furniture in last night. I'm sure Casey will want to change a few things once we're settled in, but it will do for now."

"She'll be proud of what you accomplished. You didn't have a lot of time."

"No, we didn't, but at least I don't have to evict all the ranch hands from the bunkhouse tonight so Casey and I could use it for our honeymoon."

Nick laughed, remembering his threat. "That's why

everybody was working extra hard to help you get your house finished."

"Shall we go?" Frank suggested.

Every detail had been seen to. All that remained was for the wedding to take place.

"It's time," Elizabeth agreed.

The church was already beginning to get crowded when they arrived. They positioned Frank's wheelchair in the side aisle at the front of the church. Elizabeth sat in the pew next to him. Michael and Nick went to meet with Reverend Harris.

"Your big day has finally arrived," Reverend Harris told Michael with a smile when they found him in a small room off to the side of the altar.

"Yes, it has," he agreed. "Is Casey here yet?"

"I haven't seen her, but I'm sure she'll be along. Why don't you two wait back here? I'll let you know when it's time to begin."

He left them alone as he went out to make sure everything was going smoothly.

"It won't be long now," Nick remarked with a grin.

"No, it won't," Michael agreed. In only a matter of minutes, Casey would be his wife.

"I never imagined when I came west with you that I'd end up being best man at your wedding."

"Neither did I."

"I know we've never talked about this, but I think Casey is the best thing that's ever happened to you," Nick told him.

"You do?"

"I liked her from the first time I met her there at the stable, and then once I found out more about her . . . well, I think she is one special woman. You're lucky to have her."

Michael was thoughtful. Casey had been a part of his life for a long time. Things were never dull when she was around, that was for sure. Her transformation from looking like a ranch hand to the lady she'd been the night of the dance was nothing short of amazing. He didn't know how this marriage of theirs was going to work out, but he planned to do everything in his power to make sure they had as good a life together as possible.

The terms of their agreement played in his mind, along with the memory of her kiss. He knew she expected him to honor the deal they'd made—that theirs would be a marriage in name only—but it wasn't going to be easy for him.

"You're right, Nick. She is special."

As he spoke, the organist began to play, signaling that the time had come for the wedding to begin.

Reverend Harris returned for them. He led Michael and Nick out to stand at the end of the aisle with him as they awaited Casey's coming.

Jack stood with Casey and Anne in the vestibule of the church.

"I wish your mother could see you now," he told Casey, his gaze lovingly upon her.

"She's watching us," Casey said with certainty.

"You're sure?"

"Absolutely."

Jack pressed a kiss to her cheek, then helped her adjust her veil.

The wedding march began.

"Ready?" Anne asked Casey as she handed her her wedding bouquet. The flowers for Casey's bouquet and her own had come from her mother's garden.

"Yes. I'm ready," she replied.

Anne walked ahead of them and started down the aisle.

Jack took Casey's arm and drew her to the door.

The church was full of family and friends. Everyone turned to watch as Anne began to walk slowly down the center aisle.

Anne looked even more beautiful than usual today. The demure pale blue gown she was wearing was suitable for church. It was high-necked and long-sleeved and trimmed in white lace. Anne had styled her hair up away from her face, and she was carrying a small bouquet of fresh flowers, trimmed in blue ribbon.

Anne reached the front of church and smiled at Nick, who was waiting there for her. They faced the minister, then moved apart as Michael stepped forward to wait for Casey to come to him.

Jack appeared with Casey on his arm at the far end of the aisle. They slowly made their way to the front of the church.

Casey lifted her gaze to see Michael standing with Reverend Harris, waiting for her before the altar. Her heartbeat quickened at the mesmerizing sight of him, so tall and handsome. As she walked with her father down the aisle, she was aware only of Michael.

Soon, they would be married.

Soon, she would be his bride.

They reached the front of the church. Casey felt only an instant of panic as her father prepared to hand her off to Michael. She turned to her father and kissed him. Tears burned in her eyes as she realized this was the end of her life as she'd known it.

Michael was her future.

Casey turned to the man who would soon be her husband.

Michael took her hand in his. She was a vision of beauty as she stood before him. She looked angelic in the wedding gown. Their gazes met. He could see the sheen of tears in her eyes and the shadow of uncertainty that was haunting her, and he wanted to reassure her. He smiled.

Casey hadn't thought Michael could look any more handsome, but when he smiled, he was even more devastating. She smiled tremulously back at him, and then they faced the minister, ready to begin what was to be their life together.

"Dearly beloved, we are gathered here today to join this man and this woman in holy matrimony," Reverend Harris intoned.

John McQueen was in attendance, only because he knew his absence would have been noticed in the tight-knit community. He was sitting toward the back of the church, silently raging to himself.

He didn't want to be there. He didn't want to watch Casey marry another man. He wanted her, and her ranch, for himself, but it wasn't going to happen.

She really was going to go through with this marriage to Michael.

John knew he was going to need a few stiff drinks after this wedding was over.

"Do you, Cassandra Turner, take this man, Michael Donovan, to be your lawfully wedded husband, to have and to hold from this day forward, to love and to cherish, in sickness and in health, for better or worse, until death do you part?" Reverend Harris asked, looking straight at Casey.

"I do," Casey answered without hesitation.

"Do you, Michael Donovan, take this woman, Cassandra Turner, to be your lawfully wedded wife, to have and to hold from this day forward, to love and to cherish, in sickness and in health, for better or worse, until death do you part?"

"I do," Michael said, his voice deep and certain.

"The ring," Reverend Harris urged him.

Michael took Casey's hand. He slipped the wedding band that went with his grandmother's engagement ring on her finger, claiming her as his for all eternity.

"By the power vested in me, I now pronounce you man and wife," the minister concluded. "What the Lord has joined together, let no man put asunder. Michael, you may kiss your bride."

Anne came to Casey's side and helped her lift her veil, then stepped away.

Michael smiled down at Casey as he took her in his arms for a chaste, cherishing kiss, right there before God and everybody.

"Ladies and gentlemen, may I present to you Mr. and Mrs. Michael Donovan," Reverend Harris announced.

The music began again.

Michael glanced to his parents and gave them a quick smile as he started to escort Casey down the aisle. She stopped him, though, and went to kiss her father one more time. Michael shook hands with Jack. Then Casey went to Elizabeth and Frank and kissed them, too.

"Welcome to our family, Cassandra," Elizabeth told her, smiling brightly at her new daughter-in-law.

"Thank you for everything," Casey said feelingly.

She turned back to Michael, and they made their way down the aisle and out of the church into the bright sunlight.

Anne was smiling as she stood with Nick, watching Casey and Michael greet everyone as they filed out of the church.

"The wedding was so romantic," she sighed. "I would never have dreamed they would end up together, but I think they're going to be very happy."

"I hope so."

Anne had hesitated to bring up the subject, but she

couldn't avoid asking him any longer. "Will you be going home now?"

"Soon, I guess. I'll have to talk to Michael about it, but things have settled down enough that I think he'll be all right without me."

Anne was usually a very self-possessed young woman. She was never forward or too outspoken, but at that moment, she couldn't help herself. "I won't be all right without you."

Nick glanced down at her, caught off guard by her remark. "You won't?"

"No, I won't."

Before he could say more, Anne was called away to talk with some of the townsfolk.

Anne realized she'd said too much, but she didn't care. In the short time she'd known Nick, she'd found herself falling desperately in love with him. She knew it was crazy. They had known each other only a matter of weeks, but there was something special about him that touched her in a way no other man ever had.

Now that the wedding was over, Nick would soon be gone unless she could find a way to make him stay.

Chapter Twenty-nine

The reception was held in the church hall. Elizabeth had taken care of all the arrangements, and everything went perfectly.

The music began, and Michael escorted Casey to the center of the dance floor and took her in his arms. Everyone looking on as Michael twirled her around the room thought they made a most handsome couple and that they were completely and utterly in love.

John sat at a table watching them dance. He realized now that the hope he'd held on to until the very last that Casey would come to her senses had been ridiculous. His opportunity to acquire the Bar T by marriage was over, but he still had Jack's bank loans to consider. Glancing around, he saw Allen Foster across the room, and he walked over to him.

"Foster, I need to talk with you," John declared.

"Of course," the banker said. He made his excuses to the people he was with and went to speak with John.

They moved off to a more private area.

"What is it, John?"

"I know you gave Turner more time, but I want you to revoke that extension and call in the loans on the Bar T Monday," he said coldly. He planned to move in as quickly as possible to claim the ranch.

"I can't do that," Allen answered reluctantly.

"The hell you can't! You work for me!" John snarled. "You'll do what I tell you to do."

"I know I work for you, but I can't call in the loans. Frank Donovan paid them off this morning. He has the paperwork to give to Jack Turner."

"Donovan did what?"

"He paid off every cent that Jack owed. The Bar T is free and clear of debt."

"What good are you to me?" John swore viciously under his breath. "Get out of my sight!"

Forcing himself to appear calm, John mingled for a few minutes longer, then left the reception. His mood was too black to continue smiling at people he couldn't stand.

Casey and Michael made the rounds of the hall, greeting their guests and thanking them for attending. More than once, someone remarked on how surprised he or she was that the two of them had married and that their parents seemed to be getting along. Reverend Harris remarked that it proved prayer really did work.

Jack was sitting at the same table as Elizabeth and

Frank. Now that the wedding had taken place, he felt that a great weight had been taken off his shoulders. He watched Casey with Michael and knew she would be safe from now on no matter what happened to him.

"Frank?"

Frank looked over at him. "What?"

"I want to thank you for convincing Michael to go along with my plan. I think everything will be all right now."

"You're right. It will be. Here." Frank took the papers Allen Foster had given him out of his pocket and handed them to Jack. "This is Casey's wedding present from us."

Jack unfolded the papers and read them. When he looked up at his former adversary, his expression was strained. "I never thought I'd say this, but you are a man of your word. Thank you."

"Whether we like it or not, we're family now, Turner."

Jack gave a short laugh. "You're right. We are."

Both men looked back at their children.

"Shall we dance again?" Michael invited his new bride. He knew it was almost time to leave, and he wanted to enjoy one last dance with her before they departed, for once they left, everything was going to change between them.

"I'd love to," Casey accepted.

The wonder of the melody and the pleasure of being in Michael's arms swept through Casey and left her smiling. For just this period of time, she could pretend that Michael did truly care about her and that their marriage was a real one. It was a fine fantasy, but she knew it couldn't last. He had agreed to the marriage for business reasons only.

Casey thought of the night to come and wondered what they were going to do about their sleeping arrangements. With only one bedroom in the house, she wasn't sure where she would be spending the night. She decided this was not the time to speak of it, though. She wanted to enjoy their time as bride and groom. She wanted to pretend for just a little while that this man holding her in his arms really did care about her and had married her for love.

Nick sat alone at a table near the back of the hall. His mood was troubled as he tried to figure out what was bothering him. He looked up, staring at the couples on the dance floor, and saw Anne dancing with another man.

Nick didn't know who the man was, but that didn't matter. What mattered was he didn't like Anne dancing with anyone else.

In a flash of sudden insight, Nick recognized that he might be jealous.

He'd never been jealous before.

The possibility surprised him.

He frowned, considering what it meant, for if he was jealous, it meant he cared.

His frown deepened.

Do I care about Anne?

The thought gave him pause.

He never cared about just one woman. He enjoyed all women, and they enjoyed him. He'd never allowed himself to get serious with any of them; there was too much pleasure to be found in the multitude to tie himself down to any single female.

Nick looked up at Anne again.

She was laughing at something her dancing partner had said.

His irritation grew.

The whole time at the reception she'd studiously avoided him except for moments when they'd had to act as part of the wedding party.

But that was about to end.

Getting up from the table, Nick went straight out onto the dance floor to cut in on Anne and her partner. He tapped the man on the shoulder.

"What?" the man asked.

"I'm cutting in."

Nick smoothly took his place when the man stepped away from Anne.

"Nick, what are you doing?" Anne demanded, surprised by his boldness.

"I'm dancing with the prettiest girl at the reception," he complimented her.

Anne looked up at him skeptically. "I bet you say that to all the girls."

"You're right. I do." Nick was being his most debonair, and he was surprised it wasn't working. Anne seemed almost immune to his charm. He added, "And generally it makes them smile."

Anne finally laughed, impressed by his honesty, but when she looked up at him, her expression was a bit defiant. "But I'm not just one of your many girls."

Nick became very serious as he gazed down at her. "I know that, Anne. Believe me. I know."

Nick maneuvered them near the side door. Then, without a word, he stopped dancing, took her hand and led her outside, away from everyone.

It was early evening. The shadows were deepening.

"Where are we going?" Anne asked.

"I wanted to be alone with you," he told her honestly as he looked around in frustration at the people on the streets.

All her life, Anne had been responsible and mature in her decision-making. In that moment, though, she suddenly felt as if she were living a scene from one of her dime novels. The man she wanted had just swept her away, and he wanted to be alone with her! Her heartbeat quickened at the thought, even as her conscience warned her: *Nick will be leaving soon, returning to his life back East. There could be no future for us.*

"I know where we can go," she said, casting discretion to the winds, not caring that they would only have this one night together.

They slipped away together, and Anne led him to the store's back entrance and opened it using the key her parents kept hidden there.

"Come on," she invited in a soft voice, leading the way inside the darkened store.

Nick followed Anne, then closed and locked the door behind them. He turned back to her, and she went into his arms.

Nick held her close and kissed her. It started softly, but passion erupted between them at that first embrace.

Anne had never known such excitement. Nick's kiss sent a thrill to the depths of her very soul. She had kissed a few of the men she'd been seeing around town, but none of their kisses had ever affected her as Nick's did. She gave a soft moan of delight as she responded fully to his embrace.

She was with Nick!

It was her dream come true!

Suddenly it didn't matter that he would be leaving soon.

It didn't matter that they had no future together.

It only mattered that they had this moment.

Nick, too, was caught up in the power of their attraction. Something about Anne aroused him as no other woman ever had. He deepened the kiss and began to caress her.

Anne stiffened at his touch, for she had never known such intimacy before, but then she relaxed against him as excitement shivered through her. A hunger to know more grew deep within her. The last shred of conscience was cast aside as she drew him through the darkened store and up the steps that led to a small loft area. She kissed Nick again, then quickly spread out one of the heavy blankets stored there. She knelt down and lifted her hand to Nick in invitation.

That simple gesture was all he needed. Nick took her hand and joined her on the blanket.

There was no need for words between them as he took

her in his arms and kissed her. His kiss told her everything she needed to know. The passion Nick had tried to deny overwhelmed them, and they came together in a blaze of glory. Kiss after heated kiss stoked the flames of their desire.

Anne had never known such ecstasy. She responded fully and without reserve.

She wanted this.

She wanted Nick.

When he began to work at the buttons on her dress, she helped him and slipped it from her shoulders. Nick pressed kisses to her throat and then moved lower to explore the pale silken flesh exposed above the top of her chemise.

Anne gasped at the feelings his intimate touch aroused. She stirred restlessly, wanting—no, needing more. She reached down to draw him up to her.

For an instant, they gazed at each other in wonder and excitement, and then their desire overwhelmed them. Nick bent down to her and claimed her lips in a passionate exchange that told her without words of the power of his desire for her.

Each touch, each kiss, stoked the fire that burned between them. Soon it flared out of control.

Anne had never known such ecstasy. She was mindless in her need to love him.

Nick's passion overwhelmed him. He wanted Anne as he'd never wanted another woman. A vague and distant warning sounded in his conscience, but he ignored it. He was driven on by his need to be one with her.

Each kiss and caress took them higher and higher until

they could bear the barrier of their clothing no longer. Nick helped her slip out of her gown, and she shivered in anticipation of what was to come. She was shy before him.

But only for a moment.

"You're beautiful," Nick told her in a husky voice, visually caressing her.

Anne reached for him to help him shed his clothes. She felt brazen as she ran her hands over the width of his hard-muscled chest and shoulders. "So are you."

Nick took her in his arms, and the heat of his naked flesh upon hers seared her.

"If you want me to stop, Anne, tell me now," he said in a low voice, barely in control of his passion.

"No, Nick. I love you." The words escaped her.

There was no time to say more.

Nick responded with a searing kiss that sent the flames of their desire out of control. He moved over her to make her his, and his body was a searing brand upon her.

An innocent in the ways of love, Anne held him to her heart as he claimed her as his in all ways. When Nick breached the proof of her innocence, she gasped in pain.

Nick had been caught up in the overwhelming beauty of her love, but he went completely still when he realized the magnificent gift she had just given him. He drew back and looked down at her, his expression one of awe.

"Anne—"

She gazed up at him, her eyes shining with the glory of her love. "I love you, Nick," she whispered.

He bent down and captured her lips in a tender exchange.

"And I love you," he answered, finally realizing the truth of his feelings for her. They hadn't known each other long, but there was no denying what was in his heart. Anne was special. He wanted her.

They came together in rapture's promise then.

One in heart.

One in mind.

One in body.

They loved.

When ecstasy burst upon them, they clung together, caught up in the power of their love.

Moments passed in silence as sanity returned.

Nick knew what he had to do.

He drew away from Anne.

"We need to get dressed."

She felt bereft as he left her. She also felt uneasy and frightened by the power of what had just happened between them and by the reality she now faced. Nervous, she clutched at her clothing, disoriented and wondering what she was supposed to do next.

Nick sensed her inner turmoil and reached out to touch her cheek in a gentle caress, smiling tenderly at her. "How far is it to the justice of the peace?"

"What?" She was shocked by his question.

"We're getting married. Now. Tonight."

"But . . . are you sure?" She was still confused.

He smiled and leaned toward her to press a sweet-soft kiss on her lips. "I'm sure. I love you, Anne, and I want to spend the rest of my life with you."

"I love you, too."

Chapter Thirty

It was growing late.

The time had come.

Casey knew it.

She and Michael had to act the happily married couple as they left the reception to spend their wedding night together.

Casey knew what everyone would be thinking. They would be thinking that she and Michael were blissfully in love, but sadly she also knew that wasn't true.

The night ahead loomed dangerously before her, for she wasn't sure what to expect. In her heart, she wanted this to really be the perfect wedding night. She had fallen in love with Michael, and she wanted their life together to be one of devotion and love. Casey thought back over the time they'd spent together and remembered his kiss from the night of the dance. It had been heavenly until John had interrupted them.

She wanted to know the ecstasy of Michael's love.

She wanted Michael.

But Michael didn't want her. He had agreed to their arrangement and seemed happy with the way things had been set up.

And so, the long hours of the wedding night to come stretched before Casey. She would be alone with Michael in their new house—in their marriage bed.

Needing to distract herself, Casey looked around for Anne and Nick. She wanted to tell them good-bye, but saw no sign of them anywhere in the hall. She wondered where they'd disappeared to, but had no time to worry about it, for Michael appeared at her side.

"The carriage has been brought around front," Michael informed her.

"It's time for us to go?"

"Yes."

"We need to say good-bye to our parents first," she suggested, trying to delay the inevitable as long as possible.

Michael agreed, and they sought out Jack, Frank and Elizabeth.

"Be happy," Elizabeth told them.

"We will be," Michael assured her.

"Good night, darling," Jack said, taking Casey in his arms and holding her to his heart.

"Good night, Pa." She kissed him tenderly on the cheek, then went to hug Elizabeth and Frank.

Before Casey knew it, they were in the carriage, waving good-bye to everyone as they drove away.

Michael was her husband.

They were married.

They were alone.

Michael sat beside Casey in the carriage, preparing himself for the night to come.

They had an arrangement.

He'd agreed to it.

Theirs was to be a marriage in name only, and he had to remember that, tonight and every night from now on. He almost admitted to himself that he regretted agreeing to her proposition. Not that it would matter. Casey had made it clear from the start what she thought of him. Theirs would be a peaceful coexistence, but never anything more. That was the way she wanted it.

Michael wondered why that knowledge was bothering him so much as he drove off into the darkening night with his beautiful bride by his side.

John was drunk, and he planned to get much drunker. He'd deliberately gone to the Full House saloon tonight. He hadn't wanted to see Rosalie yet, after what had passed between them the last time they'd been together.

At the time, John had thought he'd passed out in her bed from all the liquor he'd drunk. When he'd gotten up in the wee hours of the morning, Rosalie had been nowhere to be found and he'd had a terrible headache. He'd left straight for the Royal, not bothering to look for her. It had only been later, after he'd returned to the ranch and sobered up a bit that he'd realized his savage headache had been from a lump on the back of his head and not from liquor. Rosalie had hit him.

Women—they were all stupid sluts!

At that moment, John hated all females, but Casey and Rosalie most of all. If he could have gotten his hands on either of them, he would have given her a taste of his fury.

The longer John drank at the Full House, the better the idea sounded to him.

"Welcome home," Michael said to Casey as they pulled up in front of their house.

"The house is wonderful, Michael," Casey complimented him.

He climbed down and helped her out. They walked up the short path to the door. Michael opened it, then scooped Casey up in his arms. Casey had been expecting it, but she still gasped at his ploy. She looped her arms around his neck to steady herself as he carried her across the threshold. The pleasure of being in his arms ended far too quickly as he set her on her feet and went to light a lamp.

"What do you think?" he asked, turning to watch her reaction to her first look around. She hadn't been there since his mother had helped him arrange the furniture.

Casey stared around in surprise and delight. A settee and two chairs were grouped before the stone fireplace. A small table and chairs were set off in the kitchen area.

"It's wonderful. Thank you, Michael."

"You can thank my mother, too. She helped me get everything ready."

"It's perfect."

"And here's the bedroom." He led the way in and lit the lamp on the nightstand.

Casey tensed as she stopped in the doorway to stare at the bed that dominated the room. There was only one bedroom and one bed, just as she'd known there would be. The settee was too small for either of them to sleep on comfortably.

"Where are you going to sleep?" she asked, trying to sound innocent as she posed the dreaded question.

"Right here," Michael answered. He didn't let on, but her question annoyed him.

"If you're sleeping here, where am I going to sleep?"

"Right here with me," he answered easily.

"But . . ." Her nervousness was definitely showing. Did Michael really want her? Was he ready to forsake their arrangement and love her as she loved him? Hope blossomed within her as she looked at him. "But what about the deal we made?"

"What about it? Just because we're sleeping in the same bed doesn't mean anything is going to happen between us. I gave you my word that this would be a marriage in name only, and I plan to stick to that."

His tone was so cold and indifferent that any hope Casey had had that things could be different was dashed. He didn't love her, and she believed he never would. "All right."

"I'll go see to the horses," Michael said in a flat voice, and he left her alone.

Casey wanted to get undressed before Michael returned, so the minute he went outside, she went to find her nightgown. She'd sent a trunk with her personal things over a few days before, and she found her nightgown neatly folded in one of the drawers in the bureau.

Elizabeth had had Sissy include a silken negligee with her fancy underthings, but there was no use in wearing that.

Michael wasn't interested.

She would wear her high-necked cotton gown.

Hastily Casey tried to shed her wedding gown. The process started off smoothly enough, but when she tried to undo the buttons midway down her back, frustration overwhelmed her. She was trapped in her dress. Short of forcing it off and risking tearing it, or sleeping in it, she was going to have to ask Michael for help.

The thought unnerved Casey. She had hoped to be in her chaste nightgown, in bed with the covers up to her neck, when Michael returned from the stable. She'd even thought she could fake being asleep so she wouldn't have to deal with the situation tonight, but now there was no way out. Michael's hands were going to be upon her. She shivered in anticipation, then struck the thought from her.

Michael had made it plain to her.

He didn't care.

There was nothing to worry about.

* * *

Michael took his time with the horses. He and the men had built a small makeshift stable some distance behind the house, and he lingered there as long as he could. The thought of being alone in bed with Casey bothered him.

She didn't love him.

She never had and she never would.

He'd told her he would stick to their agreement, and he planned to do just that.

He was not going to touch her or kiss her tonight.

With the horse taken care of, there was no reason to stay away any longer. Michael started back up to the house. He girded himself for the dark hours of the night to come. It was going to be a long one.

What Michael expected to find when he reached the house and what Michael got were two very different things.

"Help," Casey said the minute he came through the door. She was standing in the middle of the main room, holding up the bodice of her gown, the back of the garment partially unfastened. "I can't reach all the buttons."

She went to him and presented her back.

Michael swallowed tightly as he stared down at her exposed flesh. "Let me wash my hands first."

He went to the sink and washed his hands in the bucket of water there, stalling for as long as he could.

Casey appreciated his thoughtfulness. The gown was precious and needed to be handled delicately. When he'd finished washing and was drying his hands, she went to him again and waited.

Michael carefully began to unfasten the small buttons.

It was a tedious task at the best of times, and right then, it proved torture to him. With every button he unfastened, more of Casey's back was exposed to him.

True, she was wearing a chemise, but his imagination was in good working order—too good for his own peace of mind.

A sudden unbidden image of Casey standing before him unclothed seared through his thoughts and left him swearing under his breath. He dropped his hands away for a minute.

"What's wrong?" Casey asked in all innocence.

"These buttons are hard to work with," he growled.

"I know. Anne helped me get dressed, and she had quite a time with them, too," she answered, completely unaware of his dilemma.

Michael gritted his teeth and started again.

Casey controlled a shiver as his fingers brushed against her through the chemise. The silken fabric only heightened the sensuality of his touch.

He continued to work at the buttons, denying his desire to turn her around in his arms and kiss her. He offered his self-denial up to God as a sacrifice, but the voice in his head taunted him with *But she is your wife.*

Michael slaved away and finally finished. The gown gapped open all the way to her hips. He stared down at the sweet line of her back revealed to him there, then lifted his gaze up to her neck.

A driving urge filled him to press a kiss to the juncture of neck and shoulder. He told himself "no." He fought against the desire. He knew it would lead to nothing but frustration, but he was, after all, only a mortal man.

Michael slowly bent down to her and pressed a soft kiss to her bared shoulder at the nape of her neck.

Casey had been waiting for Michael to announce that he'd finished unfastening her. She'd been holding herself stiffly in spite of the touch of his hands at her back. She'd fought against the shivers that had wracked her every time his fingers brushed against her. She was proud of the control she was showing. She didn't want to appear weak before him. There was no point in even thinking about Michael that way. She might be aroused by his touch, but he was only doing a job—nothing more.

And then his lips caressed the sensitive skin of her neck.

Casey gasped and stiffened in shock as excitement radiated through her.

Michael felt her reaction and thought she was angered by his daring. He stepped away from her, needing to put a distance between them.

Casey glanced over her shoulder at Michael, wondering what had prompted him to do that, but his expression was stony and revealed nothing.

"I'll go finish changing," she said, moving toward the bedroom.

"You do that," he growled to himself.

Michael went to the cabinet in the kitchen and took out the bottle of whiskey he'd left there for moments such as this. He'd known they were coming, and he'd made sure he was prepared. After pouring himself a stiff drink, he sat in one of the chairs before the dead fireplace. He drank slowly and deliberately. He wanted to give Casey all the time she needed to get into bed. The last thing he needed was to see her in any further state of undress.

Taking a deep drink of the potent liquor, Michael enjoyed its power as it burned through him.

He wanted to forget Casey's kiss.

He wanted to forget the way she'd felt in his arms when they'd danced together.

He wanted to forget the need that burned deep within his body.

Michael tried to think logically. He was a man. She was a pretty woman. It was normal for him to be attracted to her. He'd been attracted to other women in the past, and it had never troubled him this way.

You've never been married before. Casey's your wife.

The thought haunted him.

His wife.

He was her husband.

They were going to live together forever.

In name only!

Michael gave a disgusted shake of his head and took another drink. He tried to reason it out, but there was no denying the truth. He desired Casey. He could accept his feelings, but he could not act on them.

He downed the rest of his whiskey, then realized it had gotten very quiet in the bedroom. He set the glass aside and put out the lamp.

A lamp was still burning in the bedroom, and he walked into the room to find Casey in bed with the blanket drawn up to her chin, her back to his side of the bed, her eyes closed. He stood there in silence, staring at her for a long moment.

So this was to be his life—his existence.

He was Adam in the Garden of Eden, and Casey was his temptation.

Michael extinguished the lamp, stripped down to his underwear and climbed into bed.

Michael did not know that Casey had opened her eyes and was watching his reflection in the mirror.

Illuminated by the pale moonlight coming through the window, Casey had watched in silent awe as Michael undressed. He was beautiful. There was no doubt about it. His shoulders were broad, his chest tightly muscled, tapering to his lean waist and—

She'd dragged her gaze back up higher, not wanting to risk seeing more of him than she could handle right then. Only when Michael had climbed into bed with her did she shut her eyes. She lay tense and unmoving for long hours, waiting for sleep to overtake her, but haunted by the fiery, erotic memory of the touch of his lips on her neck.

Michael lay on his half of the bed, staring up at the ceiling and trying to ignore Casey's nearness. At first, he'd resented the pillow between them, but now he realized it was a good thing. He didn't need to wake up in the middle of the night and find her curled up against him. He would keep to their arrangement. He was a man of his word, but he finally admitted to himself that he was only human, after all.

Sleep was long in coming for Michael.

* * *

"I now pronounce you man and wife," said Brian Kennebeck, the justice of the peace in Hard Luck as he completed the ceremony that united Nick and Anne in matrimony. He smiled warmly at the couple. "I hope you'll be very happy."

"We will be," Nick assured him.

Nick looked down at Anne, who stood by his side smiling up at him. He took her in his arms.

"Mrs. Paden," he said softly before he kissed her to seal their vows.

"I like the sound of that," she said.

"So do I."

They left the office and stepped outside into the night. It was late and the town was quiet. Everything seemed peaceful.

Nick and Anne shared a knowing look.

"There's nothing I want to do more than take you back to my hotel room right now, but I think we'd better go find your parents and give them our news first."

"You're right. It wouldn't be good if my father came looking for you with a shotgun tonight."

Nick drew her close and kissed her hungrily one last time. Then they hurried off toward her home, eager to share the joy of their good news.

Anne knew now that sometimes fairy tales really did come true.

Chapter Thirty-one

Rosalie was tired. It had been a long day, and she was more than ready to retire for the night.

"The Donovan wedding really cut into our business tonight," Bill said as they closed down the saloon.

"Big weddings like that don't happen often in this town," she remarked. "Everybody who was invited must have shown up."

"Things will be better next weekend. It's payday."

"We could use a little excitement around here."

"*Good* excitement," Bill cautioned, thinking back to the previous weekend and her trouble with John McQueen.

"You're right about that."

"Good night, Rosalie. I'll see you tomorrow."

"Good night."

She locked up after he'd gone and went on upstairs to her room. It was dark as she let herself into her private quarters, but she wasn't worried. She knew where everything was and went over to the dresser to light the lamp there. As the flame flickered to life, she lifted her gaze to the mirror and went completely still at what she saw reflected there.

John was sitting on her bed behind her, and he was watching her carefully.

"John!" she gasped, startled. She spun around to face him.

"I've been waiting for you," he said quietly as he got up and walked toward her.

"How did you get in here?" she demanded.

He laughed coldly at her. "I've been here often enough to know how to get in without being seen."

Rosalie watched him coming toward her, and she wasn't sure whether to try to run away or stay. She'd loved John for so long that it was hard for her to accept that he truly was as vicious as he'd been the past weekend.

"What do you want?" she asked warily.

He stopped before her and smiled thinly. "You, of course."

The week before, she would have fallen into his arms, but now she held herself back. "Why?"

"What do you mean, 'why'?" he asked, reaching out to her. "I haven't seen you in a week. I missed you."

Rosalie could tell he'd been drinking heavily, for his words were slurred. She deliberately eluded him and kept a distance between them. "I'd like to believe that. I want to believe that, but—"

"But what?" he asked, his barely controlled fury growing even hotter. How dare she reject him this way?

"After what happened between us, I don't know if I can trust you anymore."

"Of course you can trust me," he insisted smoothly, already fantasizing about what he was going to do to her when he got his hands on her.

"Then marry me, John." She threw the words at him in a demand. "We've been together for a long time now, and I've always hoped that one day we would get married. So, if you really care about me, marry me."

"What?" He stared at Rosalie as if she'd lost her mind. "You expected me to marry you? Why would I? You're nothing but a slut! You're a whore."

"Why, you—" All the anger she'd felt toward John erupted then. She swung at him and slapped him across the face.

Rosalie felt good for a moment, but her moment of triumph was brief.

John reacted with a violent rage. He grabbed her arm and jerked her to him.

"Who do you think you are?" he snarled. His grip on her was bruising. The hatred he felt was evident in the threatening look on his face.

"Let me go! Get out of here before I scream!"

"You can scream all you want. There's no one to hear you," he said, yanking her even closer to him. "We're all alone here."

Rosalie managed one cry for help before John began to beat her. His intent was vicious and savage. She represented everything he hated; she was the embodiment of Casey and her rejection. He was going to make Rosalie pay for the sins of all women.

"Why are you doing this?" she whimpered, cowering weakly on the floor before him.

"Because I hate you!"

"But, John—"

"I hate you and all the other stupid women in this world!" he spat at her. "How dare Casey marry Donovan!"

"You cared about Casey Turner?" Rosalie was trying to understand his full-blown fury, hoping to find a way to reach him and make him stop.

"I cared about her ranch! It was bad enough that Frank Donovan didn't die in the ambush, but—"

"You're the one who shot him?" Rosalie gasped.

"There are people who can be hired to do the dirty work," he sneered, dragging her up to her feet. He liked seeing the terror in her eyes. He liked having this power over her.

He hit her again with all his might. Rosalie fell backwards and crashed against the nightstand, hitting her head. She collapsed onto the floor and lay unmoving.

John stared down at her, seeing the blood seeping from the injury to her head, and he smiled.

He turned and left the room.

Rosalie was dead, and no one would ever know he was responsible. His only regret was that she wasn't Casey Turner.

John left the saloon by the back way. No one saw him.

* * *

Casey awoke with the dawn. She was still exhausted, for she hadn't fallen soundly asleep until the wee hours of the morning. Michael's presence beside her had made rest next to impossible. And she was supposed to spend the rest of her life this way. He was sleeping soundly, so she slipped out of bed and went into the other room to dress. She had no doubts about what she was going to put on now that it was daylight. She donned her usual work clothes.

Ready for the new day, Casey considered her spotless kitchen and wondered what she could make for breakfast.

Bill Clark always came by to check on Rosalie on Sundays. He was surprised to find she wasn't up yet when he let himself into the Sundown late that morning. He moved around downstairs, looking things over, then decided he'd go up and knock on her door to make certain everything was all right.

The fact that she didn't answer troubled him. Bill thought she might have gotten up and gone out early, but he somehow knew that wasn't the case. Worried, he opened the bedroom door and stood stock-still for a moment at the sight before him.

"Rosalie!"

He ran to kneel beside her and took her in his arms, fearing the worst. Relief flooded through him when he realized she was still breathing.

"Thank God."

He laid her back down and ran from the building. He

encountered two men on the street and directed one to get Dr. Murray; the other he sent for the sheriff. Racing back to Rosalie's room, he waited by her side for them to show up.

Dr. Murray arrived first. The two men carried Rosalie to her bed and he set about tending her injuries. She had just regained consciousness when Sheriff Montgomery got there.

"Sheriff," Rosalie said in a voice barely above a whisper.

The lawman hurried to her side.

"Who did this to you?" he asked, kneeling beside the bed so he could hear her answer.

"McQueen—and, Sheriff—" Rosalie was so weak she could barely get the words out. "He's responsible for the Donovan shooting, too."

"How do you know?"

"He admitted it to me last night." She collapsed back on her pillow.

"So McQueen's the one who shot Frank Donovan," Sheriff Montgomery said in amazement.

"No," Rosalie whispered. "He hired someone."

Dr. Murray took over again as Bill walked out of the room with the sheriff.

"McQueen hired someone to kill Frank, and he beat a defenseless woman almost to death," the bartender ground out, wanting to seek some revenge of his own.

"I wonder if Frank Donovan has left town yet," Montgomery said.

"We can check at the hotel. Do you want me to ride with you to get McQueen?"

"Yes. Thanks. I've got a feeling I'm going to need all the deputies I can get today."

The two men made their way to the hotel.

"The Donovans are still here," Ernest Williams said.

"What room are they in?"

The clerk told him, and they went to tell Frank the news.

"I don't believe it!" Elizabeth exclaimed, looking from Nick to Anne as they visited her in her room that morning. "You eloped last night!"

"That's right," Nick affirmed. "Mr. Kennebeck married us."

"This is so exciting!" she went on, giving Anne an impulsive hug. "What did your mother say?"

"She was thrilled for us, too," Anne answered.

"You'd better wire your parents right away," Elizabeth told Nick. "They'll be delighted for you, too. And, of course, you have to let Michael and Casey know."

They were all discussing the best way to handle everything when a knock came at the door. Nick answered it to find Sheriff Montgomery outside with the bartender from the Sundown saloon.

"I need to speak with Frank," the sheriff announced.

"Come in, please," Nick invited, holding the door wide.

"I've got some news for you."

Frank was suddenly worried, for the lawman's expression was very serious. "What's happened?"

"We've just learned who was behind your shooting."

Frank went still as he stared at the sheriff. "Who was it?"

"John McQueen." Sheriff Montgomery quickly explained what had happened overnight and what he'd learned from Rosalie.

Elizabeth gasped in horror at his news. "McQueen? But why? Why would he want to kill Frank and hurt Rosalie so badly?"

"I don't know yet, but I'm on my way to the Royal to make some arrests. I wanted to let you know."

"I'm riding with you," Nick insisted. "Is there time to stop at the Circle D and get Michael? I know he'd want to go along with us, too."

"Yes. We can do that," Sheriff Montgomery agreed. "You have a gun?"

Nick nodded. "It's in my room. I'll be right back."

Anne went with him. She waited nervously as he strapped on his gun belt. She had never seen him so grim.

"Nick, be careful." She went to him and pressed a desperate kiss to his lips.

"Don't worry," he said as he put her from him. "I will be. You stay with Aunt Elizabeth and Uncle Frank. I'll meet you at the Circle D once we're done."

It was late when Michael awakened to find Casey gone from their bed. He was surprised that he'd slept so long, considering how restless he'd been all night. He got up, dressed and went looking for his bride.

Michael didn't know why, but he was surprised when

he found her dressed in her working clothes down at the stable taking care of the horses.

"Casey?"

"Oh, good morning, Michael," she said, looking up from where she was cleaning out a stall.

"What are you doing?"

Casey shrugged and came out to speak with him, carrying the pitchfork. "Working. Why?"

"You're my wife now," he began. "Wives don't—"

"This wife does," she interrupted him.

Frustrated, he asked, "What's for breakfast?"

"I think we've already had this conversation," she said, and she couldn't help laughing as she finished, "Breakfast is whatever you're going to fix for us."

"Come on. We'll fix it together. With both of us working at it, something is bound to turn out to be edible."

Casey followed him from the stable to the house. She happened to glance out across the land and noticed riders in the distance.

"People coming," she told him, pointing.

Casey and Michael stopped in front of the porch to watch the trio ride in.

"It's Nick and Sheriff Montgomery and Bill Clark," Michael remarked when the riders got closer.

They were both edgy as they waited for their visitors to arrive.

"How are you newlyweds?" Nick asked as they reined in before them.

"We're fine," Michael answered, "but I know that's not

why you're here." He noticed Nick was wearing his sidearm. "What's going on?"

Sheriff Montgomery quickly explained everything.

"How is Rosalie?"

"She will recover, but she is badly injured."

"And you're certain John McQueen is responsible?" Casey said in complete and utter surprise.

"That's right. He admitted it last night to Rosalie. We're heading to the Royal now. Nick thought you'd want to come along with us."

"You're damned right I do," Michael said quickly.

"*We* do," Casey put in.

"It's going to be dangerous. There's no telling what he might try once we have him cornered," the lawman said, trying to discourage her from going.

"Then you'll need me along for the extra gun." She wasn't about to let Michael go without her. "Give us a minute to get our guns and horses."

It wasn't long before they were ready to ride out.

"There's one thing I forgot to tell you," Nick began, looking over at Casey and Michael, who were riding beside him.

"What's that?" Michael asked.

"Well, last night . . ." He looked at Casey.

"Yes?" she urged.

"Last night, Anne and I eloped," he finished.

"You what?" Michael looked at him in amazement.

"We got married."

"Nick, that's wonderful!" Casey exclaimed, delighted.

"Yes, it is," he answered. "I love Anne very much."

"Congratulations," Michael told him.

"Thanks."

"Are you going to stay here or go back to Philadelphia?" Michael asked. "I can always use your help on the Circle D."

"We haven't talked about that yet," he told them with a grin. "But you know my father does need me back there to help him with the company."

"I don't think Anne will mind moving to Philadelphia at all," Casey reassured him. "She's always dreamed of traveling and seeing the world."

"I'll just have to oblige her, then," Nick said. "I was supposed to go to Europe. Maybe that can be our honeymoon."

"She'll be thrilled."

"What about you, Casey?" Nick asked her. "Did you want to go to Europe for a honeymoon?"

"No," she answered honestly. "I'm happiest when I'm right here on the Bar T."

Michael didn't doubt that for a minute.

They started off for the Royal ranch, armed and ready for any trouble McQueen might give them.

Chapter Thirty-two

They reached the Royal ranch and dismounted in front of the main house. It was a large, impressive, two-story home that bespoke its owner's wealth and status.

Michael, Nick and Sheriff Montgomery went up on the porch while Casey stayed back with Bill Clark. The sheriff knocked on the door, but no one answered. Nick went to take a look around the side of the house while Michael looked in the front windows to see if he could see anyone indoors.

"The place looks deserted. Let's walk down to the bunkhouse and see if he's there. If nothing else, some of his men might know where we can find him," Montgomery suggested.

As they all started in that direction, they saw John and the ranch hand Sid come out of the stable.

"All right, be ready. This could be trouble," the lawman cautioned.

John had seen them ride up and wondered what they were doing at his ranch. He especially wondered why Casey was with them. He worried for a moment that they'd learned he was the one who'd killed Rosalie, but he knew there was no evidence to tie him to her death. They had to have come about something else, but what?

"Stay back a little and keep an eye on things. I don't know what they're after, but it's not good, whatever it is," John warned Sid in a low voice as he walked on ahead of him to meet the visitors.

Sid did as he'd been told, lingering back where he could watch all that transpired and have a clear shot if the need arose.

"Afternoon," John greeted them. "What brings you out to the Royal today?" He looked at Casey and then at Michael. "And you even brought the newlyweds. This must be important."

Michael stiffened, not liking McQueen's arrogant attitude.

Sheriff Montgomery stepped forward to confront the rancher. "John, I need to take you in to town. There are some things we have to talk about and set straight."

"Like what?" he asked, playing the innocent.

"I know you're the one who tried to kill Rosalie," the lawman said.

"I tried to *what?*" He pretended outrage at the accusation, but his fury was really over the fact that Rosalie wasn't dead. He could have sworn she hadn't been breathing when he'd left her.

"Rosalie told us what happened. She's alive, and she will make a full recovery, but—"

"I don't know what you're talking about."

"I think you do, John," Montgomery insisted.

John knew he was in trouble. Panic threatened. "I am a well-respected citizen in these parts! Are you saying, you'd take a whore's word over mine?"

"You son-of-a-bitch! Rosalie is no whore! She's only a fool for loving you!" Bill launched himself at John. He landed a solid punch to John's jaw before the sheriff could stop him.

"Easy, Bill," Montgomery told him, restraining the bartender until he calmed down a bit.

"Are you going to let him get away with that?" John demanded, rubbing his jaw.

"You're lucky I stopped him, McQueen," the sheriff said. "I'm tempted to do more than that to you. We also learned from Rosalie that you're the one responsible for Frank Donovan's shooting, that you hired somebody to try to kill him. I'm placing you under arrest, and I'm taking you in." With those words he stepped forward, ready to put his hands on the arrogant rancher.

"Sid!" John shouted.

A shot rang out, and the sheriff fell, wounded. Michael, Nick and Bill drew their guns. Nick got off a shot in Sid's direction as they all dove for cover. Sid screamed as Nick's shot found its mark.

Michael, Nick and Bill turned their guns on John, but

he reacted too quickly for them. Unarmed and desperate now without Sid to back him up, he knew he was trapped. He had only one hope to escape.

In a frantic move, John grabbed Casey just as she was drawing her gun. He held her around the neck as he snatched the gun from her hand and pointed it at her head. He faced down the men.

"Now you're going to let me ride out of here without any trouble," John ordered in a commanding voice.

Michael had been ready to take a shot at John, but he'd moved too fast for him. Now Michael had no clear shot at the man without hitting Casey.

"Let Casey go, McQueen!" Michael ordered.

"You worried about your little wife?" he taunted. "You should be. It won't bother me in the least to cause her pain. She deserves it for all the hell she's put me through!" he threatened, tightening his grip on her.

Casey was furious. She prided herself on always being ready for anything, but John's attack had caught her completely off guard. She was helpless in his grasp, and she didn't like being helpless.

"Put your guns down, boys," John ordered, "or I might just have to hurt Casey."

"Don't listen to him, Michael!" Casey cried.

"Shut up, bitch!" John jerked her painfully against him. "But maybe you're too stupid to know when to shut up. I know you're too stupid to understand what you threw away when you married him! We could have had everything! We could have had it all!"

"I do have everything," she defied him, looking at Michael. "I married the man I love!"

Michael was startled by her words. As he stared at her being held hostage by John, the truth of what he felt for her was finally revealed to him.

He loved Casey.

Michael didn't know how it had happened or when.

He only knew that it was true.

He had fallen in love with Casey. She meant everything to him, and somehow he was going to save her from McQueen.

"I was smart not to look at you," she goaded her captor, resisting with all her might as he tried to drag her backwards. "You're a fool!" Casey hoped to make him so mad that he'd make a mistake.

John was tempted to shoot her right then and there, but he knew that would be signing his own death warrant. He continued to back up, forcing her along with him.

Casey realized the time had come. She looked at Michael. Their gazes met across the distance. She gave a slight nod as she lifted her elbow and with all her might jabbed it into John's stomach.

John had expected her to resist him, but he hadn't known she could hit that hard. His grip on her loosened for just an instant, and that was all the time Casey needed to make her move.

"Michael!" she screamed, tearing herself free and throwing herself to the ground.

Michael got off his perfectly aimed shot.

John stood, stunned, as the bullet took him square in

the chest. He staggered backward. He tried to bring his gun to bear on Casey, wanting to punish her for all she'd done to him, but darkness and pain overwhelmed him. He fell to the ground.

Michael ran to Casey as Nick went to check on John and Bill rushed to see to the sheriff.

Nick took Casey's gun out of John's hand and rolled him over to make sure he was dead.

"Thank God, you're all right!" Michael said as he swept Casey into his arms and held her to his heart.

The sound of the gunshots had brought some of John's hired hands at a run to see what was going on. They'd drawn their weapons, thinking they were going to have to defend the ranch, but they holstered their guns when they saw Bill helping Sheriff Montgomery to his feet. The lawman had been shot in the shoulder, but his wound wasn't fatal.

"What happened?" the hands asked, staring in shock at the sight of John and Sid lying dead in the dirt.

"I tried to take your boss in for attempted murder, but he and Sid resisted arrest," Montgomery managed. He looked over at Casey. "You all right?"

"Yes, I'm fine," she answered, trembling as the realization of what could have happened tore through her. She lifted her gaze to Michael. "Thank you."

Michael didn't say a word. He just kissed her tenderly, sweetly. When the kiss ended, Michael still didn't release her but held her close.

"I love you, Casey," he told her solemnly, remembering

the power of the emotions that had filled him. "When I thought I was going to lose you . . ."

Casey lifted one hand to caress his cheek. "I meant what I said to John, Michael. I love you, too."

They stood together, enraptured by the final acknowledgment of their love for one another.

Nick smiled as he watched the two of them together. "I always knew you were perfect for each other."

"You're right," Michael agreed, looking up at him and grinning. "And, by the way, that was good shooting, Nick." Nick's accuracy had surprised Michael, considering how badly he'd done during the target practice he'd put him through.

"Yes, that was very good shooting," Sheriff Montgomery spoke up, holding his shoulder to try to stop the bleeding as he leaned on Bill for support. "Thanks."

"Let's get you down to the bunkhouse, Sheriff. We'll bind you up, so you can make it back to town to see Doc Murray," one of the ranch hands suggested.

Bill helped him go along with the men.

Nick handed Casey back her gun, and she slid it into her holster.

Michael looked over to where John lay, and he shook his head in disgust. "It's so hard to believe that he was the one responsible for Pa being shot."

"Greed is a deadly sin," Nick said grimly. "McQueen found that out the hard way."

The three of them followed after the others.

They were still shaken by all that had transpired, but relieved that it was over.

Justice had been done.

* * *

Nick returned to town with Sheriff Montgomery and Bill, while Michael and Casey stopped off at the Circle D to tell his parents what had happened. Frank and Elizabeth had been shocked by the revelation of McQueen's involvement in his shooting, but they were also relieved that the mystery had been solved and the threat was over.

It was growing late when Michael and Casey finally returned home.

"I should let my pa know, too," Casey was saying as they rode up to the house.

"We'll pay him a visit tomorrow. Right now . . ." Michael looked over at her, the intensity of what he was feeling reflected in his gaze.

"Right now?" she repeated.

"I need some time alone with my wife."

"I like the way you think," Casey said, excitement racing through her from the heat of his regard.

They reined in before the house and dismounted. Michael quickly went to pick Casey up in his arms.

"What are you doing?" she asked breathlessly, clinging to him.

"I'm going to carry you over the threshold again."

"But what about the horses?"

"They'll be fine. They're not going anywhere."

"But—"

He silenced her with a passionate kiss as he strode up to the house and carried her inside. He did not set her on her feet, but carried her straight to their bed and laid her upon its softness.

"I love you, Casey Donovan," Michael said with deep emotion.

Casey decided to show him rather than tell him of her love. Brazenly she reached up and drew him down for a hungry kiss.

The moment was rapturous for them both. They were caught up in the whirlwind of their desire. With eager hands, they stripped away their clothes. They took the time to explore the beauty of each other's bodies.

Each caress, each kiss, heightened the power of their need to be one. Michael pressed hungry kisses to her lips, then traced a fiery path down her throat. She arched in ecstasy against him and cried out his name as he sought the sweetness of her breasts. Deep within the womanly heart of her, Casey ached to know his love more fully. She ran her hands over his shoulders and back, urging him on, wanting to be one with him.

Michael could deny himself no longer. He moved over her and made her his own, breaching the proof of her innocence.

Casey went still for a moment, glorying in his loving invasion. She surrendered to his full possession and responded hungrily to his passionate kiss.

They came together.

Loving.

Sharing.

Worshiping.

Adoring.

Giving each other the most perfect gift—the gift of their love.

When at last they reached the height of desire's delight, they crested together.

Wrapped in each other's arms, they clung together, one in body, one in spirit, one in love.

What God had joined together, no man would put asunder.

They loved.

Epilogue

Three Weeks Later

The going-away party for Anne and Nick at the Circle D was festive. The couple would be departing for Philadelphia the following day.

"Nick is going to show me the world," Anne said in delight as she gazed adoringly at her husband. "And I can't wait to meet his parents."

"I'm sure they'll be thrilled to meet you, too," Elizabeth said, knowing how lucky her brother was to have such a wonderful daughter-in-law. He was almost as lucky as she was with Cassandra, she thought with an inner smile.

"We'll be in Philadelphia for a few weeks, and then we'll set sail for the Continent and our official honeymoon," Nick said.

"That sounds wonderful," Elizabeth said.

"Hey, Nick!" Tom and Harry called him over to join them.

"Excuse me." Nick left Elizabeth and Anne and went to see what the two ranch hands wanted.

"Here's your money," Harry said, handing him a large wad of bills.

"What money?" Nick asked, surprised. It was a goodly sum.

"We're men of our word here in Texas. We made you those bets that day in the bunkhouse about Michael and Casey getting married, and it turns out you were right. You won."

Nick was smiling. "Thanks."

"What bets?" Michael asked as he came up on them.

"Oh, nothing." Nick and Harry and Tom shared conspiratorial looks.

Harry and Tom moved away, leaving Nick and Michael together.

"I'm going to miss you, Nick. Thanks for all your help. I appreciate your coming out here with me," Michael said.

"If I hadn't come to Hard Luck, I would never have met Anne."

"So you enjoyed your stay here?"

"Oh, yes, and I'm sure we'll be back to visit regularly."

"I hope so. I'll miss you."

"No, you won't. You've got Casey now. You're never going to have a dull moment in your life with her around."

"You're right." Michael grinned. "And I love every minute of it."

* * *

Frank was sitting in his wheelchair across the room from them with Jack standing at his side.

"I would never have believed things could work out this way."

"Neither would I. Life is good," Jack agreed. His health was holding up, and just knowing Casey was happy made all the difference in the world to him.

It was just before sundown when the party broke up.

Michael and Casey promised Anne and Nick that they would come into town the next day to see them off.

On their way home, Michael drove their buckboard off the road down toward the river.

"What are you doing?" Casey asked, puzzled.

"Well, it's been a long hot day."

"Yes. So?"

"So I was thinking it would feel real good to take a swim on our way home."

"But we don't have anything—"

"I know," he said, grinning at her.